A MIDWAY, A CORPSE, AND TOO MANY SECRETS

The carnival has come to Delphi, South Dakota—injecting a dose of seedy excitement into the smalltown routine.

Plump, razor-tongued, forty-something waitress Tory Bauer makes her living serving the local eccentrics at Delphi's main watering hole. Now Hamilton Bogner's International Extravaganza has brought new faces into her town—some merely strange, some vaguely sinister . . . and one that Tory later sees drained of life, and swinging from a fun house beam.

The police see nothing unnatural about the unfortunate carny's death. Tory Bauer, however, thinks otherwise. And she's determined to follow her hunches into the dark, sordid shadows behind the midway—where murder may not be the worst of sins.

KATHLEEN TAYLOR

SEX AND SALMONELLA

AVON BOOKS NEW YORK

SEX AND SALMONELLA is an original publication of Avon Books. This work has never before appeared in book form. This work is a novel. Any similarity to actual persons or events is purely coincidental.

AVON BOOKS
A division of
The Hearst Corporation
1350 Avenue of the Americas
New York, New York 10019

Copyright © 1996 by Kathleen Taylor
Published by arrangement with the author
Library of Congress Catalog Card Number: 96-96023
ISBN: 0-380-78355-X

First Avon Books Printing: August 1996

AVON TRADEMARK REG. U.S. PAT. OFF. AND IN OTHER COUNTRIES, MARCA REGISTRADA, HECHO EN U.S.A.

Printed in the U.S.A.

RA   10   9   8   7   6   5   4   3   2   1

For Ken and Lona Prater and Curtis and Matthew Taylor, my parents and my children—who all waited, not too impatiently, for me to finish just one more page

ACKNOWLEDGMENTS

I would like to thank the following people for their assistance—though I am entirely responsible for the story that follows, it would not have come into being without their help: Jody Weisflock, Lorah Houser Jankord, Kris Hansen, Jane Stimson, and the Dianes (Willis and Jankord) for chapter-by-chapter enthusiasm; Betty Baloun at the library; R.E. (who didn't want to be named) for the Latin translation; the wonderful Jane Dystel and her staff for finding this book a home; and especially Terry T, whose support saved me from having to find a real job a long time ago.

Prologue

You know how mysteries work—the main character, after a series of unlikely circumstances and odd coincidences, stumbles across a dead body. This same character has already seen or heard something important but doesn't realize it, comes to a couple of wrong conclusions in the middle chapters, and finally solves the mystery on the second to the last page, thanks to the fact that he or she happens to be precisely the right person in the right place at the right time.

There are some who would debate the notion of my being the right person at any particular time or place. But there is no doubt that I found the body, that I saw and heard something that I didn't, at first, realize, and that I drew mostly erroneous conclusions and yet more or less solved the mystery.

I am not particularly fond of carnivals. They're loud, crowded, and dirty, and the food is even worse than what Aphrodite cooks at the cafe. Rides hold no attraction for me; being flung upside down at great heights and even greater speeds is not my idea of a good time.

Unfortunately, this carnival was set up in the vacant lot just west of our trailer. With the dust and noise sifting in continually from the time the rides were fired up until the last shrieking teenager was sent home, it was just as cool, quiet, and comfortable outside in the heat and dirt as inside covering my ears.

So, I wasted some off-time seeing the shabby sights of Hamilton Bogner's International Extravaganza.

There is every possibility that I would have been somewhere on the grounds, nibbling sticky cotton candy, safely off center stage at zero hour. If I had been, I could have clucked like everyone else, feeling sorry for the dumbshit who spotted the body.

Actually, I do feel pretty sorry for the dumbshit who spotted the body, since I was the sweating fool in the third turn of a low-rent fun house maze, bored with seeing a zillion shorter, fatter reflections of myself multiplied around and disappearing into infinity, who looked up into the closely spaced stainless steel girders of the ceiling of the semitrailer.

Once I did that, I had no choice but to see her up there, crumpled into a dark crawl space above the mirrors so that only her face peeked over the edge, tendrils of greasy blond hair partially covering the wide surprised eyes and open mouth. No choice but to see her sad, still, dead face and the cheap turquoise cross necklace, whose chain was looped loosely around her closed fist.

Unfortunately for me, here is where those "unlikely circumstances" come into play. If Stuart McKee hadn't been married, I would never have gone into the fun house to begin with. And if my cousin Junior Deibert hadn't the misfortune to serve and eat an improperly stored chicken, I would never have recognized the dead girl.

And if not for the odd coinciding of those two facts, I would not be in the position I am right now.

So for the story that follows, which began a week ago

or more, blame bad timing and unlikely circumstances and odd coincidences.

Blame sex and salmonella.

1

....

Shoop Shoop

When you live in a small town in a big empty state, you are expected to volunteer your time, money, and expertise to any and all causes. If you happen to fall short in those categories, you can still cheerfully perform gofer duties for committees that pour out of the woodwork any time there happens to be a barn raising or bake sale.

Debate may rage elsewhere over a lack of commitment to social issues, but here in the Midwest, community service is alive and thriving. It's one of the punishments for living in small-town America. Or at least it is in small-town South Dakota.

Unfortunately, there are plenty of occasions to endure humiliation in the name of raising money. I don't mean minor embarrassments like being dunked and kissing pigs. I'm talking actual debasement: mud wrestling, donkey basketball, Spink County's Biggest Butt Competition (which I took as a personal affront, even though I was not asked to compete). And our own

5

contribution to Community Service Hell, the Delphi Phollies, a talent show that was organized to cap the closing-night festivities of our fifty-fourth annual three-day celebration, Delphi Daze.

For weeks, faded and curling flyers and posters had dotted the windows of local establishments, including Aphrodite Ferguson's Delphi Cafe, inviting one and all to attend Friday's Rocky Mountain Oyster Feed and All-Night Street Dance, Saturday's Men's Over-30 Slow-pitch Game, and Sunday's performance of the Phollies.

And if the locals could stand any more excitement, Hamilton Bogner's International Extravaganza, a carnival running the length of the festival, agreed to donate part of its profits for some community project.

This year's money is slated for the Neil Pascoe Memorial Swimming Pool Fund, named for our young local millionaire because he seeded the trust with a hefty donation, not because he is dead. Although he may well die before enough additional money is raised to begin construction.

Neil would gladly have given the whole amount to the city himself, but his offer was refused.

"It'll feel much more like *our* pool if we *all* work together to get it built," said NPMSPF committee chairperson, wife of the Lutheran minister, my first cousin, and all-around pain in the neck Junior Deibert, who was usually spruce but looked a little green and shaky today. She'd done nothing more than pick at her lunch, though that wasn't unusual. The food at Aphrodite's rarely met Junior's exacting standards.

"This way everyone contributes toward a shared goal. And speaking of contributions . . ." She paused and repressed a small shudder.

I didn't know if she was genuinely feeling ill or just leading up to some especially unsavory suggestion. Nor did I particularly care.

"No," I said.

I've always been a hard sell for the solicitation crowd.

"I already bought two tickets to the talent show, one

for the street dance, one for the baseball game, and five on the car drawing," I said over my shoulder as I picked up a couple of lunch specials for the booth next to Junior's.

Actually, the car drawing ticket wasn't community altruism—I didn't have a car, and could use even a junkheap prize like a dented silver '79 Pacer, though that was beside the point.

"I can't sing, I can't dance, and unless waitressing counts, I haven't a single talent that can be put on display."

"I wasn't thinking of you being *on* stage," Junior said. She dabbed her napkin across a damp forehead. "We could use a few more volunteers for carnival crowd control and cleanup—"

"Sure, I bet Tory's ambition in life is to run the carnival cleanup crew," said Del, who, along with the rest of the noon crowd, was eavesdropping in the good-hearted spirit of small-town nosiness. "I wish I could help shovel half-eaten hot dogs and empty pop cups too. But I just know I'm going to be busy."

Flashy, red-haired Del is my late husband's first cousin. We shared a trailer just on the edge of town, overlapping shifts at the cafe, and her twelve-year-old son.

We also both disliked Junior, though Del was a bit more vocal.

I pretended to swab the counter on the other side of the cafe's long wall, across from the booths with a short row of tables in between as a buffer. It was wise to be at a safe distance if Junior and Del were going to start.

"You interrupted me. Those were just examples," Junior said firmly, if faintly. "I didn't mean for Tory to think—"

"Well, that's just what Tory thought," Del said, leaning over the divider between the cafe and the kitchen, clipping an order to the stainless steel carousel hanging from the ceiling and giving it a spin. "Isn't that right, Tory?"

"I'm not paid to think," I said, trying to stay out of it.

"I'm paid to take this cheeseburger and fries to Stu McKee, and that's all I'm paid to do. Right, Aphrodite?"

In the kitchen, cafe owner and chief cook Aphrodite Ferguson grunted around her cigarette and continued flipping burgers.

Stu smiled and squeezed my elbow, which caused me to sternly repress a blush. Which caused me to turn to Junior and ask exactly what she had in mind.

Which was a mistake.

"It goes without saying that not everyone belongs onstage," Junior said, then, seeing my face, added a hasty disclaimer. "I'm not performing either. There are important jobs for those of us who don't have obvious talents."

With compliments like that, who needs insults?

"Hey, Tory does so have talent. In fact, she's *going* to be onstage," Rhonda Saunders, our other waitress, said from the back of the cafe where she had been whispering in Del's ear on and off during the entire conversation. "With me."

Rhonda's newest fashion incarnation was adapted directly from the late sixties. These days, she looked a little like a young Gloria Steinem, if Gloria had ever been a corn-fed, gum-chewing, nineteen-year-old waitress with big boobs.

I looked from Rhonda, who tucked her straight, center-parted blond hair behind one ear, to dark-haired pale Junior as she licked her white lips, to Del, then Stu, and the ten or so others in the cafe, who were all grinning expectantly.

Delphi loves a show.

"No," I said to Junior and Rhonda. "No," I said to Del and the rest. Except for Stu. I didn't say anything to him.

"Come on, Tory," Rhonda and Junior said at the same time, which proved Junior really was ill—she never lapsed into whiny slang.

While this was going on, I continued to pick up empty plates and refill coffee cups. I would have run the till, but no one left. They were all too busy watching, even though the noon hour was officially over.

"We'll be called Waitresse." Rhonda pulled a wrinkled sheet of notebook paper from her leather vest pocket and smoothed it on an empty table. "See?" She pointed at three inexpertly drawn figures. "Aren't the uniforms great? Just like fifties carhops, with little satin shorts and caps and roller skates and everything. You and Del will be the backup singers. I'll do the lead—"

"Whoa there," I interrupted. "I am not singing, and I am not roller-skating, and I will never wear satin shorts."

"But you gotta," Rhonda wheedled. "I need you there. Del's going to do it."

Like that was some sort of incentive. Del does all kinds of things that should only be attempted by professionals.

"Thanks," I said to her.

"Hey." Del smoothed her hands over her snug jeans and shrugged. "I thought it sounded like fun. Besides, it's an easy song to learn."

"What's that got to do with it? Lyrics aren't the problem. You've heard me in the shower." Not only has Del heard me, she has been known to complain loudly every time I try to sing. In the shower or out.

I had the feeling this conversation was getting out of hand, that everyone was forgetting a major point.

"I can't sing and I don't wanna," I said.

"Sing for us, Tory," a couple of guys called from a back booth. "Please, please."

"Yeah," chorused everyone else. Rhonda and Del were the loudest.

"All you have to do is glide around a little and go 'Shoop shoop' in the background, and do these little hand swoops like this," Rhonda said, demonstrating something that looked like it belonged on American Bandstand. In 1959. "There's hardly any singing, really." She grinned and refolded her drawing.

"*What?*" I asked, thoroughly confused.

"We're singing the shoop-shoop song, dummy," Del

said, picking up a burger plate from the counter. "In Rhonda's girl group called Waitresse. For the Delphi Phollies. This Sunday."

"Waitress?" None of this made any sense at all.

"No," she said patiently, "Waitresse, with an accent on the last *e*. And you know the song." She sang a couple of lines.

My mind reeled with the nightmare vision of my blobby self on roller skates, packed into satin shorts, onstage in front of everyone I knew, asking if it was "in his eyes."

"I don't want you to go onstage or anything public at all," Junior said quietly.

I turned to her gratefully. Maybe she would get me out of this.

"I just want you to drive me up to Webster this afternoon to check out the carnival before it gets here tomorrow morning."

This was a weird request—Junior and I aren't exactly close. She has always been too trim and pretty and fastidious and fussy for me. I am none of those things.

We tolerated each other politely at family reunions, and I took her hamburgers back for Aphrodite to throw on the grill a little longer. That was about it.

"What do you want me along for?" I asked, intrigued in spite of myself. "Besides, I don't have a car, you know that."

"Can't you borrow Del's? Clay has ours for the day, and we can talk about the rest later," she said quietly, glancing around.

"My car's in Ron's shop," said eavesdropping Del, peering at Junior's pale face. "You don't look like you're going anywhere anyway. What's the matter with you?"

"It's nothing, just a little headache. It doesn't matter," Junior said, swallowing several times. "Today is the last chance to check the carnival out before they set up here. It's my responsibility to do that since I recommended them. I have to go."

"Ooh, sounds really interesting," Del said, totaling up Junior's ticket. "What kind of dirt are you looking for?"

"We're not looking for any dirt," Junior said, exasperated. "Someone I know in Mobridge mentioned that we might want to keep a close eye on this particular carnival, that's all. So I intend to do just that, and afterward I want to have a little talk with the owner. It's nothing serious. I thought a witness would be helpful, on the off chance that I do see anything untoward."

Junior was the kind of person who actually used words like *untoward* in general conversation. Even when she didn't feel well.

"So, will you help?" she asked me quietly.

The whole thing sounded boring as hell, but I did get off work in less than an hour and had nothing important planned for the rest of the day anyway.

"Oh, all right, just give me a minute after work to run home and change. What car are we taking, by the way?"

Webster was a good forty miles north and east, a bit of a hike on foot.

"I don't . . ." Junior said as she stood up, then crumpled to the floor, unconscious.

Over the general confusion, with everyone on their feet trying to pick Junior up and call for help and milling around and making noise, I could hear Del.

"Jesus Christ, she only fainted. She's not dead. Give her some room to breathe."

It appeared that Del's diagnosis was correct; within seconds Junior was struggling to sit up and talk.

"Lie back down," Del said. "We'll get you some water. Rest a second."

Junior searched the faces bent over her and caught my eye. "Tory," she whispered, and crooked a finger for me to kneel down and listen.

I could barely hear her. "Go to Webster without me."

"I can't, Junior, I don't have a car. How will I get there?" I wasn't trying to weasel out of going. I was just stating fact.

"You can ride with me," someone said.

I looked up into Stu McKee's gorgeous green eyes with the laugh wrinkles at the edges. I was slightly horrified.

"I have to go to Webster this afternoon anyway for a Wheat Growers' meeting at the Super 8. I can drop you off at the carnival and pick you up after the meeting." Stu and his father ran the local seed and feed store, across the street from the cafe.

I searched the other faces but no one seemed to think Stu's offer was untoward. No one except for Del, who was grinning madly, if a little maliciously.

"Go with the man," she said wickedly. "It seems like a great solution to a sticky problem."

It was. That was the problem.

For over a month, Stu and I had been very careful not to be seen in public together except at the cafe, making awkward conversation, showing the whole world that I was just a waitress and he was just a customer and that we were emphatically *not* having an affair.

In a town with antennae tuned specifically for just such shenanigans, no one who didn't know from the start has caught on. Especially not Stu's wife, whose existence I tried to ignore, if not forget outright.

Here, then, was a perfect excuse to be seen with him in public. A reason to go out of town with him. To spend the afternoon at a motel, no less.

"That's perfect," said Junior weakly, still on the floor but getting a little color back, and some of her natural bossiness. "Go with Tory and look around too; see if you spot anything unusual."

I glanced at Stu, with his slightly receding sandy brown hair, sparkling eyes, and big smile. "No problem, I'll be happy to look things over with her."

He said this directly to me, holding out a hand to help me up. No one even noticed us; they were all fussing over Junior, who stood up shakily.

I looked away, not sure this was such a good idea, and thought of something to ask Junior.

"What exactly are we supposed to be looking for?"

Quietly she said, "You'll know it if you see it. Talk to the owner afterward. Tell me what he says."

"Tell you what he says about what?" I was sorry I'd ever agreed to go.

"Just watch," Junior said. "Please."

Rhonda was staring at Stu with narrowed eyes. "What time is your meeting over?" she demanded suspiciously.

"Six, six-thirty most likely," he said.

"Okay." She rattled the beaded fringes on her vest, obviously calculating. "That should get you back here in plenty of time, even if you walk around the carnival for an hour or so."

"Back in time for what?" I asked.

"Rehearsal." She grinned. "We got a lot of work to do before we sing on Sunday."

Shoop shoop.

2

....

Bauer and McKee

The eastern South Dakota map looks a little like a cross-stitch graph designed by a minimalist, nothing much on it but small towns every ten miles in all directions, with the odd ghost town gap as a reminder of our perpetual hard times. The ruler-straight north-south and east-west roads are broken only by the occasional curve thoughtfully provided to give drunken teenagers the opportunity to crash head-on every couple of years or so.

Like the rest of civilization, our two- and four-lane highways, and most of our county roads, are paved, though road construction is a never-ending process since no one has come up with a substance (outside of Aphrodite's lasagna) durable enough to survive the double whammy of 115-degree summers followed closely by −30-degree winters.

Narrow township roads, sometimes not much more than an unmarked path through a pasture, are gravel, a surface much better suited to the climate and population. Granted, gravel roads are dusty, pocked with

holes, impassable in the spring when rain turns the hard
pack into six inches of mush, and guaranteed to chip the
factory paint job of fools who drive good cars out in the
country. But the traffic is light enough (and the Highway
Patrol appropriation small enough) to render the 55-
miles-per-hour speed limit moot as long as you keep a
roving eye out for the various species of suicidal wild-
life.

Sometimes, you can drive sixty miles of back roads
and never meet another vehicle. But sometimes, by
unspoken agreement, every farmer in the county de-
cides to haul hay, transport cattle, or drive the John
Deere to the other field, all on the same day.

And if you happen to be traveling in the middle of one
of these agricultural migrations, it is an especially good
idea to remember that, in a state where everyone knows
everything about everyone, there are few people as well-
known, and easily recognized, as the local seed and feed
dealer.

And if you happen not to be married to this particular
seed and feed dealer, it is a really good idea not to look
as though you were enjoying riding in the same hot
pickup cab on the back county roads, meeting and
greeting a half dozen farmers, all of whom know the
aforementioned dealer, and most of whom I have
waited on some time or other.

Actually, it wasn't too hard to mask my enjoyment,
because I wasn't having a particularly good time.

By now, our relationship was past most of the un-
dressing in the dark/Was it good for you? awkwardness.

Unfortunately, our meetings were hard to arrange,
and so fraught with unspoken guilt that we rarely wasted
precious time out of bed. Talk was usually limited to the
kind of pre- and post-sex goofiness that passes for
conversation in couples who don't know each other well
enough to talk about the really important stuff yet. Like,
say, books and music.

My jeans were tight, and I was hot and uncomfortable
bouncing along the uneven roads in the noisy,
burgundy-upholstered truck cab, thinking it was a mis-

take to have agreed to ride anywhere with Stuart
McKee.

I shot a sideways glance at him. He lounged behind
the wheel, driving effortlessly with one elbow propped
out the open driver's side window, Keltgen Seed hat
pushed back on his forehead a bit, his soft, sandy hair
just long enough to be stirred by the wind.

He caught me staring and grinned, laugh lines etched
around his deep green eyes. Embarrassed, and suddenly
self-conscious, as though being together like this was
somehow more intimate than stolen afternoons, I
turned to watch the endless acres of nearly ripe wheat.

We'd traveled fifteen miles already without speaking.
If the silence wasn't exactly tense, neither was it exactly
easy. It seemed the perfect opportunity to have a Real
Conversation. If I could only think of something to talk
about.

"You got any music?" I asked, pleased for the brainstorm, if not the grammar. If we couldn't talk *about*
music, we could at least listen *to* some. "You know,
cassettes or something?"

"Sure, in the cubbyhole." He waved in the general
direction of the glove compartment. "Plug in anything
you like."

I sorted through wrinkled invoices, dust-coated
cough drops, and dented Hot Wheels cars, knowing that
there would be no Mozart or Gilbert and Sullivan or
New Age Jazz Fusion, but hoping against hope that we
shared some common musical ground. Like early Billy
Joel, or mid-career Simon (Paul or Carly), or any
vintage James Taylor. Even late Willie Nelson would do.

"Oh," I said.

"It's mostly country stuff." Stu shrugged. "Sorry."

"Don't apologize; it's your truck and your music," I
said, studiously not wondering why I was attracted to a
man with such pedestrian musical taste. Pedestrian
musical taste and a Bush-Quayle bumper sticker.

Stu's music collection was comprised entirely of Top
Ten Pop Country—Wynonna, Reba, Garth, Clint, and

the Travii (Tritt and Randy), none of whom could I listen to without cringing.

At least there wasn't any Elvis. Or Billy Ray Cyrus.

"Wait a sec. Here's another one." I fished a cassette from under a refolded North Dakota map and held up plaintive folkie Nanci Griffith. My good friend and future swimming pool namesake Neil Pascoe and I both loved her voice. This was an encouraging sign. I smiled.

"Oh," Stu said. "That one's Renee's."

"Oh."

That's what I said, anyway. What I meant was: Oh shit, son of a bitch, god damn. "Why don't we just listen to the radio?" It was tuned to a country station, of course.

Conversation stalled while Dwight Yoakam yodeled his way through a twofer and I tried to think of a subject, any subject, that wouldn't lead us back to Stu's wife.

"This is great, isn't it?" he asked out of the blue. I must have looked surprised, because he continued, "I mean, actually spending some real time together."

"I don't know," I said carefully.

He turned to me, eyebrows raised, grinning. I sorta remembered why I was attracted to him.

"Well, yes, of course, it's great," I rushed. "But aren't *they* going to think it's weird? I mean us going off together. In the same vehicle. And all."

They, of course, was all of Delphi. *They* watched everyone like hawks. *They* picked up on the slightest irregularity in a relationship. And *they* reported it to each other at the speed of light.

There was no need to explain to Stu who *they* were.

"*They* aren't going to think shit," he said calmly. "*They* will assume that I'm a nice guy for offering. And *they* will know you're a dip for letting Junior hornswaggle you into agreeing to go. Right?"

"No kidding."

"And *they* will expect us to spy properly and come back with something juicy for Junior."

"I'll be damned if I can figure out what it is Junior wants us to see," I said. "What do you suppose she expects us to find? The only thing I can think of is Health Department violations."

"You mean old grease in the corn dog fryers?" Stu asked, waving at a passing farmer. "That's too easy. If people were getting sick from carny food, we'd have heard by now."

"Cheating on the midway games?" I hazarded.

"Nah, that's SOP. Everyone knows those booths are rigged. And only an idiot plays them."

"What, then?" I drew a blank.

"Drugs, I suppose. And prostitution. That's the kind of thing that gets a minister's wife worked up, isn't it?"

"I'll grant you, Junior sees illicit sex in the woodwork and wants it all stopped," I said, "but that's too much of a stereotype. Besides, who would actually *pay* to have sex with the sleazy women who work in carnivals?"

"Who's stereotyping now?" Stu asked with a laugh. "Not everyone who works in a carnival is sleazy. Besides, isn't it possible, on a purely hypothetical basis, of course, that a young man with a taste for adventure just might be lured by the bright lights into taking one of the girls out for a date? So to speak? Hypothetically."

I considered this during the radio weather report, which predicted, surprise, more hot muggy weather.

"So how would a hypothetical young man go about arranging a 'date' with a nonsleazy carnival hooker?" I asked—hypothetically, of course. "And exactly how old were you? And who were you with? And what did it cost? And did you catch anything?"

Enquiring minds want to know.

"You sure you want to hear this?" That was a patently stupid question, and he knew it. "It's not exactly a pretty story."

"You brought it up," I said primly. "Let's just think of it as research—preparation for our undercover work at the carnival this afternoon."

I was amazed. This was the longest out-of-bed conversation we'd ever had, and what were we talking about? Stu having sex with someone else.

"Well," he said, lifting his hat so the air could blow under it, "it was the summer after I graduated. Me and Pete and Pat Jackson were down at the state fair. Eighteen-year-olds could still drink three-two beer then, and we spent most of the afternoon at the beer garden, when we decided to stroll down the midway a while. We were pretty well lit, and we thought we were irresistible."

He grinned and shrugged in a you-know-how-kids-are way.

Though Stu was a couple of years ahead of me in school, and I was too busy being infatuated with my future late husband to care much, I still could not have avoided noticing him.

Twenty-some years ago, before the slight paunch, with a full head of hair, when the laugh lines were just tracings, he *was* irresistible.

Unfortunately, he was still pretty much irresistible.

"Anyway," he said, "we stopped at the balloon pop booth. The woman in charge seemed really old, but was probably all of thirty-seven. She let us know in no uncertain terms that she was available to show us a good time. For a price."

"She said it just like that? With no preamble?" I asked, unbelieving. "What did the people in line think?"

"There wasn't anybody else in line. And I hardly think that hookers worry much about subtlety, Tory."

"I suppose not. It's not very romantic, though," I said.

"We were young, drunk, and horny," Stu said patiently. "Romance wasn't exactly our prime consideration."

"I suppose not," I said again, chewing a lip. "What then?"

"We drew straws. Pat won. I came in second, and Pete was last. Fifteen bucks for a quickie behind the booth, scared to death that someone was going to stumble into us." He looked over at me with a small smile. "Not the best experience of my life. Pete loved it, though. Pat too. They went back three or four times. And tried to get me to go along with them." Stu paused for a second. "He's back, you know," he said, changing the subject abruptly. "In Delphi, I mean."

I assumed he meant Pete, since Pat had never left town.

"On parole again? Or has he been out for a while? It's hard to keep track."

As kids, identical twins Pete and Pat Jackson got into the kind of trouble that most rural boys get into. The kind that gets taken care of under the table—petty theft, break-ins, underage drinking. Corner any grown-up South Dakota boy and you'll hear the same story.

Not too long after their carnival adventure with Stu, Pete and Pat found serious trouble. They borrowed a case of beer and a fifth of Lord Calvert from a neighbor, along with his '58 Olds.

A night of joyriding wouldn't have been treated too severely in those days, since DUIs weren't handed out like flyers the way they are now, and the twins intended to return the car, with a couple of extra miles on her but no worse for the wear.

Unfortunately, on their last swing down Highway 281, an ill-kempt two-lane in those days, they blew a tire at upwards of 95 miles per hour, lost control, and smashed into an oncoming car, killing the driver, his wife, and three of their four children.

Those days also preceded air bags and automatic seat belts.

In the inexplicable way some accidents happen, Pete and Pat both walked away with only minor injuries—right into the arms of the police, who charged Pete with grand theft auto, burglary, driving under the influence, and five counts of vehicular homicide. Pete pleaded guilty, spent the next eight years in the penitentiary, and has been in and out for minor and major offenses in several states since.

Pat completed one hundred hours of community service (which was much more like hard labor back then) and married Patricia Rhorbach, Pete's old girlfriend. The Pats now run Jackson's Hole, Delphi's only bar. And Pete flits in and out sporadically between stretches in jail and other unknown adventures.

"Isn't he always on parole?" Stu asked. "Or probation?"

"Whatever. Doesn't it strike you as odd that they get along so well? I mean, Pete never seems to mind that Pat missed going to jail *and* married his old girlfriend."

Delphi would not be Delphi if considerable time wasn't spent dredging up old grudges and remembering past scandals.

"Nah." Stu shrugged. "Ancient history. Pete and Pat always raised hell. If they hadn't got caught then, it would have happened sometime. It's too bad they took a whole family along."

"Yeah," I said glumly. So much for lively conversation.

We bounced along on the uneven road, not speaking, nearly hypnotized by the almost-amber waves of grain.

Stu sat up suddenly and lunged for the dials on the radio, which had been droning the hourly news.

"What's going on?" I started to ask, but he shushed me as he adjusted the volume.

I hate being shushed, and was going to say so, but something the radio announcer said stopped me.

". . . a series of break-ins last week in Mobridge and surrounding areas. Mostly small, portable items such as jewelry and home and car stereos have been taken, though the total in lost items and damage has now exceeded ten thousand dollars. Anyone having information about these thefts is asked to call the Mobridge city police department." The announcer rattled off the number to call.

"Why does Mobridge ring a bell?" I asked.

"Don't you remember? Junior said someone from Mobridge told her to keep an eye on our carnival. That's why we're on our way to Webster—to check out the carnival for your unconscious cousin before it sets up in Delphi"—he grinned—"and robs us of all our small portable valuables."

"So we're supposed to look for stereo-toting bad guys, huh?" I wondered. "Hookers and druggies and thieves, oh my."

"Ah, but it's a clue for the famous detective team of McKee and Bauer to unravel."

"No, you discover clues and unravel mysteries," I corrected. "And for your information, it's Bauer and McKee."

"And are *McKee* and Bauer going to meet somewhere to compare notes later this afternoon?" He waggled his eyebrows, a goofy expression that struck me as adorable.

I squashed a grin. "That all depends—Bauer has reserved Room 238 at the Webster Super 8 Motel for the express purpose of clue comparison. If McKee has anything interesting to show Bauer, he may bring it along to the Clue Room after his meeting, which Bauer presumes will actually end before the previously stated six o'clock time frame."

"Before five." He laughed, eyebrows wagging again. "And McKee intends to show Bauer something *really* interesting."

I hoped so.

3

....

Hamilton Bogner's International Extravaganza

A good many experiences seem better on paper or on the big screen than in Real Life. Take sex in a bathtub, for instance—it sounds so warm and cozy and romantic. And sexy. Kevin Costner and Susan Sarandon sloshing around among the candles fueled many a fantasy.

Unfortunately, reality is a whole other story. Sure, with a lot of jockeying for position and tight-lipped concentration, you can actually get the job done. But believe me, unless you have gills and cast-iron kneecaps—and think pruney skin is sexy—you aren't going to enjoy it.

Most of high school belongs in that category too. Do you know a single person who enjoyed going to a prom? Even in my time, when guys wore their own suits and girls sewed up scoop-necked, short-sleeved, empire-waisted confections, the main objective was to get laid before curfew or get drunk trying. The dance itself was incidental, a flashbulb-popping ordeal to be endured before the real festivities.

As far as I can tell, the only difference now is that kids often get the sex portion of the evening out of the way first, and then drink until they throw up on their rented designer formal wear.

Undercover detecting seems interesting in print too—Kinsey Millhone and any number of interchangeable Dick Francis heroes make it all look so romantic and dashing.

I had a sinking notion that the reality might not be quite so much fun. Kinsey, et al., usually knew what they were looking for. And they got paid.

I had only Junior's cryptic instructions for my volunteer mission, and not a clue as to where to begin. I seriously considered faking it, telling Junior that everything at Hamilton Bogner's International Extravaganza was hunky-dory.

And I would have done just that, but Webster is a small town, and its diversions were too similar to Delphi's to be tempting. Besides, I had two hours to kill before the big rendezvous back at the motel.

"Just wander and observe," Stu had suggested. "You never know what you'll see."

So I wandered and observed.

What I mostly observed was the nifty system carnivals have for jacking up the price of a spin on a rusty ferris wheel. You don't pay cash for individual rides anymore. You buy a book of coupons, and each ride requires a set number of coupons as the price of admission. The smaller and less popular the ride, the fewer coupons needed. A ride that goes really high or really fast—or, conversely, is slow and gentle enough for parents to accompany small children—takes more. Mid-terror rides like the Tilt-a-Whirl and Scrambler, and juvenile attractions like the fun house and the fortune-telling booth, are cheaper.

The beauty of this system is that the coupons cost an unwieldy amount (say, twenty-seven cents apiece) that doesn't lend itself easily to mental addition, so most people don't realize they're paying $1.32 to be flung upside down in the Zipper for two and a half minutes.

And though the rides always cost an even number of coupons, the coupons are always packaged in odd-number lots. You may save money by buying in bulk, but you're always left with an extra ticket at the end, and of course, nothing on the midway costs one coupon.

Since Junior hadn't offered to reimburse my under-cover work, I decided to keep expenses to a minimum; an easy task since I'd rather set my feet on fire than ride on a roller coaster.

I am, however, a sucker for cotton candy, so I bought a froth of pink spun sugar from a shaggy young fellow with the name "Larry" stenciled on the breast pocket of his black HBIE T-shirt. Larry may or may not have been his actual name—I had already noticed "Moe" and "Curly" running the Wheel of Fortune and the carousel. I suspected the merry folks at Bogner International had a whimsical attitude when it came to identification.

To be honest, this particular carnival was a little larger and a little cleaner than I had expected. I squinted in the bright afternoon sunshine and counted more than a dozen rides, the ones you'd expect in a small traveling midway ("International" notwithstanding). While the rides were obviously not new, or newly painted, they still looked to be in good repair, at least to my totally untrained eye.

Nothing actually fell over or came to pieces while I wandered, and the customers, mostly teenagers, seemed to be having a good, if noisy, time.

The carny people, all wearing identical black Bogner T-shirts and blue jeans or shorts, ran their rides or hawked cheap souvenirs or tried to tempt passersby to win enormous purple pseudo-Barney dolls. They also shouted back and forth to each other, carrying on conversations in the dust.

It was easy to imagine that these people were a small community and that we, as customers, were just walk-ing wallets. Necessary economically, but otherwise a pain in the butt.

Kind of like cafe customers.

I strolled past the fun house, which appeared to be an unhooked semitrailer on wheels. Lurid paintings and signs promised such horrors as the Evil Hall of Mirrors, the Lair of the Giant Spider, and the Walking Dead. Since sincere-sounding screams, shrieks, and thumps came from inside the trailer, the terrors must have been marginally realistic.

As I stood and watched, a group of maybe eighth or ninth grade girls thundered out the back door and down the stairs, blinking at the bright sunlight, a little pale, but giggling and obviously enjoying themselves.

Two of them whispered to the others and pointed to something across the walkway. The others giggled and then huddled, whispering furiously to each other, all the while peeking over their shoulders and squeaking in that supremely annoying pitch only adolescent girls can reach.

I wondered what had caught their interest. The only ride in that area was the ferris wheel, a midway standard with twenty or so rusting gondolas swinging between two thirty-foot rotating rings. The very notion of twirling up and around on one made me shudder. Then I saw what made them giggle.

They had spotted the wheel operator, leaning laconically against the brake handle, toothpick hanging from the corner of his mouth, arms folded, squinting in the sunshine, and smiling in their direction.

No wonder the teenies were unnerved—this young man was no stereotypical carnival employee.

With shoulder-length curling black hair tucked under an HBIE cap, rippling muscles shown to perfection in a T-shirt at least two sizes too small, and jeans tight enough to assure that the muscles weren't acquired in compensation for any physical shortcoming, he was handsome enough to attract even my attention.

Not that I have any interest in young men with smoldering eyes and great buns. But these girls certainly did, and as I walked past, they dared each other to go over and talk to him.

"You do it."

"Why don't you? You're the one who thinks he's so cute."

"Oh, and like you don't think he's gorgeous too, Angela. Give me a break. Go on."

"Oh jeez, he's looking over here. No, don't look!"

"Shit, he knows we're talking about him. What do we do now?"

There was a minor panic as the girls huddled and blushed. I wanted to lean over and tell them to go home and play with their Barbie dolls.

That's what I did when I was thirteen.

They would probably not work up the courage to start a conversation with the hunk, and it wouldn't do any good for me to say anything anyway. Foisting unsolicited advice on the youth of America isn't my forte.

Mentally shrugging, I shot a glance at the young man. He caught my look, stood at attention on the platform, swept his hat off into a low bow, grinned, and beckoned me to ride.

I shook my head no.

He patted his chest in the general area of his heart over the name "Marko" on his pocket.

"Free rides today for big, beautiful women like you," he said with a laugh.

Big, beautiful women like me can usually deal with pseudoflirtatious arrogant young men.

Even really handsome arrogant young men.

"Thanks anyway," I said, fixing him with what I like to call the Mother Look. Even though I've never had children of my own, I practice plenty on Del's twelve-year-old Presley.

The Look usually sends males between the ages of eight and twenty scuttling, with the irresistible urge to do homework or clean up their rooms.

It didn't phase Marko.

"It'd be the ride of your life," he shouted after me, a comment that amused several eavesdroppers.

"I'd go for it if I was you, honey," called a woman with bad teeth and seriously big hair behind the counter of a souvenir booth festooned with T-shirts and ugly hats, just down and across from the ferris wheel. Her T-shirt was also about two sizes too small. "Believe you me, Marko's got what it takes to satisfy."

She puffed on a cigarette and cackled lewdly. I didn't check, but I thought I could hear Marko hooting faintly behind me.

There was no way to get out of a situation like this gracefully, so I just hitched up my dignity and continued on.

At least I had something to report back to Junior now—the ride operators were impertinent. Unfortunately, I didn't think rudeness interested Junior. But so far that was all I'd found.

The noise level on the carnival grounds was intense, with mechanical clankings and groanings and the high motor whine of the rides competing with wheezing Sousa marches that blared from speakers at each site.

The crowd was still sparse, though I knew that later in the evening, when temps cooled a little, it would be jammed. Even so, the screaming was constant, a background blanket of sound.

There were already a few young couples pushing strollers and trying to corral enthusiastic toddlers. They looked fresh and enthusiastic themselves, spending some quality time with the kiddies.

Give them an hour or two here in Parent Hell and see how they look.

The funnel cake booth was calling me, the hot smell of cinnamon-and-sugar-coated fried dough reminding me I'd forgotten to bring my toothbrush along.

Stu should be happy I didn't crave onion rings.

As I waited for Daisy to finish my order, and hoped she would continue to turn her head as she sneezed, a small voice spoke near my ear.

"Don't pay any attention to Midge."

The speaker was a youngish, frail-looking blonde about my height, wearing a carny T-shirt. She nodded toward the souvenir booth. "Midge has a nasty sense of humor and just likes to embarrass people."

"Don't worry about me, ah"—I paused and glanced down—"Lily."

This chest inspection routine could get awkward.

"Besides, Marko over there started it," I said.

Lily blushed. "Oh, no. Marko's really nice, he didn't mean anything at all. It's Midge who turns everything around and makes it sound bad."

So it wasn't just town girls, or the very young, who were smitten by Marko. Midge was mid-fifties if she was a day, and my best guess put Lily in her early twenties.

"Whatever," I said. I wasn't willing to argue. I wasn't expecting to get to know these people well enough to care who had the worst manners.

Lily stood there, still gazing longingly back at the ferris wheel. This seemed like a good opportunity to slip away. I get enough impromptu conversation with strangers at work and don't look for it on my off-time.

When I turned to go, Lily caught my arm and fished inside her T-shirt. "I'm not supposed to show anyone this, but see what Marko gave me."

She flashed a cheap-looking turquoise cross on a chain. I'm no judge of jewelry, fine or otherwise, but it looked like an ordinary necklace to me, though it obviously meant a lot to Lily.

In fact, if Lily was indiscreet enough to show her treasure (after being warned not to, apparently) to someone she just met, she would probably be a good source of inside information on the workings of the carnival.

Lily was still gazing at her necklace, and it occurred to me that she was likely just a lonely kid. Somewhere in the Book of Ethics, there was probably a rule against grilling lonely kids under false pretenses for officious first cousins.

On the other hand, she seemed to want to talk.

"So, do you like working in a carnival?" I asked, a general enough question. Continuing down the midway seemed a good idea. Midge was frowning in our direction.

"It's okay," Lily said, hands pushed into the back

pockets of her jeans. "This is my first summer with the troupe, and it takes a little time to get used to being on the road." She pulled her hands out and tucked the cross back inside her shirt.

"What do you do? I mean, what is your particular job? With the troupe?"

See, I'm picking up carnival lingo already.

"Well, uh, um . . ." She scratched her head and thought for a second. "I guess you could call me a floater. Yeah, a floater."

She nodded, agreeing with her own terminology.

"So, what does a floater do?" I asked. "Exactly."

A small grin played at the corners of her mouth. "Well, floaters don't have a specific workstation; we take over when the booth regulars need a break or something. And do other stuff."

"Do you run the rides?"

"No, only men run the rides, except for the little kid ones, like the merry-go-round. Most of us women aren't strong enough to pull the brake handles. I know I'm not."

She flexed her skinny arm for me.

"We're just kind of around, in general, whenever anyone needs us. We get assignments on and off during the day."

"Sort of like the relief girls at the cafe where I work," I said.

"Yeah." She laughed. "We relieve people. Do you work here in Webster?"

Turnabout is fair play. I could answer a question or two.

"No, I live and work in Delphi."

That stopped her short.

"I've always wanted to see Delphi," she said, and was quiet for a minute. Then she smiled. "We're going there tomorrow, you know, maybe I'll see you again."

"Well, I'm not much of a carnival person," I said, "but if you come to the cafe in the morning, I'll treat you to a piece of pie."

Aphrodite doesn't encourage freebies, but I felt sorry

for the kid. She looked like she could use the calories to bulk up those muscles a little.

We walked a little farther, stepping carefully over the electrical cables that crisscrossed the pathway. Up ahead was the manager's trailer, my next stop on this wild-goose chase.

I was going to say good-bye, or gently suggest that Lily must have some work to do, when a small, middle-aged guy with a droopy mustache, wearing a cowboy hat and glasses, poked his head out the door of the square ticket booth and hollered.

"Hey, Lily, you're on."

"Oops." She giggled. "Got to go relieve someone." She waved and skipped off, and then stopped and turned around.

"Maybe we'll run into each other. In Delphi, I mean."

4

....

Ham and Cheese

I want it known that I don't like to lie and I've never liked lying.

Lying makes me nervous. It makes my neck itch and my nose drip. It makes me say stupid things that I always regret.

One time I told Willard Hausvik that his hero, Fran Tarkenton, was my all-time favorite quarterback too. I actually thought it'd shut him up for a while.

What it got me was the shy offering of a different football fact every morning at the cafe. For a month, I was bombarded with Tarkenton statistics, Tarkenton photographs, and Tarkenton play-by-play recounts as viewed through the elderly Hausvik perspective.

In desperation, I finally said I believed that sportswriters pretty well agreed that Joe Montana was King of Football—and a whole lot cuter than Fran to boot.

To which an aggrieved Willard muttered something about not always believing what you read, and moved to one of Del's tables to bore her for a while.

It's not just lying that bothers me. It's the lies themselves—oily half-truths and blatant misstatements that, once uttered, become woven into the fabric of our lives.

Like Nicky solemnly vowing (in front of several witnesses, including my mother) to "forsake all others," a promise he never had any intention of keeping.

Even worse are the lies we tell ourselves.

My being here in Webster, pacing back and forth in front of Hamilton Bogner's trailer, was a case in point.

I could pretend all day that I was doing Junior a favor, but I'd never willingly done Junior a favor in my life and would not have started now if I hadn't needed a cover story for a late-afternoon tryst with a married man.

And I was trying to concoct another while blending into the milling crowd. Neither was an easy task.

I couldn't very well knock on the door and tell Mr. Bogner (if indeed Mr. Bogner was not a Betty Crocker–style invention) that my cousin sent me to ask something, except she fainted before she could tell me what.

I considered saying I was a magazine writer doing undercover research, but decided against it mostly because I suspect undercover writers rarely announce their presence.

I chewed my lip and considered an idiotic story about a lost wallet. A lost child.

A lost self-respect.

I wandered back and forth, deciding finally to give it up—to tell Junior the truth, that the whole idea was stupid—when the door to the trailer swung open.

A very large man with a very large shiny bald head leaned out and said, "You're wearin' a path out there, honey. I been watching you through the winda for the last fifteen minutes, waitin' for you to make some kinda decision. I finally said to myself, 'Ham, this woman wants to talk to you and she can't bring herself to walk right up these stairs and knock on your door.' Am I right or am I right?"

He saved me the trouble of answering by continuing almost immediately.

"Hamilton Bogner here," he said, holding out a huge right hand which I shook gingerly. "Owner, manager, proprietor, public relations director, and father figure to this marvelous array of American capitalism at work."

He grinned widely and said, "Call me Ham."

I guess I had pictured Hamilton Bogner to be a smallish, graying, hesitant man, sort of like the Wizard of Oz.

I hadn't expected a hearty, moving mountain wearing a polo shirt and plaid polyester pants of the type and color seen usually on older amateur golfers.

And I especially hadn't expected him to be sitting at the window of his office trailer, watching me.

He turned and went back inside, motioning for me to follow.

Since I'd already blown the incognito part, I decided to find out what I could the direct way—by asking questions and telling the truth.

He pointed to a swivel office chair opposite a metal desk littered with papers and an adding machine whose tape looped and spiraled across the desk and down to the floor. On top of some irregularly stacked ledgers at the corner closest to me sat a Melmac plate with a few slices of cheese whose edges cracked and curled slightly. Colby, by the look of it.

Old Colby.

"Have a seat. I was just about to get myself a cold one," he said, rummaging in an upper cabinet for glasses and then in the small refrigerator. "Want some?"

"No thanks," I said, uncomfortably swiveling the chair back and forth.

I was hot. There was an inefficient ceiling air unit running, but the temp in the trailer had to have been in the high eighties anyway. No wonder the cheese was curling.

"I can see I'm interrupting some bookwork. I'd better go."

"Nonsense," he said as he turned sideways to get past and behind the desk to sit down. He carried a bottle of wine and two small juice glasses. Beads of condensation ran down the bottle.

"The French don't drink wine from stems anymore, you know. They use regular glasses to allow the bouquet to develop fully."

The French also eat snails, I thought.

I said, "You're not from South Dakota, are you, Mr. Bogner?"

He twisted a jointed metal corkscrew down onto the bottle. It made me think of a guy called the Unknown Comic, whose shtick included twirling the top of a corkscrew in imitation of the Linda Blair headspin in *The Exorcist.*

"Ham, I told you, call me Ham." He poured both glasses three-quarters full of some kind of white wine and set one down in front of me. He sniffed his glass, swirled it around a couple of times, then downed the contents in one gulp.

"Great stuff." He sighed exaggeratedly, then leaned back in his chair, fingers laced on his stomach. "How'd you know I wasn't from around here?"

"In South Dakota, 'a cold one' always means beer." I smiled, pointing at the wine bottle.

"Good call. What are you, a detective?"

"No, Mr. Bogner—"

"Ham," he warned genially.

I sniffled a little and thought furiously. The truth, Tory, I commanded myself. Just the truth.

"I'm, um, a writer." I scratched my neck. "With *Newsweek.*"

Anyone have a gun? I could just shoot myself right now and get it over with.

"I'm doing a feature on carnival workers. You know, how they live. Where they come from. What they do on their off-time. You know"—I faltered—"that sort of thing. The kind of personal stuff that really interests people."

Did I mention that I also babble when I lie?

Ham raised an eyebrow and poured himself some more wine.

"Is that so?" he asked neutrally.

Even though I'd decided against drinking wine in a hot trailer with a newly acquainted carnival owner/father figure, I took a sip to give myself time to come up with a brainstorm that would get me out of this ridiculous situation.

"Wow, this is really good," I said, meaning the wine.

"Clos du Bois, chardonnay, Alexander Valley, 1991. Fruity with a nice oak finish," he said, presumably in wine code. "I like it too. Here, have some more."

He refilled my glass before I could protest.

"I don't believe I've ever met a magazine writer before," he said, meaning me.

He was plainly having a hard time accepting that a reporter from a major newsweekly would show up on his doorstep unannounced.

"Well, I'm not really a magazine writer." I sipped again, thinking furiously. "Not yet, anyway. I'm just sort of working freelance right now. Hoping to get enough information on carnivals in general to sell a story. Somewhere. Because they really interest me. Carnivals, I mean."

I sounded so sincere, I started to believe myself.

Apparently Ham believed me too; he relaxed and smiled and offered me a piece of stale cheese.

"So, what do you want to know?"

"Tell me a little about your outfit—how long have you been the owner? Have you always been on the road? How large is your circuit?"

I figured a freelance wannabe would ask the obvious questions first. I'd read that getting the interviewee to talk about himself is always a good idea.

"Hamilton Bogner's International Extravaganza was established in 1973 when I bought and combined two smaller shows," he said.

They'd have to have been real small shows if HBIE was the sum total.

"We've been on the road ten months a year since and have traveled to many countries and performed for heads of state on four continents."

I'd have been more impressed with this if I hadn't already seen a faded carnival poster pinned to the bulletin board proclaiming in large letters HBIE's visits to THREE WESTERN CONTINENTS—CANADA, THE UNITED STATES AND MEXICO.

"Do most of your people stay with you the whole season, or is turnover high?"

Ham crossed his arms over his ample chest and leaned back in his chair, which gave a protesting creak.

"We get a lot of carny groupies each season; some of 'em are just unhappy kids who think life on the road is some sorta romantic journey instead of just plain hard work in the hot sun. Runaways who hate their parents or small-town life or have had a run-in with the law and need a fast ticket out. Most of them give up and go back home in a couple weeks.

"But there's a few with traveling in their blood, and generally they sign on and stay the whole season and come back the next. Some of my people have been with me for going on twenty years.

"Say . . ." He sat up and narrowed his eyes at me. "Are you recording?" There was accusation in the voice and real displeasure.

"Huh?" I asked, feeling like a kid caught with a hand in the cookie jar. I should have known I could never fool anyone into thinking I was a writer.

"Recording," Ham said slowly, pointing at my purse. "Taping this conversation with one of those little foreign cassette things."

I laughed, nervous but relieved. "No, I'm not recording anything."

I held up my hands to show him they were empty.

He relaxed back into his chair. "Well, then, aren't you going to write any of this down for accurate quotes?"

Shit, I'd forgotten all about note taking. I'd never even make Jimmy Olson, much less Lois Lane.

"Um, yeah, uh, sure," I said, rummaging in my purse for anything even remotely resembling a notebook. All I could find was a nearly full pad of unused green tickets from the cafe.

I sat up straight, trying to look more like a writer and less like a waitress taking an order, and wrote "Hamilton Bogner" under the Delphi Cafe logo.

Ham had poured himself another glass of wine; almost half the bottle was gone already. "Where were we?" His hearty good humor had not exactly evaporated, but he was certainly more wary.

"Carny groupies," I wrote without looking up. "Law trouble."

"How about health care?" It seemed a logical question. Who treats hookers with gonorrhea? "I mean, I know if there's an accident or something, you'd use whatever local hospital. But for everyday things—colds, sprains, and stuff like that—do you have a doctor on call?"

"Dr.?" I wrote.

"We are very lucky to have a doctor traveling with us this summer. Dr. William Aker, from Harvard Medical School and Johns Hopkins, takes care of all our medical needs."

An awfully fancy pedigree for a seedy little carnival, I thought. They probably picked him up somewhere on that Mexican continent.

I wrote "Wm. Aker—Harvard/Hopkins Rx."

I was warming up; I even had a question I was genuinely curious about.

"What about floaters?" I asked.

"What about floaters?" he repeated flatly, perhaps tired of the Q & A.

"Well, I was talking to Lily, one of your employees, earlier, and she told me that floaters are sort of on call, ready to relieve other workers whenever they're needed. It sounds interesting. How many floaters do you need in addition to the regular staff?"

Ham pulled a pair of half-glasses from his shirt pocket and arranged them on his nose. "Lily Mitchell is one of those troubled youngsters I was talking about earlier," he said coldly. "She joined us just over a month ago, and frankly, I don't think she'll be with us much longer." He peered over the glasses at me. "However, that particular bit of information is strictly off the record."

He frowned as I wrote "Lily Mitchell—trouble—gone soon," but nodded when I drew a line through it.

It was past time to end the pseudointerview and I hadn't picked up a single usable piece of information for Junior, though I could show her the notes to prove at least I had tried.

Ham wasn't waiting for me to get around to ending it officially. He punched a string of numbers into the calculator. The already long tape grew longer, with many of the totals printed in red.

He paused and looked up. "It's been pleasant talking to you, Miss . . ."

I had forgotten to introduce myself. "Bauer, Tory Bauer."

Actually it's Mrs., but if I was pretending to be a writer, I could just as well pretend I'd never been married. Or widowed.

"Miss Bauer, I am terribly busy today. Please send me a copy of your article when it's printed. And come back to Bogner's International Extravaganza any time and bring your friends. Have a couple of complimentary ride passes."

The hearty father figure had been entirely replaced by the owner/manager.

The busy, humorless owner/manager.

He handed me a thin red booklet of tickets and shook my hand.

"Thank you for taking the time to talk to me," I said, "and sorry for—"

The door suddenly slammed open and the man in the booth with the drooping mustache, the same one who had called Lily away, burst into the trailer. "Doc" was stenciled on his HBIE shirt.

"Yes?" Ham asked him impatiently. "You need something?"

Doc glanced back and forth between us, crumpling his cowboy hat between sweaty hands, and swallowed.

"It's Marko again," he said to the floor. "You'd better come."

"Son of a bitch," Ham muttered through clenched teeth as he opened the upper-right desk drawer with one hand and slipped something small from the drawer into his pants pocket. I tried to peek over the desk unobtrusively into the drawer, but Ham closed it too quickly.

A thin mournful man with thin scraggly hair, Doc nodded imperceptibly at me. Or maybe at Ham. It was hard to tell since he was still looking at the floor.

If Doc was the mythical Dr. Aker, he sure didn't fit my image of a Harvard man.

"I have to go immediately, Miss Bauer. Thank you and please let yourself out." Ham slid past me and was out the door before I could say anything more.

I sat for a second in the empty trailer, pretending to put my notes away before leaving. This time I didn't even fool myself.

Lying is something I try to avoid, but snooping is another matter entirely. Delphi citizens pride themselves on knowing as much about each other as we possibly can, and that knowledge is not always honorably obtained.

Granted, our Delphi style of snooping is not usually so blatant, but as a native, I have a reputation to uphold—and a first cousin to impress.

I was curious about what had sent Hamilton Bogner scuttling, of course, but I was more curious about what he'd taken from the desk. And what was left in that drawer.

With a sideways glance at the still-open door, I slipped behind the desk and rubbed my fingers together. My heart was pounding. I had a good view of the entire midway from Ham's window and could see a gathering crowd in front of the ferris wheel. No one was looking in my direction.

Ham had a strained headlock on a furious and dusty Marko, who tried to swing at a similarly dusty and furious young man with a bloody nose being held back by Doc and Midge.

Ham's desk looked pretty much the same from his side, except for open ledgers and a silver picture frame engraved "To the Boss," dated a year earlier. Among the twenty or so seedy-looking people lined up and posed in the shot, I recognized several current workers, including Midge, Doc, and a considerably less muscular Marko.

Figuring I had a couple of minutes before the fight broke up, I slowly slid the desk drawer open and peered inside.

And was thoroughly disappointed.

There was nothing inside but a folded newspaper section from the *Mobridge Tribune* and an official-looking square white pad with the name "Dr. William Aker" printed across the top of each sheet.

Blank prescriptions for the Harvard grad, huh?

Like the good detective I was pretending to be, I wanted to take a page from the pad, but they were numbered so I reluctantly decided against it.

Through the window, I could see that tempers evidently had cooled. Marko, head down, shuffled his feet in the dust as Hamilton Bogner, again the hearty public relations director, laughed and put a beefy arm around the other young man and handed him a small red booklet.

They were walking back toward the trailer as I closed the door softly behind me, nibbling a piece of stale cheese I had absentmindedly grabbed from the plate.

5

....

South Dakota Snailing

Eastern South Dakota is essentially one very large small town. Our boundaries do more to bind us together than keep us apart. Our similarities are instantly recognizable, and even our differences are the same—we belong to the same mainstream churches, we harbor the same starboard list regardless of political party. And when we defiantly do none of the above, we're still recognizably South Dakotan because the personality trait we prize above all others is a fierce and stubborn independence.

Thanks to inbreeding and the dearth of new blood for the collective gene pool (South Dakota's minimal population growth is due mostly to its own birth rate), we even look alike.

We squint in the bright sunlight. We talk with our mouths full. We love to hate mandatory seat belt laws. And we all keep an eagle eye on each other.

Sort of like the Delphi five hundred times a million. Or more accurately, times a thousand.

As a waitress, I have no choice but to meet an

extraordinary number of people, but even I'm amazed at how many people in-state I recognize.

Unfortunately, an even larger number recognize me. It is nearly impossible to travel inside a three-hundred-mile radius from Delphi and not run into someone you've met.

"I know you, you work at that restaurant in that little Greek town," I was told once at Mount Rushmore by a large loud woman who had perhaps attended the Tammy Faye Bakker Messner School of Makeup Application. "East river town, in the middle of nowhere, right? Only cafe in town, right? Terrible food, right? Me and my husband had heartburn for a week." She patted me on the shoulder in commiseration. "Small world, huh?"

Here in South Dakota, there are plenty of places to run, but nowhere to hide.

Which is why I spent ten minutes skulking around the corridors of the second floor of the Webster Super 8 Motel in the vicinity of Room 238, hoping desperately to avoid bumping into any of my 500,000 friends and acquaintances.

The license plates of several pickups and cars in the motel parking lot bore the lead number "57," indicating Spink County residents. Though I didn't recognize any of the vehicles, that was no guarantee.

We South Dakotans change trucks the way other people change their hairstyles.

Most of the visitors were probably here for the same reason Stu was. Or at least for his official reason, anyway.

One might wonder why I was so nervous. After all, I am a single woman and can, theoretically, see whomever I please wherever it suits me.

To which one might answer—Don't be an idiot. Delphi might not care overmuch what I was doing, but they'd certainly be interested in who I was doing it with.

When you get right down to it, they'd be just as interested in what the hell I was doing too.

So I carefully let myself into Room 238, relieved until

I remembered that I'd need to cross the hall again for ice.

Hamilton Bogner's white wine intrigued me, and I'd tried to buy some to share with Stu. A suitably romantic gesture, I thought. And romantic it would have been except the liquor store sold no wine that Ernest and Julio didn't bottle.

My request for "Clos do something, chardonnay" netted me a constipated expression from the clerk, so I settled for the local paper and a warm four-pack of Bartles & Jaymes.

Which meant I had to venture out again.

Key in hand, I tiptoed across to the chrome ice machine and quickly scooped up a bucketful of mostly cold water with a few random cubes floating in it, and was just closing my door when another door, a couple rooms down on the other side of the hall, opened.

"Lemee just get some more ice, babe, then we can reeealy start to party," hollered an obviously inebriated man whose voice sounded vaguely familiar. I heard the sound of sloshing water (ain't motel soundproofing grand?) and then a grunt of anger.

"What is this shit?" he bellowed, not rhetorically, since another voice told him to "Hold it down."

"Nothing but fucking water," the first voice shouted. "No fucking cubes."

An object that sounded suspiciously like the plastic ice bucket thoughtfully provided for the convenience of motel patrons bounced several times past my room and down the hallway toward the stairs.

I'm too short for the fish-eye to do me any good, and while I debated the wisdom of peeking just to satisfy my own curiosity, the man lumbered back to his room and slammed the door.

I listened and very carefully cracked open my door, but saw only an empty hallway and heard only the muffled laughter of two, or maybe three, people float across the hall.

I shrugged and shook out the soft two-piece outfit I'd

rolled up and stashed in my purse before leaving Delphi.

Though they couldn't blatantly market these things as sex clothes, especially not in my size, I still couldn't see anyone ever actually wearing something like this under regular clothing. Or trying to sleep in it.

Luckily for me, I had no intention of sleeping.

I'd barely put the finishing touches on my makeup (and despaired, again, of ever doing anything even remotely stylish with my hair) when I heard a soft knock on the door.

"Yoo hoooo," a quiet singsong voice intoned. "Message from the desk for Room 238." The tapping got a little louder, as did the voice. "Let me iiin, or I'll huff and I'll puff—"

"Ssh, someone's in the room across the hall," I whispered, and pulled Stu in and replaced the chain, safe now against prying eyes. "They can probably hear you."

"Oops," he said more quietly. He smiled and kissed me lightly on the nose. "Look what I got for you." He handed me a full grocery sack, took something off the top, and squashed it on my head.

I reached up with one hand and carefully removed it, trying not to mess my hair, though a glance in the mirror opposite the bed told me it was too late.

"Gee, thanks," I said, inspecting the DeKalb cap with the famous Flying Ear logo. "Just what I always wanted."

"I knew you'd like it. There's plenty more in the sack if you want them too. Also jackets, fridge magnets, and T-shirts."

Feed and seed dealers are walking boutiques, veritable cornucopias spouting freebies of the kind that will be classified as collectible fifty years from now but for the present are just plain tacky.

As a dealer, Stu was pretty well obligated to wear assorted agricultural logos on nearly every article of clothing. Currently, my favorite fantasy involved finding him dressed in a crisp white shirt with rolled-up cuffs, plain blue jeans, and not a single company name in sight.

"Wine coolers?" he asked with a raised eyebrow.

"Well, I wanted to get some good wine, but they didn't have any. I thought we might try these instead."

He turned the cap off one bottle and took a swig, grimaced, shrugged, and drank again, then handed the bottle to me.

I sat cross-legged on the bed, hoping he'd say something nice about the outfit I had on. Or better yet, something naughty.

"So . . ." He leaned on his elbow and traced cold circles with a finger on the bottom of my foot. "Did you see anything interesting at the midway this afternoon?"

"Oh, romantic chitchat. I love this part," I said, laughing.

"Hey," Stu protested, "we're supposed to be spying together, remember? I thought it'd be a good idea if we got our stories straight."

"Aren't we going back to the carnival, um, after, if you know what I mean?"

"I don't suppose we'll have enough time, um, after, if you know what I mean." He grinned and unbuttoned his shirt. "It's getting late."

I'd already seen more carnival than I cared to. This was a much better way to spend my time. I gave him an abbreviated rundown of the afternoon's action while he undressed.

"They're calling it 'floating' these days, huh?" Stu smiled.

"What do you mean?"

"Think. It'll come to you," he said over his shoulder.

I was too busy watching him to do anything else at the moment. Like Scarlett O'Hara, I'd think about it tomorrow.

"So how about we just say all that stuff happened while we roamed the grounds later?" He stood up and unzipped his jeans.

I still don't like lying, but this was a pretty minor request, considering.

"All right," I said only a little dubiously. "I also remembered to pick up a local paper. I'll check later to see if there's anything carnival-related. That should please Junior."

"Good idea, Sherlock. By the way," Stu said from the end of the bed, where he was neatly stuffing his socks into his shoes, "I have a surprise for you."

"If you're talking about that"—I pointed primly toward his general lower midsection area—"too late. I've already seen it."

"No, no, no," he said, crawling up to me on the bed. "It's not something you see, it's something you feel." He waggled his eyebrows.

"Sounds interesting," I said. "If you plan to make a lot of noise, I feel I should warn you that the walls here are not soundproof."

"Nope," he said. "No noise. No special equipment."

"Let's get to it, then. I haven't got all day, you know."

"Ah, but we can't ignore the preliminaries," he said, sliding a warm hand over the smooth fabric. "Soft," he mumbled, locating and circling the one area that wasn't.

"About time you noticed," I said. "One hundred percent silk. Romantic visions for the full-figured woman."

Large ladies have a secret corner in Lane Bryant behind the support hose and panty girdles—a section of lacy, frilly underthings. User-friendly lingerie, Del would say. Designed especially for the woman whose inhibitions are naked but whose body demands some sort of cover.

Stu should be impressed. It had cost a fortune in tips.

"I wasn't talking about the material," he said, nipping gently through the fabric. "I was talking about you."

"Oh, gee, thanks for reminding me," I said, exasperated. "You know, it's pretty hard to maintain a romantic mood if you're going to bring up body fat."

"Will you cut that out?" he said, fixing me with a stern look. "I meant it as a compliment. Don't be so sensitive. I like you just the way you are." He rolled back on one hip. "See?"

I looked. He was right.

"I hope this surprise of yours doesn't involve complicated positions. I can't stand on my head, and my legs aren't long enough to do anything really interesting," I said truthfully.

"You don't have to do a thing." He slipped his hand under the camisole and then raised it. "Your job is to lie there and enjoy." Each word was punctuated with a noisy kiss.

That was one advantage of a motel. We didn't have to be quiet or worry about being interrupted by my housemate or her noisy twelve-year-old son. Or Stu's wife.

At least that was the theory. In practice, we never quite relaxed anywhere. But we worked hard at it.

Stu nibbled and smooched his way back toward the end of the bed. "It's show time," he said softly, deftly undoing assorted snaps and ties.

I propped myself up on my elbows to look down at Stu's head, his soft brown hair brushing my inner thighs.

It was an interesting view, though not as interesting as the one in the large mirror on the opposite wall.

He paused and glanced up at me. "It won't be as much fun if you play Observation Team."

"I thought I'd take notes," I said, "so I could tell my other boyfriend about this wonderful new technique."

Stu smiled. "Let him do his own research. Lie back now, and close your eyes."

I did. And before very long, I was extremely glad to have taken Stu's advice.

"Good Lord," I said unevenly. "What do you call this?"

"The South Dakota Snail," he mumbled happily. "Nice, huh?"

"No kidding," I panted.

"What's that?" I asked a few moments later, finding barely enough air to speak.

"The antennae," he said. "Don't worry about it. You can figure it all out later."

"And that?" I asked.

"I just threw that in," he said, laughing, "to see if you were paying attention."

"Thanks," I said gratefully, and swallowed. "You know there are no snails in South Dakota."

"Will you please shut up and let me do my job?" he asked in mock disgust. "How's a man supposed to accomplish anything when talkative women interrupt him all the time?"

"Okay," I said, I think.

And very soon, I would have been unable to say anything at all.

Except "Wow."

6

....

The Clue Room

I've always thought that Erica Jong's Isadora Wing had her "zipless" fantasy backward. Isadora wished for aseptic encounters in which clothes melted magically away and conversation was unnecessary, where every detail was perfect and fabulous sex ruled the day.

Not too shabby, as fantasies go, though of course, by the end of that book, even Isadora realized that zippers and moods (and noisy air conditioners and voices in the hall) can't be wished away.

They can be ignored for a while if your mental filtration system is good, but sooner or later reality intrudes, bringing with it a messiness not included in anyone's fantasy.

Personally, I'd rather the aftermath be "zipless." How nice it would be to get out of bed already washed, dressed, and deodorized. No awkwardness, no wet spot, no fumbling for shoes and socks.

The reality was that we were on a tight schedule, on the second floor of an out-of-town motel, with two hallways and a parking lot to navigate without being recognized.

"I'll go down to the conference room first and pick up a couple more Frisbees," Stu said to the mirror, combing his hair. "I doubt if anyone even noticed that I was gone, but I can casually mention that we spent the last hour looking over the carnival, doing our civic duty."

He grinned. Some duty.

"You got about twenty minutes or so to get dressed and, um, whatever," he fumbled, "then we can meet at my truck in the front of the parking lot."

"No problem," I said, sitting up, sheet pulled neatly to my chin. "I'll shower and sneak out the side door, go down a block, and walk back to the parking lot from the direction of the carnival."

"Perfect." He flashed a wink back in my direction. "See you in twenty." He nodded and strode purposefully out.

I held my breath, listening carefully for doors to open along the hall as Stu's footsteps faded safely toward the staircase.

Relieved, with my hair pinned up (it wouldn't do, after all, to arrive home from a carnival with a wet head), I showered quickly and dressed, then stuffed the wrinkled silks back into my purse and resisted the urge to remake the bed.

Unopened newspaper tucked under an arm, the room keys prominently left on top of the TV, I put my ear to the door, listening, over the sound of my own pounding heart, for people in the hall.

I tiptoed out, with a quick backward glance to make sure I hadn't forgotten anything, then firmly and quietly pulled the door closed behind me. Leaving the keys inside saved the embarrassment of checking out just two hours after checking in.

However, it also meant that I was stranded in the open, no longer able to retreat to the safety of the room, and in sudden and utter panic because a door across the hall banged open.

Hysterical shouting from several voices, male and female, echoed along the hall.

In total confusion, I ducked across to the ice machine and hunkered down beside it, hoping that whoever these people were, they'd be too engrossed in their own troubles to notice me.

"Stay back! You keep away from me," a young voice warned, crying and shouting at the same time. "Leave me alone," she sobbed, "please just leave me alone."

"No, wait," a man pleaded, voice loud and slurred.

It was the same voice I'd heard before, tantalizingly familiar. Familiar and dangerous. And if I recognized the owner of that voice, he would more than likely recognize me as well.

I pushed back as far as I could, willing myself to be invisible. Or at least a lot smaller.

A crying girl, blond and frail, in a black T-shirt, miserable face streaked with mascara, clutched at her chest, holding what I knew to be a cheap turquoise cross on a chain.

Astonished, I watched Lily Mitchell run past me to the staircase.

"What the fuck are we supposed to do now?" the man in the still-open doorway asked.

Low voices conferred quietly for a minute. Two people, I thought in despair. Two upset, familiar people about to erupt into the hallway.

Two very good reasons to stay put.

"Okay," the same voice said, calmer now. "I'll go see if I can stop her before this gets out."

He took a couple of steps in my direction and then paused. "Oh, and Pat," he said, "why don't you straighten this mess up if you can? No point in drawing any more attention than we have to."

He waited for a murmured assent as the door closed, then turned and trotted, slightly unsteadily, down the hall. A grim stocky man with a Fu Manchu mustache and long dark hair tied in a thin ponytail. He wore a plaid shirt with the sleeves cut out, and looked neither right nor left.

I knew him. And I knew who else was in that room. Then I realized what Stu meant about floaters.

I had only a couple of minutes to get out of the building before the other one came out of the room.

Quiet didn't matter now, only speed. I walked quickly to the stairway and down two flights, then out the side door into the blinding late-afternoon sunlight.

Panting and anxious to tell Stu what I'd just seen and heard, I hurried as fast as the heat would allow around our prearranged one-block detour and ambled nonchalantly to the motel's front parking lot from a side street.

Stu's pickup was still in the same spot, next to a dusty blue Ford with Colorado plates. He was already there, leaning against the box on the far side, his back to me.

"God, you'll never believe what just happened," I said breathlessly, rounding the back of the truck.

"Tory, it's about time you got back here," he said with a wide-eyed stare that was unnerving but conveyed no actual meaning. "Look who I ran into."

My heart sank as I shaded my eyes and saw, finally, that Stu had been talking to someone who was leaning against the cab of the aged Ford.

A man with long dark hair, wearing a sleeveless plaid work shirt.

"Pete." I swallowed, forced a smile, and extended a hand. "Pete Jackson, I heard you were back. Haven't seen you in the cafe yet. Del will be glad to know you're home again."

That was a safe assumption, since Del was glad to see any breathing male.

I glanced pointedly at Stu and raised my eyebrows.

"Pete here needs a ride back to Delphi, and I told him it'd be no trouble for him to ride along with us," said Stu brightly. "I already told him I was taxiing you and that one more didn't matter. You don't mind, do you, Tory?"

"Shit no, why should I mind?" I lied cheerily. "Are you having engine trouble, Pete?"

"Naw." He patted the Ford. "This baby's gotten me through fourteen states so far this summer. But I gotta get back home for my shift at the bar. Pat can drive the truck home later."

He grinned as though that was a perfectly logical explanation.

"I better leave a note, though," Pete said, wafting smoke fumes with a beer undertow my direction. "Say that I'm going ahead with you."

He patted his pockets and then looked at Stu. "Got any paper? I'm fresh out."

Stu patted his pockets also and shook his head. They both turned and looked at me.

It was like being at a mime convention.

"Sure," I said, wearily digging in my purse, hoping the crumpled silks wouldn't pop out onto the pavement.

I tore a sheet off the pad and handed it to Pete. "Need a pen too?" I asked.

7

....

News Notes

People who are addicted to big stories on a global scale can turn to TV for an instant hit—there's never more than a twenty-minute wait for a complete update of the world's major catastrophes. That's why God and Ted Turner invented CNN (though I'll bet neither takes responsibility for Larry King).

The ones who enjoy a more leisurely perusal of yesterday's headlines can take their time with any one of the zillion daily papers. There, the latest outrage in the Middle East is only a section away from Heloise's newest method for removing ketchup stains from upholstery and Ann Landers's perpetual harping on chastity.

But if you want real news, the stuff that makes a prairie heart go pitter-pat, go directly to the small-town weeklies.

Where else would you find an up-to-date total of the year's rainfall, a detailed account of the latest attempt by the school board to sneak organized prayer back into the classroom, and a grainy photo of a smiling grandpa holding up both a proud grandson and a string of bullheads, all on the front page?

Of course, the juicy stuff is on the inside—the police reports, the court news, hospital admissions, obits, births, reactionary letters to the editor, delinquent property tax lists (not only naming the owners but giving the addresses and the total in arrears), and the minutes from contentious county and city commissioner meetings.

A small-town paper takes its mandate seriously; there is no piece of information too trivial to be included. Therefore, endless social columns, from the city proper and outlying communities, detail who visited whom, which granddaughter is on what honor roll, and every baby shower including the gifts and attendees.

Unfortunately, Delphi doesn't have a paper of its own, so Willard Hausvik's wife, Iva, compiles a column called "Delphi Doin's" for the Redfield paper. You have to watch what you say in front of her unless you want all of Spink County to know that Uncle Albert ate too much meatloaf at your house last Thursday.

Iva takes her writing seriously and has lately begun calling herself a journalist. She has an unfortunate talent for sniffing around the edges of stories that participants would rather keep quiet.

But it's not necessary to be acquainted with individuals to enjoy reading the intimate details of their lives (which explains the popularity of *People* magazine).

So even though most of the names in the *Webster Reporter and Farmer* were unfamiliar, I still relished the details of the 4-H livestock judging and little Marjorie Kwasniewski's prize-winning Suffolk ewe.

I'd been home for about a half hour, having shooed Presley, Chainlink Harris, and John Adler from the living room, where my stereo had been vibrating the trailer walls, to Pres's room, down the hall, where his stereo was now vibrating the trailer walls.

I sat at the Formica kitchen table, sipped a diet Coke, and concentrated on the police reports.

There wasn't much that seemed related to the carnival; a couple of break-ins looked promising, one at the liquor store where I'd bought the wine coolers and another at a residence. Nothing much of consequence was taken—a case of beer from the former and some cash and a couple of rings from the latter.

This was typical small-town crime—and there was no real reason to connect any of it with Hamilton Bogner's Extravaganza except the vague reports of break-ins from Mobridge that Stu and I had heard on the radio and Junior's cryptic warning.

Nothing in the *Reporter and Farmer* looked promising, at least in regard to the carnival. There was the usual article about the midway with the standard photo of the ferris wheel and the normal advertisements for the Monday-to-Wednesday run with a coupon for half-price ride tickets for senior citizens.

In fact, the only really interesting piece of information was Patricia L. Jackson's ("age 44, Delphi, South Dakota") fifty-five-dollar speeding ticket.

I had just finished enjoying a letter to the editor detailing the dangers of "Liberal Thought" and "World Values being taught in our schools today." I especially liked the part where "global harmony and cooperation" was compared to the "Cultural Molestation of our Young."

It was exactly the sort of nonsense that Junior loved to spout at public meetings, which reminded me that I'd better check in to let her know how the spying went.

With a sigh, I stood and dialed the avocado wall phone and sat down again, anticipating a typical tedious Junior-type conversation.

"Hello," a quiet voice answered.

"Oh, Tres," I said, surprised. I hadn't expected Junior's eight-year-old daughter to answer. "This is Tory, is your mom around? I need to talk to her."

"Mommy doesn't feel very good. She's lying down right now. I'm not supposed to wake her up unless it's something really important," Tres said. "Is it really important? Do you want me to get her?"

"Nah," I said, "it can wait till tomorrow. Are you baby-sitting the trips?"

This was our shorthand for Junior's younger offspring, a set of three-year-old triplets so well behaved that another three-year-old could easily have been left in charge.

Tres giggled. "No, they're all sleeping," she said in a low, conspiratorial voice. "I'm supposed to be reading but I turned on the TV real quiet and I'm watching MTV."

Though usually impeccably behaved, Tres shows an occasional spark of normal kid-ness, which drives Junior crazy.

I encourage this behavior whenever I can.

"Well, keep the volume low and listen real careful so you can turn it off before your mom catches you."

"I will," she said.

"Just tell her I called and that I'll get hold of her later," I said. "Oh, and Tres, don't let those music videos rot your brain. Your mom would never forgive you if that happened."

She giggled and hung up. I sat down and continued reading until Presley poked his head into the hallway and hollered over the stereo noise booming from his bedroom.

"Hey, Tory, did you find the note?"

"Where?" I shouted, glancing back at the telephone. If there'd been a note posted there or on the fridge door, I would have noticed. Nothing was tacked up in either place.

He answered, but the noise from his room garbled the sentence into something like "Overboard the amazing plan."

"What?" I asked, thoroughly confused.

I still couldn't hear his reply.

"Turn down the music so I can understand you," I mouthed carefully.

He grinned and ducked back into the room. The booming sound reduced considerably, and he reappeared.

"That's better," I said. "Now, where do I find this note?"

"On the counter, over by the Raisin Bran," he said with mock impatience.

"Of course, why don't I ever think to look under cereal boxes for notes? So much safer than putting them out where one could actually see them."

"I didn't want it to get lost." Pres shrugged, dark curly hair tousled and eyes sparkling. "Mom said it was important." He vanished back into his room and turned the music up again, though not quite as loud as before.

The yellow Post-It note written in Presley's handwriting said: "Tory—Mom, Rhonda, Home—RIGHT AWAY—Bar," which made no sense whatsoever.

Since the music was still plenty loud, I figured it would be easier to go to Pres for an explanation, even though it meant walking past Del's velvet Elvis wall hanging, which gave me the creeps because his beady little velvet rock 'n' roll eyes seemed to follow me everywhere.

Presley, Chainlink, and John were kneeling, in the center of his room, over some kind of book. Evidently they didn't realize I was in the doorway leaning against the jamb.

Pres's room looked like every other twelve-year-old American boy's bedroom, with clothes and damp towels strewn everywhere except in the open dresser drawers. Jars and empty pop cans and marbles and radios and candy wrappers and Nintendo game cartridges littered the floor. The walls were entirely covered with Freddy Kreuger and rock star posters, interspersed with the odd Cindy Crawford or Claudia Schiffer: proof that puberty was about to raise its ugly head.

"She does too have the best ones," pudgy Chainlink, with the Coke-bottle glasses and buzz haircut, said. "God, I wish one of those shells would slip. Then we'd get a good look."

"Get outta here," replied John Adler, who blinked and looked a lot like his father, except with more chin.

"Everyone knows that Jasmine has the best bod. Ariel's just a fish."

"Bullshit," said Presley. "Belle's the babe of the bunch. Just think about her and the Beast getting it on."

That notion overwhelmed them, and they sat for a moment in silence, three twelve-year-old boys leering over the sexual activities of Disney cartoon characters.

"I still think Ariel has the best tits," Chainlink insisted.

I cleared my throat loudly, startling all three, who turned with guilty smiles and slightly flushed faces. Pres scrambled over to the stereo and turned it off.

"It might behoove you, when discussing tits, to make sure there aren't any standing behind you," I said severely.

"What?" asked John, blinking.

"She means: Either keep the door or your mouth closed," Pres explained.

"Then why doesn't she say so?" Chainlink asked.

"She always talks like that." Pres shrugged. "We're used to it."

"I didn't mean to eavesdrop," I apologized, "though it certainly was a fascinating conversation. I just want to know what the hell this note means."

I handed the slip of paper to Pres, who shrugged.

"Mom and Rhonda are up at the bar and they want you to go up there as soon as you get home," he said, as though that should have been obvious to me from the beginning.

"Why didn't you tell me this earlier?" I asked.

"I forgot," he said. "Say, Tory, you aren't really going to sing in the Phollies, are you? Up onstage, in front of everybody?" He shuddered slightly.

The idea gave me the shakes too.

"Your mom and Rhonda seem to think so," I said. "Though I'm going to do what I can to get out of it."

"Good idea," he said to John and Chainlink. "You ought to hear her in the shower." He put a hand over his heart and yodeled a line from "You've Got a Friend" in a falsetto at the ceiling.

I scooped a wet towel from the floor and lobbed it at him, though he ducked it easily.

"Or worse yet," he continued, laughing, holding a pillow up as a shield, and launching into a pretty good imitation of me imitating the Cowsills singing "Hair."

I caught him square in the teeth with a pair of scuzzy underwear just as he opened wide for the finale.

Coughing and spitting and laughing, all three boys collapsed and rolled on the floor.

"Actually, it'll be all right if you sing with Mom and Rhonda," Pres said, sitting up again. "That way we'll win first prize."

"What do you mean, *you'll* win?" I asked.

"We're entered in the contest too," Pres said. All three stood up, curled their lips in a sneer, assumed a wide-legged stance, and bungled a couple of pelvic thrusts. "You're looking at the Sons of Elvis, baby," he said in a fair imitation for a kid whose voice has not yet changed.

Never-married Del has always insisted that Elvis (the *real,* dead Elvis) is Presley's father, a story patently absurd, but one she sticks to nonetheless. Of course, no one believes her, but no one challenges her either.

Del's fiction doesn't seem to bother small-boned, wiry Pres one way or another anymore.

"Are you sure that's a good idea?" I asked.

"It's a *great* idea," he said. "If we don't win on our own talent, we'll win because the judges will feel too sorry for me not to give us the prize anyway. It's a great plan. An easy hundred and fifty bucks."

The other two nodded solemnly.

"Besides," Pres went on, "we're going to win because we're good. Right, Sons?"

"Right, baby," they all sneered together.

No matter what they sounded like, the Sons of E had to have a better stage presence than the baton twirlers and the Belly Button Whistlers and the elderly accordion duet who played "Lady of Spain" every year.

And they were better looking too. Like his namesake, Pres had always been irresistibly charming. And the other two, though still goofy looking, were the kind of goofy looking that presaged adult handsomeness. Or at least adult presentableness.

I was about to point that out, at least the part about the accordion duet, when the phone rang.

"Prince Charming drove off forty-five minutes ago," Del said loudly into the phone over the background TV noise, "so I know you're back. Why the fuck aren't you here?"

"Sorry, I just now got the message," I said. "What's up?"

"Nothing's up," she said. "Rhonda and I were having a beer and we thought you might like to join us."

A likely story, that. I'm sure they intended to get me tootled enough to agree to this singing group fiasco.

"I don't really want to go anywhere," I said. "I'm tired."

"I'll bet," Del said, a little nastily. Del is one of two people in town who know that Stu and I are seeing each other, though I refuse to share any of the details and that irritates her.

Especially since she generously shares all of her exploits with me.

I could hear someone in the background hollering "Don't buy a vowel now, you idiot" while several others hooted in derision.

"Come have a beer and tell me about your day," Del said in her nicest voice. "Rhonda will be so disappointed if you don't show up."

I really didn't want to go out again. I was tired and not anxious to dispel what was left of the afternoon magic in the secondhand smoke and country music at Jackson's.

Not that much magic was left after the long and very uncomfortable ride home sandwiched between Stu and Pete, while the conversation revolved around how drunk Pete was last week and how drunk Pete intended to get this week and how drunk Pete would like to have been right at the moment.

Which also reminded me of a question.

"Is Pat back yet?"

"Mr. or Mrs.?" Del asked.

That was how we kept them separate in conversations since they had the same first name.

"Mr.," I said.

Someone on TV apparently hit the $5,000 spot on the wheel and called for *D*'s, of which there were several, according to the cheering.

"Neither one was here for a while," Del said, pausing to think for a moment, "but they're here now, and they're testy." She hesitated. "Actually, something unusual did happen, now that you make me think of it."

I waited for her to continue.

"But if you want the scoop, you'll have to come up here to get it."

I could imagine her calculating smile. It was not necessarily a pleasant sight.

"Oh, for Christ's sake," I said, "you're really going to make me trudge uptown?"

"Yup," she said smugly.

"All right, I'll be there in a minute. This better be good."

"You won't be disappointed." Del laughed.

8

....

Jackson's Hole

Here in South Dakota, underage drinking may be rampant, but since grown-ups own the bars, grown-up music is all you'll find in the dimly lit, poorly insulated establishments where sloping floors don't inhibit dancing and neon beer signs are seriously appreciated.

Unfortunately, here, grown-up music consists of singers who make Stu's collection of cassettes look hip.

You want George Jones? You got him. You want Hank Williams (Sr. or Jr.), plug in your quarters. Got a hankering for Loretta Lynn, Tammy Wynette, or Jeannie C. Riley? Plop yourself down for an hour or two and wallow.

It was small consolation to know that our enjoyment of a cold one was never going to be interrupted by the banshee wailings of Sinead O'Connor or by an incoherent Bob Dylan.

Until quite recently, if grown-ups of my particular age group foolishly wanted to listen to music from, say, our own adolescence, we were quite simply shit outta luck.

"If you were marooned on a desert island," my neighbor and good friend Neil Pascoe said to me a little more than a month ago, "and could only take four albums with you, what would they be?"

"This would be your typical desert island," I replied, "complete with electricity and functioning turntable, I presume."

"Actually, it would have a state-of-the-art CD sound system," Neil said, tilting back in his chair, with his feet planted firmly on the massive oak desk.

"Well, if it has all that, I want Mel Gibson, and to hell with music."

We were sitting in the main room of Neil's library, the one he runs from the first floor of his restored Victorian house, drinking diet Cokes and eating warm chocolate chip cookies.

"Nope, you only get music. No sex," he said, pushing his glasses up on his nose. "And only pop music. No classical. You're going to spend your time being entertained, not elevated."

I considered carefully, though it might have looked like I was eating another cookie.

"I find Gilbert and Sullivan entertaining," I said finally, licking chocolate off my fingers. "But if I must be marooned, I'm not going anywhere without James Taylor or Paul Simon."

"Good, I like them." He propped a tablet on his knee and scribbled.

"Why are you taking notes?" I asked, trying to peek at what he was writing.

"You'll find out soon. Get busy. We have to come up with two more names." He grinned and ran his fingers through his short hair streaked with premature gray.

"What's this 'we' shit? Are you marooning with me?"

Though he was nearly ten years younger than me, Neil was my friend. We liked the same books, the same music, and the same warm chocolate chip cookies. If I was going to be marooned, I'd want him along.

"All right, drop the desert island scenario. I"—he paused dramatically and sat up straight—"have sweet-talked Pat Jackson into letting us select four CDs for her new jukebox at the bar."

"You're kidding," I said, flabbergasted.

That jukebox, packed with eighty-eight of the most unlistenable country hits, was Pat's baby, you almost had to ask permission just to play the damn thing.

"I'm trying to picture you 'sweet-talking' Pat into anything," I said. Pat was a taciturn woman with a short fuse and absolutely no sense of humor.

"Well"—Neil laughed—"a contribution toward new uniforms for the softball team helped."

"Ah, now I understand."

While the male Jacksons loved good times and spending money, the female third was downright cheap, and she generally controlled the purse strings.

They only sponsored the softball team because it was a nice tax write-off. The jukebox was the first brand-new piece of equipment ever purchased for the bar. And that only after Pat was convinced it would be a money-maker.

"I also had to promise we'd feed quarters into it on a regular basis." Neil laughed again.

"Fine by me," I said, "as long as there's something worth listening to. How about Carly Simon as number three?"

He suggested Carole King's *Tapestry* instead.

In honor of summer, I thought we should go with a goofy one like *The Muppet's Beach Party* as the fourth choice.

Neil countered with the Broadway cast album of *South Pacific.*

We split the difference with Jimmy Buffett, whose "Why Don't We Get Drunk (and Screw)" was now a bar anthem, punched up often after the former was already accomplished and the latter increasingly unlikely.

As my eyes adjusted to the murky interior of Jackson's Hole, Paul Simon earnestly insisted from the "new" jukebox that we call him Al. I was suddenly sad, and lonely for Neil, whom I hadn't seen or spoken to in a month.

Paul Simon was obviously Del's opening move to butter me up. Unfortunately for her, it would take more than music.

She waved from a table behind the pool players. I threaded my way back, saying "Hi" here and there, though most of the patrons were not given to idle chatter when there were beers to drink.

Two empty beer mugs and a full one sat in front of Del, and a couple more empties were across the table. Rhonda's purse dangled from the back of the chair, and I spotted her up front, talking on the phone, a hand over one ear to muffle the blare of the TV.

I caught Pat's eye and signaled her over. Pete was laughing and talking loudly with a group of guys at the end of the bar near the door. He peered over at Rhonda, still in hippie garb, and said something to the group, who all laughed lewdly.

On my way in, I'd noticed the blue Ford pickup with the Colorado plates parked in the alley beside the bar. An old and greasy popcorn machine lay partly covered by a tarp in the truck box. Obviously, Pat made it back to Delphi, though he was presently nowhere to be seen.

"Well, how was it? That Super 8 aphrodisiac still working?" Del asked, stabbing a butt into the already full ashtray. The fact that I wouldn't tell her any juicy details didn't keep her from trying to pump me anyway.

It was her own fault. Del, who never took her own advice, always said, "If you want to keep a secret, don't tell anyone. Ever."

Of course, she didn't think I'd take her quite so literally. And though Pete's sudden appearance this afternoon, and his and Pat's involvement with Lily, were certainly noteworthy, I couldn't talk about it without giving away more than I wanted to.

"I had a lovely time," I said. "Very uneventful."

Del snorted and lit another cigarette. "I'll bet."

"You want something to drink, Tory?" Pat Jackson stood ready to take my order, a tall woman with linebacker shoulders and no waist, who emphasized both by wearing tight blue jeans and a strapless terry cloth tube top.

"I'll have a Tom Collins," I said.

"With or without?" Pat asked, unsmiling. Her pallor and raspy voice bore witness to years spent in dark smoky places.

"With," I said. I happen to like the maraschino cherry and orange slice.

Pat frowned. The drink cost the same either way, so she lost money on the fruit and the plastic sword.

"Wanna roll?"

"Nah, I'll just pay for it," I said. Patrons could roll dice for free drinks, if they were willing to take the chance of paying double when the numbers came up wrong.

"Anything for you or the kid?" Pat said to Del, pointing over her shoulder at Rhonda, who was still yakking animatedly on the phone.

At nineteen, it was illegal for Rhonda to buy or drink liquor, but the Jacksons would sell to minors if they were accompanied by an adult who did the buying.

"I'm fine, but you can bring another mug for Rhonda," Del said to Pat. "I'll get Tory's drink too."

That actually brought a small smile to Pat's impassive face. Money exchanges always made her feel better.

Scratching her head through the frizzy blond perm with a pencil, Pat demanded, "What the hell is that godawful music?" Plainly holding me responsible for it.

"It's from *Graceland*," I said, hoping she wouldn't have it banished from the bar.

"That don't sound like any Elvis I ever heard."

"It's some of his early stuff," Del said.

Del takes her Elvis seriously, and was probably offended at the notion that anyone could mistake Paul Simon for her idol. But for some reason she was willing to play along.

Pat looked at both of us for a moment, shrugged, and left to get the drinks.

Does she know that Mr. Pat is cheating on her? With

carnival hookers, and his twin brother as an accomplice, no less?

Contrary to popular assumption, the wife is generally not the last to know. I always knew when Nicky was cheating on me.

But then, Nicky never took much trouble to cover his tracks, and Junior made sure I got the scoop when he did.

I wondered how well Pete and Pat had covered their tracks.

Del sipped her beer and said, "So don't you want to hear what happened?"

I had decided on the hot walk from our trailer that, since Del noticed Stu drive by, she must also have seen Pete get out of the pickup and that was her mysterious news.

But in revenge for being dragged out against my will, I decided to spoil her fun.

"I already know," I said smugly. "So there."

Del smiled and raised an eyebrow but said nothing because Pat was back. She set my drink on a napkin printed with Ole and Lena jokes, and stood a small placard on the center of the round table.

In script it read: 7:30–9:00 BEFORE THE DANCE FRIDAY NIGHT, OUTDOOR ROCKY MOUNTAIN OYSTER FEED, ALL YOU CAN EAT $4.95 PER PERSON, BEER SERVED.

Across the bottom in bold print ran the motto: IF YOU HAVE THE BALLS, WE HAVE THE BALLS.

Farmers would wash and freeze their harvest each spring, and once a year pool the cache for a public feed. The Jacksons did the cooking and the money went toward a current community project.

Rocky Mountain oysters tasted mostly like batter-dipped, deep-fat-fried chicken gizzards rolled in slime. That is, if you could forget that they were actually bull testicles.

I was never quite able to forget. And I didn't even want to think about how they were "harvested," though in that I was in the minority. Rocky Mountain oysters were an inexplicable favorite around here.

"You're coming to the feed, aren't you?" Pat asked me as she counted change for Del.

"Anything on the menu besides oysters?" I asked.

"Pat's deer sausage, as usual," she said on the way back to the bar. "For the wimps."

Mr. Pat ground and smoked his own very spicy sausage every fall after deer season, and served it on special occasions throughout the year. Nutritionists might blanch at the fat content, but so far no one has died from it.

Rhonda, flushed and smiling, sat down in her chair and took a quick gulp of beer and flashed an inquiring look at Del over the mug.

Del shrugged almost imperceptibly.

Almost. Something was up between them.

"How was the carnival?" Rhonda asked innocently. "See any cute guys?"

"I stopped noticing cute guys years ago," I said, and Del snorted.

"Actually," I said, "there is a guy named Marko you might find interesting."

That perked them up. Rhonda was between boyfriends at the moment, and Del was always looking. They spoke at the same time.

"What's he look like?"

"How old is he?"

"Probably Rhonda's age. Runs the ferris wheel, long dark curly hair, huge shoulders, lots of muscles, big smile," I said, then, remembering his attitude and the fight later, continued, "Impertinent, short-tempered, and I think he already has a girlfriend."

"Shoot," Rhonda said, disappointed.

Del smiled. Short tempers and girlfriends only sharpened her focus.

I actually thought the carnival women were more interesting, but I didn't want to get into a discussion about Lily. Not with Pete still behind the bar, staring intently in our direction.

Or with Pat, who had shorter hair and no mustache, but was unmistakably Pete's twin, finally appearing from the staircase that led to the Jacksons' upstairs living quarters.

His wife was wiping sticky liquor bottles with a damp rag. He hesitated, watching her back, an unreadably solemn look on his face.

I leaned over the table and asked Del quietly, "When did Pat get back?"

"She came in not too long after Pete," Del said.

"No, not her," I said. "Him. What time did *he* come in?"

Del sipped and said, "You know, he might have been here earlier. When Pete came in they stood looking at each other for a minute. Then Pete shrugged and drew himself a beer and held the mug up like he was proposing a toast—"

"No," Rhonda interrupted. "Pat came down after Pete, don't you remember, Del? Pete already had a beer and was laughing with Stu McKee."

"Oh?" I said, trying not to sound too curious. "Stu stopped here before going home?"

It was no big deal, I guess. I'd just assumed that Stu resented Pete's intrusion as much as I did.

Del grinned widely but waited for Rhonda to continue.

"And I'm sure it was later when he saluted with the mug, like you said," she said. "Pat came down the stairs at the exact time Renee McKee came in looking for Stu."

I nearly choked on my Tom Collins.

"What?" I croaked.

"I thought you already knew," Del said, laughing.

I said, "Renee McKee actually came into the bar? Looking for Stu?"

"Pretty weird, huh?" Rhonda asked.

Weird wasn't the word for it. In the year since Stu had moved back to Delphi to run the feed store with his father, elegant and trim Renee McKee was never, and I mean *never,* seen in Delphi. Not in the cafe, not in the grocery store, not in any of the churches. And especially, not in the bar.

"Had to have been something pretty damn important for her to set her dainty little foot in Jackson's Hole, don't you suppose," Del asked sweetly.

I ignored her.

"What happened then?" I asked Rhonda.

"Everyone sorta froze and just stared for a second."

I could well imagine. An unwilling and unhappy Minnesota transplant, Renee was a figure of great mystery.

"And Pete turned and then saw Pat standing behind the bar. I'm sure that was the order."

"And then?"

"Pete laughed out loud, and everything was back to normal, with everyone talking at once."

"And the McKees?"

"I think they left then. Stu had his arm around her shoulder."

I sat wondering what this public appearance, in the bar of all places, meant. Was Renee suspicious, checking up on Stu? Or worse yet, did she love him and just want to spend time with him?

"Did she seem upset or angry?" I asked.

"What do you care?" Del said to me, fixing me with an eagle eye.

She was right. It wasn't wise to seem too interested in Renee McKee's moods.

Rhonda stood up, slinging her purse over a shoulder, and tucked her hair behind her ears. "Come on, guys, it's time."

Del stashed her cigarettes and lighter in a snug jeans pocket and smiled.

"What?" I asked, still slightly dazed. "Time for what?"

"Rehearsal, dummy," Del said gently. "Time to practice our song-and-dance routine."

Shoop shoop.

9

....

Rehearsal Blues

Metropolitan areas have concert halls and opera houses and theaters for the edification of the general public. City dwellers tend to think they have a monopoly on culture, looking down their snooty noses on us, rustics without even an Arts Commission to guide us along the rocky path to enlightenment.

Well, we might not have a culture czar to show us the way, but here in Delphi, we do have a concert hall/opera house/community theater—it just looks, to the untrained eye, like the high school auditorium.

Delphi High was built in the heyday of the three-story, rectangular, brick, arched-window period of school architecture. With high ceilings and wide hallways and dark woodwork, the main structure is a grand old gal that at one time housed grades K–12, but now is home only to junior and senior high students.

In the first half of this century the auditorium also served as the gymnasium. Sometimes, sitting on the built-in bleachers, I try to picture prewar basketball games being played on an old stage barely large enough for a regulation court. With walls only four feet beyond the faded boundary lines on three sides, and just one foot to the orchestra pit on the fourth, shooting hoops must have been dangerous.

The new gym (as it is still known) was built while I was in grade school, so the auditorium is now used mostly for school plays, assemblies, note passing, and community functions. Like the Delphi Phollies.

There was a large poster proclaiming rehearsal times tacked to the tall French doors separating the auditorium from the school foyer.

Rhonda went ahead, saying she wanted to find our place on the roster, but was waylaid by a similarly attired group of refugees from the sixties who squealed in recognition.

"If everyone here is going to be onstage," I said to Del as we stood in the aisle between the risers, "there isn't going to be anyone left to watch."

It looked as though half of Delphi had gathered, milling aimlessly in the bleachers, chatting with each other, shouting across the room, and paying little attention to neat, small, chinless Ron Adler, who carried a clipboard, a stopwatch, and a worried expression as he blinked furiously.

"Shit, there aren't any more than sixty here now." Del grinned. "Come Sunday, this place will be packed, you know that."

She was right, the Phollies drew a large audience from surrounding communities.

The very thought made me ill.

"I feel sick," I said, jumping out of the way as two trumpet-toting boys barged between us and barreled down the staircase toward the stage. "I think I better go home. Maybe I'm contagious."

Del patted my shoulder reassuringly and turned to Ron Adler, whose nervous tic went into high gear whenever he was near Del. He'd been waiting patiently, a lovesick look on his extremely married face, for her to notice him through most of our conversation.

"You're singing with the Saunders girl. Right?" he asked Del, blink, blink, blink. He consulted the clipboard. "You're on almost at the end of the show, just after the Pee Wee Tap Club dances to 'God Bless America.'"

Jesus, this was going to be worse than I had expected.

"Sounds fine to me," Del said, placing a deliberate arm around Ron's shoulders. "Just give us a holler when it's our turn."

"Sure." Ron blushed and checked something off on his paper. "Say"—blink, blink—"did you hear?" He leaned toward Del. "Renee McKee showed up at Jackson's this afternoon."

Del shot a look at me over Ron's head and then steered him away. I could hear her: "Yeah, I was there when she walked in . . ."

Actually, Del was doing me a favor by pointedly leaving me out of the conversation. Renee McKee's unexpected appearance was already causing excited conjecture.

"I imagine she thinks he's screwing around and wants to keep an eye on him," I heard a woman say behind me.

"Who with?" another asked avidly.

That, unfortunately, would be the prime question.

"Someone in Aberdeen, I heard."

"Don't you think . . ." said another, but I hurried off before she finished, anxious to get away from the speculation, afraid to wonder how long it would take before someone stumbled across the truth.

I sat by myself, leaning as far back as the wooden risers would allow, and tried to concentrate on the stage, which was now filled with a group of young and middle-aged farmers holding huge four-foot-tall top hats. On Sunday they would strip off their shirts, paint big red lips around their hairy navels and wide surprised eyes using nipples as pupils, don the big hats, and belly-sync to "The Colonel Bogey March."

It always brought the house down.

"Kind of makes you wonder if we really are the top of the evolutionary chain, doesn't it?" Neil Pascoe asked from a couple of rows above me.

I twisted around. I hadn't seen him sitting there.

"The dinosaurs probably had talent shows too," I said, "but the incriminating evidence burned up in the comet collision."

He stood, then stepped down to my row and sat a couple of feet away from me and looked at his feet, and then up at the ceiling, wrinkling his glasses up on his nose.

"Haven't seen you at the library in a while," he said, still not looking at me.

"Yeah, well, I've been meaning to come over," I said, "but I've been pretty busy. With work and all . . ." I shrugged and faltered, feeling awkward and uncomfortable. Something I never used to be with Neil.

He finally did look over, serious brown eyes locking with mine. "I know," he said quietly.

That was the trouble. Neil was the other one who knew about Stu and me. We'd had a noisy, nasty fight about it last time we talked.

"They got you helping with this?" I asked, desperate to change the subject. Neil was always willing to help with community projects. He had plenty of free time on his hands, and another sixteen years or so before the lottery checks stopped.

"Nope," he said, "I'm performing."

"You're kidding," I said.

"You see before you Brother Pascoe, the Hypnotizing Monk, here to astound and amaze you with his mesmerizing talent." For the first time, a small smile played around his lips.

I knew he knew hypnosis, but doing it as a stage act?

"Why a monk?" I asked.

"Why not?" he countered. "I'm on just after the baton twirlers, somewhere in the middle of the lineup. The one I'm looking forward to is the closing act." His eyes sparkled behind thick glasses. "Some high school kids are doing a medley from *Hair*."

"You think Delphi is ready for the American Tribal Love-Rock Musical?"

Neil grinned. A lovely sight. "As long as they keep their clothes on."

"Party pooper." I laughed. "I'm singing too, you know."

"Ooh, that's a little scary," he said.

"Tell me about it." I sighed. "It wasn't my idea."

"It should be fun, though," he said, and was quiet again.

That was everyone's attitude.

The silence lengthened between us as the sound level in the auditorium rose. Ron gestured furiously to the men onstage.

"Is Ron running the show?" I asked.

"Sorta, he's emceeing. Gonna wear a tux and tell jokes in between acts."

I groaned. Ron's jokes were not likely to be repeatable in mixed company, and they were even less likely to be funny.

"Have we signed a collective pact to make ourselves look idiotic in front of the rest of the county?"

Neil turned to me. "You're missing the point, Tory. The whole idea is to let our hair down. To act goofy. And to enjoy it."

"There's a big difference between being silly on purpose and trying to sing when you can't carry a tune. Unfortunately, outside of breaking a leg, there's no way I can get out of it now."

We sat for a while longer, watching and sweating. South Dakota school buildings were designed to hold the scant winter heat in, not keep the summer sun out.

"Say . . ." I finally thought of another subject. "You get the Mobridge paper, don't you?" Neil's library subscribed to all the local papers and kept them on file.

"Sure. Why?"

"Junior had me checking up on the carnival that's

coming to town, and I heard something on the radio today about break-ins. Did you see anything in the paper that could be connected to the carnival?" I told him about my conversation with Ham Bogner and the furtive search of his desk.

He thought for a moment. "Nothing special; there were a couple of burglaries reported. Bad checks, speeding tickets, some kids arrested for steroid possession, the usual stuff. You think any of that connects?"

"Probably not; you know Junior. She doesn't need logic to set her off." .

I tried to frame the next question lightly. Unlike Del, Neil has no desire to hear the gory details about Stu.

"Any mention of prostitution?"

His eyes narrowed slightly. "I don't remember anything."

"Hey, Neil," Rhonda called loudly from below, taking the steps two at a time up to us.

He smiled warmly at her. "Hi, kiddo. I hear you're going to steal the show."

She raised her eyebrows and shrugged. "Now that we got a full backup section," she said, smiling at me, "we just might have a chance."

"Yeah, a chance for the booby prize," I said.

"Oh, Tory," she said in disgust. "You're always selling yourself short. Isn't she, Neil?"

"Yes," Neil said quietly. "Always."

"Anyway," Rhonda went on, "Del sent me up to get you, Tory. You're supposed to go backstage now. We're on pretty quick."

"If I must," I said, heart sinking. I could not believe I was actually doing this.

"Of course you must," Rhonda said. "Say, Neil, did you hear what happened this afternoon?"

Rhonda was ready to tell the Renee saga. As an actual witness, her version would be highly prized.

I didn't want to see Neil's reaction to the story and so started down the bleachers.

"Tory," he called after me, interrupting Rhonda.

"Come over after work tomorrow; we'll check the newspapers and see if anything interesting pops up."

"Are you sure?" I asked.

It had been a long time in between invitations.

"What do you think?" he asked.

And then he smiled.

That made me feel better. So much so that the prospect of singing onstage didn't seem quite so horrible.

Of course, in that, I was wrong.

10

Lily of the Field

As a general rule, it takes only twenty-four hours for a fresh rumor to pump its way through the Delphi circulatory system. A story, hypothetically speaking, about the reclusive wife of a well-known town businessman popping into an establishment she has been known to shun (with a shudder, I might add) would merit instant and excited repetition.

And if the reclusive wife was thought to turn up her Minnesota nose at small-town South Dakota, you just might detect a little malice in the retelling.

At the very least, you would expect it to be the hot topic at the cafe the next day.

So I was fully prepared to spend a dreadful shift feigning indifference for any wives, anywhere. But luckily for me, another juicy tidbit took precedence.

"Have you seen this?" Iva Hausvik demanded, pointing at a brand-new Delphi Phollies roster. "A group of high school children intend to sing pornographic, un-American music."

"It's disgusting. A plain insult to everyone who fought for our constitution, flag, and country in The Big One," Willard Hausvik said, looking for confirmation first to his wife, seated across from him in the booth, and then to me.

Even people my age, some of whom I distinctly remember avoiding the draft by any means available, were outraged.

"You know, Willard, the constitution you fought for guarantees freedom of speech," I said, continuing around with refill pots. "Besides, it's just a play, and the music is fun."

"Yeah, well, I don't think anyone should have the freedom to dishonor the flag," he growled into his coffee.

Iva, patting improbably blond hair off which you could bounce a quarter, nodded in agreement.

Much as I would have liked to stand and argue the finer points of constitutional interpretation with the Hausviks, there were burgers to serve and booths to clear. Rhonda and I were exceptionally busy. A steady stream of dusty, greasy carnival workers had been trickling in all morning.

"*Hair*," said a carny worker who swiveled around on his stool at the counter with a smile on his face. He held a Phollies flyer in his hand. "You're talking about *Hair,* right? Ain't that the play where they take all their clothes off and dance at the end?"

His companions, mustachioed Doc and muscular Marko, snickered.

"That might be worth sticking around for," said Marko, who actually had no choice. The carnival was scheduled to run through Sunday anyway.

The Hausviks were horrified at the thought, though Iva might have been just a little more horrified than Willard.

"Is that true?" he whispered to me as I rang up their ticket. "You think they'll really take their clothes off?"

"Well, the original ones did in New York," I said, counting change into his hand. "But this isn't New York. I highly doubt any group of kids will strip in front of their parents and teachers and ministers."

"It's out of the question," Iva said firmly. "They shouldn't allow an anti-American act in the first place. Whether they keep their clothes on or not is immaterial."

I thought Willard looked a little disappointed as they left. The prospect of a few young, naked bodies probably soothed his wounded veteran soul.

"I don't get the fuss," said Rhonda, depositing plates of the day's special, fish sticks and coleslaw, for Marko and Doc. "The human body is a beautiful thing, and no one should be ashamed to see one."

Rhonda was flirting outrageously with Marko, who flexed his biceps in appreciation.

"I'm never ashamed to see a naked human body," he said, all wide-eyed innocence.

Aphrodite clanged a couple of plates down on the stainless steel counter that divides the cafe from the kitchen, reminding Rhonda that she had more to do than discuss nudity.

"Oops." She grinned at Marko. "The polyps are calling me."

"The who?" he asked, fork halfway between plate and mouth.

"Today's special," she said over her shoulder.

Marko put his fork down slowly, as did Doc.

I was behind the counter again, fishing the last two slices of cherry pie from the cooler.

"Eat up," I said to them, and winked.

Gruff and monosyllabic, Aphrodite rarely speaks and never repeats herself. Therefore it's not surprising that Rhonda, when she first came to work with us, misunderstood her. Though it took us a while to figure out why we always had so much pollock left over.

"Polyps," Rhonda would chirp at patrons, who sometimes paled visibly. "Today's special is breaded polyps."

It became a cafe joke, resurrected whenever fish was on the menu.

It was also good for quieting impertinent customers like Marko, who whispered something in Rhonda's ear before handing her a couple of wrinkled bills at the till.

Rhonda giggled, looked at her watch, and said something to him I couldn't hear.

She turned to take an order from some guys riding through on Harleys, and so missed Marko's exit, which coincided with Lily's arrival.

They met in the doorway. Marko smiled and squeezed her shoulder. Lily stopped halfway inside the door to watch Marko leave. Her look of total adoration was painful to see.

I'm not an interferer by nature, but this combo looked like trouble for everyone.

I was so engrossed in watching Lily that at first I didn't notice her companion, a tall man with a fiercely peeling forehead, wearing an HBIE T-shirt stenciled "Hank" on the pocket.

"We'd like to place an order to go, if we could," Hank said quietly in a voice bordered with Southern undertones.

"Sure," I said. I hadn't noticed this one yesterday. "What can I get you?"

He pulled a folded sheet of paper from his shirt pocket, adjusted reading glasses on his peeling nose, and quickly read a long list of burgers, with onions, without mustard, no tomatoes, with everything, no cheese, double bacon, large fries, cheese balls, onion rings, no salt, tartar sauce, and four chocolate shakes, extra thick.

"Whoa, slow down," I said, laughing. "I can't write that fast. Maybe I should just copy your list."

"I doubt it," Hank said. "My shorthand is difficult for anyone else to translate."

He was right. The list looked like gibberish. So he repeated everything slowly for me and, at the end, turned to Lily. "Did we get your order too?"

"Actually, I thought I'd sit a while and eat here," Lily

said lightly, with a smile. "Catch up with my old friend."

She was looking at me. Hank did too, over his glasses.

"You know her?" he asked Lily, looking at me.

We both nodded. I didn't know what Lily was up to—I'm hardly her "old friend." But she looked happy, euphoric even. Much better than when I'd seen her last, sobbing and running from Pete Jackson's motel room.

"Just checking," he said. "Behold the Lily of the field, she toils not."

From what I'd seen the day before, I thought she probably toiled plenty. I wondered how much Hank knew about that side of carny business.

"I bet she doesn't spin either," I said, handing his list to Aphrodite, who frowned mightily when she saw its length.

"It'll be just a few minutes," I said to them, then attended to Presley, who was waiting at the far end of the counter.

"Wow, Tory, who's that?" Pres whispered, pointing at Lily.

"She works for the carnival," I said, deciding that Pres should have the special instead of a triple burger. "And she's too old for you."

"There's no such thing," he said, waggling his eyebrows exactly the way Nicky used to.

We have maybe another six months of peace with this kid before puberty wrecks our entire lives.

"She may not be too old," I said, "but you're definitely too young."

He hooted in response and spent the next ten minutes engaged in twelve-year-old courtship rituals: spinning around on the stool, burping loudly, and staring pointedly at Lily, who seemed oblivious to the whole performance.

I stocked a paper sack with extra ketchup and salt packets and napkins for the big order as Aphrodite bagged up a zillion burgers and fries. Rhonda totaled the order and Hank paid with a roll of dollar bills.

Carrying half a dozen bags, some with grease spots

showing already, Hank turned back to Lily from the door. "What are you ordering for lunch?" he demanded.

"Don't worry, I'm just having a plain hamburger and fries and a Coke," she said in a singsong voice, the kind kids use when being sarcastic to their parents.

"Okay," he said seriously, and left.

"So you want a plain burger?" I asked Lily. "Small or large fries with that?"

"Are you kidding?" she said, leaning low over the counter. "Gimme a toasted cheese sandwich, nice and thick with the cheese dripping out of the bread."

"I think we only use Velveeta," I said, wondering why she changed her order. "Presliced. It's not supposed to drip."

She laughed. "I don't care. I haven't had cheese for so long, any kind would taste good. Even Velveeta."

I guess cholesterol awareness starts early on the carny loop.

"Rotten damn diets," Lily said, standing and reaching into a jeans pocket. She shook a small pill from a folded envelope which she returned to the pocket.

Her hands shook a little as she washed the pill down with water.

"Is Delphi everything you thought it'd be?" I asked Lily. The crowd was thinning out finally, and I had more time for conversation.

"I haven't really seen it yet, just this main street here." Lily pointed out the window.

"That's pretty much all there is to Delphi," I said, setting her sandwich in front of her.

"Actually, it was easier to come here than I thought it was going to be," she said. "Not nearly as awful as I expected."

"I know what you mean. Delphi hits me that way sometimes, too," I said.

She attacked the sandwich, gobbling half in four big bites.

I noticed, for the first time, shiny scar tissue running the width of both of her wrists, and looked away embarrassed.

"God, that's good," Lily said. "You never know how much you miss something until you can't have it anymore."

Her cholesterol count must be sky-high.

"You want some pie?" I asked her. "We still have a couple pieces of apple left. My treat."

I felt bad for grilling her yesterday. For knowing she was probably a prostitute. For noticing her scars today.

She was obviously a troubled kid. Apple pie couldn't fix her life. But it couldn't hurt, either.

"That's okay," she said, licking the last bit of cheese from the corner of her mouth. "I have to get back anyway. I'm late. You know how it goes, work to do, people to relieve."

She giggled and blushed and wiped a sheen of sweat from her forehead.

I wondered whom she was going to "relieve" in Delphi, and if that accounted for the blush.

"You can treat *me* to a piece of pie," Pres demanded from his end of the counter.

"Your mother can treat you to a piece of pie," I said. Presley's meals always went on Del's tab. If you've ever fed a twelve-year-old boy, you know what kind of total we're talking here.

"Ice cream too," he said. "And hurry, please. I want to see them put the ferris wheel together."

I hoped that sweaty, swearing men assembling large machinery would be more fascinating to him than a frail blond girl. Though from the way Pres had watched Lily, I rather doubted it.

I'd just spiraled a loop of soft vanilla on top of Presley's pie and turned to hand it to him when the plate slipped from my hand in surprise and confusion. It shattered, sending shards of porcelain and ice-cream-coated apple slices to the floor, the shelves behind the counter, and my legs.

Piss, shit, god damn, I said to myself. Fuck.

"Good shot, Tory." Pres laughed. "Hope that's not the last piece of apple pie."

"Are you all right?" Rhonda rushed behind the counter with a rag to help. "What happened?"

"Nothing," I said. "Not a damn thing."

I gathered up my courage. More than I thought I'd ever have, or need, and walked over to the booth.

"Can I help you?" I asked, neutrally, carefully, forgetting maybe that I was a waitress and not a floorwalker at Penney's.

"I don't know," Renee McKee said, fingering the edges of the laminated menu I handed her. "Can you?"

11

....

Carny Knowledge

I imagine most lottery hopefuls, handing over dollars that could be spent on groceries or the light bill, don't dream of hitting the big one so they can open their own libraries with the prize money. But that's what Neil Pascoe did.

A book and music lover, with a penchant for fixing up old cars, Neil was different from the average South Dakota boy. Even before the money.

I was a few years out of high school, married to Nicky and waiting tables at Aphrodite's, when young Neil refused to play freshman football on Delphi's nine-man team. In a state where every kid is expected to compete in every sport, this was a major controversy.

The coach, the principal, the mayor, and even our district congressman all did their best to coax, cajole, bribe, and force Neil, who was certainly big and strong enough, into playing.

But Neil simply wasn't interested in competitive

sports, and he stuck to his guns all through high school and cheered in the stands, but did not play.

Years later, after the Iowa Lottery Commission confirmed his winning numbers, he still watches and cheers on occasion, and still politely declines invitations to play on the men's softball team, or to bowl with the guys down in Redfield, or to shoot hoops one-on-one with anybody.

Alone with two cats in a three-story Victorian house, lending books and CDs to anyone who asks, cheerfully volunteering for community projects and always pitching in to help his neighbors, Neil lives so quietly that most of the time we forget how much money he has.

A while back, before my life got so complicated, I saw Neil nearly every day. Either he would eat at the cafe or I would walk over after work, and we'd gab and laugh and look through or listen to the library's new acquisitions.

Now we have polite and careful conversations, speaking only on neutral subjects.

This was the first time I'd been invited over since our argument, and I hoped desperately that the invitation meant we could regain our easy friendship.

I hesitated a little on the hot front porch, then rang the bell three times and walked inside.

A blast of cool air stopped me in the foyer, and I stood enjoying the only efficient air-conditioning in Delphi and peered around the arched doorway into the main room of the library.

Glass-doored bookshelves lined the walls, and cozy overstuffed chairs were grouped here and there. All was quiet and empty.

"That you, Tory?" Neil's voice, muffled, came from upstairs.

"Yeah," I shouted up the wide curving staircase. "Where are you?"

This was not a library that demanded whispers.

"Up in the tower."

I trudged upstairs, through Neil's second-floor living

quarters, clean and neat as always, and up the narrow
staircase that leads to the third floor, which used to be
just attic but now also holds the entrance to the tower
recently added to the front of Neil's house.

Not for the first time, I realized a regular regimen of
aerobic exercises would be beneficial.

"You really should put an elevator in," I huffed,
sweating.

"Nah, I need the exercise," Neil said, leaning over to
turn down the volume of the portable CD player on the
floor beside him.

Scattered around the player were Lyle Lovett and k.d.
lang CDs. Mary Chapin Carpenter was singing the
lottery theme song, "I Feel Lucky."

"You going country on me?" I asked.

Neil liked all kinds of music, though I'd never noticed
an affinity for twang before.

He still hadn't looked at me.

"Those guys are only country because there isn't a
category called 'quirky,'" he said.

That comment would have netted him a smile, if he
had looked my way.

He didn't.

"If you say so," I said a little doubtfully.

The tower, finished on the outside to match the rest of
the gingerbread, fish-scale, leaded and beveled exterior
of the house, was still a construction site on the inside.

Arched windows circled the room for a 360-degree
view of the surrounding prairie, but the walls were still
bare studs with wires snaking through for outlets and
light fixtures.

Neil does all of his own carpentry and plans eventually to build window seats around the perimeter of the
tower for spectacular views in all directions.

He was sitting on a makeshift bench—a plank sus-
pended over two sawhorses—binoculars slung around
his neck, monitoring the activity below.

"Come and watch this," he said, pushing his glasses
up on his head and raising the binoculars to his eyes.
"It's fascinating."

I leaned over the plank and looked out the window. We were facing north and had a perfect view of Delphi's dusty main drag forty feet down, which made me slightly dizzy.

I hate heights.

From the tower, you could see past the two blocks to the cafe, which was the last building on the far side of the street before a half mile of farmland bordered the road to the highway.

We could also see the roof of Jackson's Hole, across the street to the west of Neil's house. My trailer was kitty-corner across the main drag.

But that wasn't what Neil found so fascinating. He was watching Hamilton Bogner's International Extravaganza set up in Delphi's only vacant lot.

The one that just happened to share the same block as my trailer, conveniently located so the carnival could keep me awake for the next three nights, and kick up even more dust than usual, and in general make my life miserable.

"You'd think a dying town like Delphi would have at least two lots suitable for a carnival," I groused.

"Oh, come on," Neil said, eyes glued to the binoculars. "The Daze are fun, and even you can use a little excitement and adventure."

"Delphi is exciting enough for me without Hamilton Bogner's International Extravaganza," I said, watching the workers scurry like ants to assemble the rides.

"So I hear," he said quietly, lowering the binoculars and turning toward me. "How's it going?"

I don't think he was just asking about Stu and me, though that was certainly part of the question. We used to talk about everything. Lately, we didn't talk at all.

"Not bad," I said.

I couldn't tell Neil that I was lonely. That afternoons were fine, but mornings and evenings were even worse now than before. That sharing bodies without being able to share lives is pretty miserable.

And I sure as hell couldn't tell him how agonizing it had been to serve a politically correct low-salt/

fat/cholesterol meal to Renee McKee, whose calm
and distant eyes locked with mine during every exchange.

"Not bad," I said again, shrugging.

I couldn't meet his eyes. He turned again to the
window and we watched together, CD droning in the
background, as the carnival began to take shape.

Using less equipment than I would have imagined
possible, the kiddie rides and Octopus, ferris wheel, and
Tilt-a-Whirl grew from the dust as workers scrambled
madly.

The ticket booth at the far end of the lot, with Ham
Bogner's trailer parked just beyond, was already in
place. Like covered wagons circling for the night, several
other small campers and trailers, as well as semitrailers
and trucks and old school buses, dotted the perimeter of
the carnival.

The merry-go-round spun in slow motion, stopping
occasionally for workers to adjust mechanisms under
the canopy.

Neil slid the window up and we could hear the faint
strains of calliope music.

Other workers strung flags and bunting to connect the
three booths that outlined the east edge of the carnival
proper, next to my trailer. Everywhere thick black
cables lay twisted, connecting each ride to portable
generators.

More to fill up the silence between us than anything
else, I recounted my carnival visit the afternoon before,
remembering to include the information about Dr.
William Aker.

"You were either really brave or really stupid," Neil
said. "Do you think that Doc is the fabled Dr. William
Aker?" He was still peering through the binoculars.

"I kinda doubt it," I said. "Not that I am intimately
acquainted with pedigrees, but I don't think he ever
parked his car in Harvard Yard."

"Just because he didn't talk like a Kennedy?"

I thought for a minute. "No, it wasn't that concrete.
And I know the accent isn't an entrance requirement. I

think it's because I never met a doctor who was hesitant to interrupt. This guy was definitely undoctorish."

Neil accepted the analysis with a shrug.

"Besides, I think his real job around the carnival is pimping," I said, carefully explaining my theory about Lily's position as a floater. Without saying exactly where or how I saw her and Pete Jackson, I told Neil as much as I could about the hallway encounter.

"Looks like both Jacksons share an enthusiasm for carny women," he said, handing me the binoculars. "Check out the ticket booth. Pat's the one with no mustache, right?"

I adjusted the focus and saw Pat Jackson, pale and clean shaven, with neatly combed short hair, leaning one elbow on the ticket booth window, genially conversing with whoever was inside.

From my angle above, I wasn't able to read lips, but I could see what perhaps no one could see from the ground. Pat casually extracted some bills from a wallet attached by a chain to a belt loop. The money disappeared and a couple of red rectangles were pushed back through the opening.

"What's he getting for the money?" Neil asked, excited.

"Ticket books," I said. "Tickets for rides. Funny, none of the rides are running yet."

"Pretty nifty system." Neil breathed. "I'll bet he turns in a couple of full books for services rendered. Give me the binocs—it's my turn to spy."

"Uh-huh." I shook my head, watching Pat nonchalantly stroll away from the ticket booth, past Ham Bogner's trailer, back toward the campers parked at the outer edge of the carnival. "This is too good. Oh, look!"

I forgot and handed the binoculars over to Neil. He hooted.

Even without the field glasses, I could see Pat glance over his shoulder both ways and then knock on the door of a small trailer. The door opened.

"Blonde," Neil said, "thin, black T-shirt. Lily?"

"Yup," I said. "What's happening now?"

"He flashed the ticket books, she nodded, and he went in and the door closed." Neil lowered the glasses, grinning. "Show's over for"—he consulted his watch—"I'd say fifteen minutes, half hour at least."

"How did she look?" I asked, remembering yesterday's sobs.

"Like a young blonde in a black T-shirt," Neil said. "Why?"

I fumbled for a second. "Just curious, I guess. I've never watched a hooker at work before."

"She looked excited; he looked nervous," Neil said, laughing.

"He'd better be nervous," I said. "If his wife catches him, he'll be singing soprano from now on."

"You got that right."

The female Pat Jackson, well-known for her muscular rages, was definitely more deadly than the male.

I didn't want to talk about angry wives, so I directed Neil's attention back to the carnival.

"Anyone else we know down there?"

"Well, the old farts are keeping track of everything, and Willard Hausvik has been yakking with anyone who would stop long enough to listen, as always. Ron Adler wandered through three or four times—maybe he's working up enough courage to tap on Lily's door too."

He watched for another minute. "And a bunch of kids, including Presley, have been there all afternoon. They seem equally enthralled with Muscle Boy running the ferris wheel and our entrepreneur in the trailer," Neil said.

"I know, he drooled over her at the cafe," I said. "Good thing he's only twelve, or we'd have to worry."

"Twelve is old enough," Neil said.

"Maybe for some," I said, "but his voice hasn't even changed yet. He doesn't have any pubic hair." I was almost sure of this, although I hadn't seen him naked for a couple years.

"Don't be too sure," Neil said. "His mother is pretty interested in Marko."

"Lemee see," I said.

Sure enough, there was Del, spiffed up in shorts and a hot-pink halter top, pretending not to gaze admiringly in the general direction of Marko's muscles. He didn't bother pretending disinterest in Del. He grinned over his shoulder often as he tightened nuts and bolts with a huge wrench.

"Remind me not to ride the ferris wheel," Neil said. "Marko doesn't look like he's paying very close attention to detail."

A circle of girls younger than Rhonda were huddled on the other side of the wheel, giggling and whispering.

"There's the big boss, I think," Neil said, pointing. "Huge fella, acres of polyester, lots of head, right?"

"Where?"

"Just came out of the trailer next to the ticket booth. He's talking to whoever's in there."

It was Hamilton Bogner, all right, gesturing emphatically. Maybe shouting, though we couldn't hear anything specific over the machinery clanking and music both inside and outside the tower.

"Oops," Neil said, "this could be interesting. I think he's heading to Lily's trailer." He watched silently for a moment.

"Come on, what's happening?" I demanded. "If you're going to hog the binoculars, you have to give a running report."

"Sorry." Neil laughed. "The boss is pounding on the door, I think he's shouting. A couple of the workers have stopped to watch."

That much I could see. Several dusty black shirts stood up and turned toward the camper, though the locals strolling and gawking didn't seem to notice anything amiss.

"So, this is either something that never happens and they're surprised," I said, "or it's something that always happens and they're amused."

The camper door cracked open and a blond head peeked out.

"Lily is flustered. Boss is angry. Lily shakes her head no and Boss is pissed," Neil reported, enjoying the scene enormously.

At the ferris wheel, Marko, who had a good view of the camper between the other rides and booths, stopped peeking at Del and leaned against the assembled machinery to watch. We couldn't see his face from the tower, but even without magnification, I could tell his shoulders were tense and his fists were clenched.

From below, a phone rang.

"Damn, I forgot to bring the cordless up with me," Neil said, handing the binoculars over. "Keep watching, I'll be right back."

He loped down the stairs noisily as the phone continued to ring.

During that exchange, I missed the end of the confrontation between Lily and Ham Bogner, who was now stomping back toward his trailer in tight-lipped fury. He didn't look much like a public relations director/father figure at the moment.

Lily's camper was quiet again, so I stole a peek back at Marko through the binoculars. Midge, of the big hair and Magic Marker eyebrows, had her arm around his shoulders, presumably speaking words of comfort into his ear.

Marko shook her arm away and turned back to the ferris wheel. Midge patted him and stole a glance at Del on her way back to her souvenir booth.

Lily's camper door opened slowly and Pat Jackson sidled out and around the back, and then innocently ambled across the street away from the carnival, shit-eating grin on his face and a jaunty lilt in his step.

Marko ignored the rest, and Ham Bogner was out of sight, back in his trailer.

Neil thumped back up the stairs, three at a time, not huffing or puffing at all.

"It's for you," he said, raising a quizzical eyebrow, handing the phone to me. And in a theatrical whisper added, "It's a man."

12

....

Clay's Dilemma

Maybe in Seattle, where it rains every second day, and if it isn't raining, inhabitants know it will be soon, people themselves are free to be a bit more unpredictable. Listen to the music that comes from that city and see if you think anyone there is sane.

Lord knows in California each beautiful day is like every other one. There the lunatic fringe is on permanent display and regularly gets elected to public office.

And you never know what to expect from New Yorkers, who live where the weather is predictably unpredictable (always awful within well-defined parameters).

But here in Delphi, an 80-degree early-spring day can be followed by a six-foot blizzard. A calm summer morning can whip up a hypnotically destructive thunderstorm in half an hour, and the temperature can swing 140 degrees between August and January (and that's without the windchill factor).

We cope with meteorological whimsy by sticking to our routines. Rain or shine, heat or snow, we can always be counted on to do the same thing in exactly the same way, every single day.

So it's not surprising that someone might track me down at the library—since it's well-known that Neil and I are friends and it certainly was my habit to visit him daily.

I was surprised, however, that there was a man on the line.

I could think of only two men who might have a reason to call me—one would never take that risk to begin with, and the other held the receiver out to me with a small smile.

"Hello?" I answered tentatively, suddenly aware of the powerfully hot sun shining through the tower windows, hoping it wasn't Stu, hoping it was Stu. Confused and uncomfortable.

"Tory? This is Clay Deibert, sorry for the interruption."

"No problem, Clay," I said, relieved and irritated at the same time.

Tall, blond, handsome, cheerful, seriously dependable, Lutheran minister, excellent father, and married to my exasperating cousin Junior, Clay Deibert was exactly the kind of person who normally set my teeth on edge—all that hearty goodwill is hard to take.

But for some reason, I like Clay, and we get along well.

Which is more than I can say for his wife.

"What can I do for you?" I asked.

Neil had picked up the binoculars and was pretending to study the carnival again, though I knew he was listening intently to my end of the conversation.

"Well, this is a little awkward, but you know that Junior hasn't been feeling well."

Clay paused, waiting, I guess, for confirmation.

"Yes, I was in the cafe yesterday when she fainted. Is she still sick?"

"The doctor says it's just a small case of food poisoning, but she's still feeling pretty weak, not well enough yet to be out and about. Which is why I'm calling you."

He paused again. This time I waited too, with a sinking feeling. If I was going to be roped into good-deeding, I wanted Clay to have to ask specifically.

He continued. "Anyway, the doctor has ordered bed rest for Junior until Sunday at the earliest, and I know she is really anxious to talk to you."

That seemed unlikely. Junior was always ready to lecture and berate, but there was little time in her busy schedule for conversation. Especially with me.

"Clay," I said patiently, "Junior doesn't even like me. Why would she want to talk to me?"

"I don't know," he said, sounding confused. "I think it might have something to do with the carnival that's setting up in town. Does that make sense to you?"

Actually, it did.

"Junior asked me to check out the carnival before it left Webster, though I never did understand why. Anyway, I didn't see anything that would interest her," I explained.

Anything that I was willing to repeat, at least.

He sounded relieved. "That must be it. Will you talk to her, then? It'd calm her down, I think, so she can get some rest."

Easy enough.

"Sure, Clay, I'll give her a call as soon as I get home."

"Well, uh, I was hoping you'd drive out to the farm and see her in person."

"Oh, Clay"—I was close to whining—"is that really necessary? You know we don't get along very well. Sometimes just seeing me agitates her."

"I know, but I'd really appreciate it if you'd go instead of phoning. Something is bothering her and maybe she'll tell you what's wrong."

"She's a good deal more apt to tell you what's bothering her," I said. "Or Aunt Juanita."

"Juanita's out of town today. Please, Tory, you know I wouldn't ask if I didn't think it was important." He waited.

Neil had given up his carnival observation pretense and was openly grinning at me. He knows how I feel about Junior. I mimed indecision and he nearly laughed out loud.

"Oh, all right," I said finally. "Del's car is back from the shop, but it'll be a half hour or so before I can leave. Neil and I still have to check the Mobridge newspapers for references to the carnival. Should I let her know when to expect me?"

"No, I'll do that," Clay said. "And thanks, Tory, I really appreciate this."

"No problem," I lied, and hung up.

"This is interesting." Neil laughed. "Clay sending *you* to find out what's wrong with Junior."

"Sounds like she's having some kind of breakdown," I said unkindly. "Probably can't get all the lint out of the dryer filter or one of the kids said a dirty word or something earthshaking like that."

"Give the woman a break, she's not as bad as you think," he said, shrugging.

"That's easy for you to say. She's not your perfect cousin."

"Just the same, I think there's another person inside all that perfection, and maybe you can help the real Junior emerge."

"You're being pretty cryptic," I said, narrowing my eyes at Neil. "What do you know about all this? Do you know what's really the matter with Junior?"

"I might." Neil grinned.

"And you're not going to tell me?"

"You're the one playing detective." He laughed and headed downstairs. "See what you think after you talk to her. Come on, let's go check out some newspapers, Inspector Bauer."

13

....

More News Notes

Like all other red-blooded Americans, we resent and distrust our police force. Our Dakota hearts skip a beat when we spot a Highway Patrol car in the rearview mirror. We bitch and moan about the double nickel and think we're being persecuted when we're ticketed for driving a paltry 75 miles per hour.

In theory, we heartily endorse strengthened DUI laws, as long as that doesn't include the six-pack consumed on the way home from a third-run movie in Aberdeen.

We are pretty good at policing ourselves and taking care of each other, and see no need for uniform intervention.

Except, of course, when the neighbor's dog barks all day. Or a kid down the street throws a noisy party on a weeknight. Or we've locked ourselves out of our own cars and homes.

Or any other situation we find annoying but don't particularly want to deal with on our own.

Then polite and official help is just a phone call away.

It is a truth universally acknowledged that we want our police to police everyone else, but to leave us alone.

How do I know this? From the police report sections in various local newspapers.

"Here's a good one," Neil read aloud, feet propped on the big desk in the main room of the first-floor library. "'A woman called to complain that rabbits were chewing the buds off her prize mums and wanted something done about it.' Bring on the Rabbit Patrol."

We were methodically searching through a small stack of newspapers from towns in a fifty-mile radius of Hamilton Bogner's carnival. Most of the papers were weeklies, issues dated the week after the carnival left.

So far, we hadn't run across anything significant. I was enjoying a relatively tension-free afternoon with Neil and almost thanked Junior and her paranoia for making it possible.

"There seems to be an epidemic of wild young men tearing dangerously around eastern South Dakota on bicycles," I said. "'A group of boys shouted obscenities at an elderly couple watering their lawn in Webster, and a mother called to report that older juveniles were handing out cigarettes to her eight-year-old daughter.'"

"In Mobridge too," Neil agreed. He sat up. "Here's something, though—'Two juveniles were questioned and released regarding possession of controlled substances, including amphetamines and anabolic steroids.'

"There's a big article about it here," he said, turning the page and adjusting his glasses. "It says that they're investigating where the kids got the drugs. No one thinks they took any, but the stuff was certainly in their possession and the police want to know who they got it from. So far the kids aren't talking."

"It's sad, but fairly common these days," I said. "You think it might have anything to do with our carnival?"

"It's stretching some, but there may be a connection." Neil peeked over the top of his paper. "I've been watching the behemoth setting up the ferris wheel all afternoon. He's pretty muscular for a kid that age."

"Young men can build big muscles in the space of a year without taking steroids," I pointed out, remembering last summer's photo of an undersized Marko.

"I know, but it takes a lot of work, lots of time, and a gym to bulk up legally."

Neil does some weight lifting himself, so he'd know.

"I talked to Marko at the carnival yesterday, and he ate in the cafe at noon today. He seemed horny and conceited and a bit intense, but otherwise okay."

"Was his skin broken out? You know, pimples?" Neil asked. "What's his hair like?"

"Long, dark, and curly," I said, "and I was too busy to count zits. Rhonda was flirting with him, so she might have noticed. That is, if she saw anything other than his big brown eyes and rippling biceps."

"Biceps don't ripple, idiot." Neil laughed. "How about the top of his head—was his hair thinning?"

"I haven't seen him without a cap. What's male pattern baldness got to do with it anyway?"

"Steroid use sometimes causes marked hair fallout and chronic acne. It can also result in uncontrolled bursts of anger. 'Roid rages, they're called."

That sparked a memory of a furious Marko being restrained by Ham Bogner. And a carny worker with "Doc" stenciled on his T-shirt saying, "It's Marko again."

"Doctors can prescribe steroids, can't they?" I asked. "I mean, they're not like marijuana and cocaine, always illegal, right?"

"Right. They have several legitimate uses—after accidents and long illnesses where patients have to rebuild their strength." He paused. "You're thinking of the mythical Harvard man?"

"Well, mostly, I don't think there is a Dr. William Aker, but there's a prescription pad with that name on it in Ham Bogner's desk. If he doesn't exist, someone is faking the credentials—and maybe picking up illegal prescriptions along the way."

Neil smiled. It was so nice to see him smile.

"At least you have something to report back to Junior now."

"I don't think I'd better repeat this—it's just speculation anyway, and you know how she overreacts. Unless we have a really good reason to suspect real wrongdoing, I'm not going to say anything. Especially to Junior."

"You're probably right," Neil agreed. "Listen to what she has to say, and if it correlates to this stuff, use your best judgment in telling her."

Unfortunately, we both had reason to think my best judgment was less than reliable.

I'd finished reading and was refolding my paper when Neil rattled his, and a picture on the front page of the *Mobridge Tribune* caught my eye.

"Shit, will you look at that." I breathed. "Here we've been searching the back sections and police reports for rumor and innuendo, when the whole enchilada was staring at us from page one."

"What? What?"

For just a second, I enjoyed knowing something that Neil didn't, a thoroughly juvenile and satisfying emotion.

And then I pointed at the bold print caption that read: HEIRLOOM ITEMS TAKEN IN BURGLARY. FAMILY OFFERS REWARD FOR RETURN.

It still looked cheap to me, but who was I to judge heirlooms?

Front and center among the other valuables in the grainy black-and-white insurance inventory photo was a turquoise cross on a silver chain.

14

....

Delphi-on-Avon

Like everything else in our society, popular first names ride in on the high tide of fashion—and six hours later vanish back into the murky depths.

When was the last time you heard a child called Myrtle? Or Mabel, Matilda, Martha, Minnie, or any other *M* name that conjures up dowager's humps and mildew?

When I was in school, Katherines abounded. Not once was I in a class without at least two variations on the theme: Kathy, Cathy, Kathie, Kathi, Kate, Catherine, Kathleen, and Katrina.

There were so many that we came to recognize how they spelled their names by their behavior: *C* Cathys were quiet and studious, straight-A students; *K* Kathys were yakkers who would pass notes in English class right under Mr. Gilbertson's nose and get away with it.

About twenty years ago, South Dakota suffered an intense Hooterville fixation. Our college campuses are now filled to the brim with girls named Billi Jo, Bobbi Jo, Amy Jo, Sarah Jo, Becky Jo, and Delphi's own Tallulah Jo.

This was followed by a brief romance with Michelle, Nicole, and Danielle, whose French influence was eroded by the Anglomania that grips us now.

You can't throw a stone in Delphi without hitting an Ashley, a Courtney, a Brittany, or a Heather.

Not to mention Joshua, Jeremy, and Jessica, all of whom I could whack pretty handily, if throwing rocks at tiny second cousins appealed to me.

Which it didn't, as a rule, though their eerie good behavior always threw me off-kilter.

Used to Presley and his noisy cohorts, I am always surprised by these three perfect toddlers.

They sat now, lined up neatly, feet barely reaching the edge of the couch, intently watching Barney or some other hypnotic TV show.

As the triplets' older sister, Tres (officially named Juanita Doreen III, after her overbearing grandmother), trotted down the hallway to tell her mother I'd arrived, I realized that Junior must be ill indeed.

The fairly new ranch-style house was not actually dirty—the table had been cleared, the rugs vacuumed, and the furniture dusted.

But Junior's attention to detail is microscopic, and she would never leave books and magazines piled haphazardly on an end table. Nor would she have left Kool-Aid fixings out on the counter, with a red-stained dishrag hanging over the edge of an open kitchen drawer.

And until now, I had never seen the triplets less than perfectly dressed and coordinated. There was no room in Junior's tidy life for mismated socks, shirts wrongly buttoned, or uneven collars.

"Mom says please go back to her bedroom, Tory," Tres said as she emerged from the hallway. "She still doesn't feel very good."

Tres looked a little frazzled herself. "Don't worry,

your mom will feel better soon," I said, giving her a quick hug on the way past.

The shades in Junior's chintz-and-frills bedroom were pulled. But even in the dim light, I could see she had a serious case of bed head. A glass of what looked to be 7Up and an open package of saltines lay on the end table.

"Oh, Tory, thank God you're here," Junior, still pale, said as she sat up in bed and pulled a wildly flowered coverlet up under her chin. "At times like this, family is such a blessing."

"Times like what?" I asked, mildly alarmed.

I had just talked to Clay, so I knew nothing had happened to him. And Junior's children were a bit disheveled, but present and accounted for.

That left our remaining family members in common—Junior's younger brother, Paul; our mothers; and their mother.

"Has something happened to Grandma?" Grandma Nillie had hovered on the brink of death for a couple of months now, stubbornly clinging on, with only my mother for round-the-clock care.

"Grandma?" Junior asked, wild-eyed, voice rising. "Has something happened to Grandma?"

"That's what I'm asking you," I said quietly. Junior is nothing if not controlled; her irrationality was starting to worry me. "Have you heard something about the family that you need to tell me?"

"Of course I haven't heard anything. How could I hear anything? I've been in this damn room for a whole day now and I still can't get up. Clay even took the phone out."

Junior reached for a cracker and nibbled on a corner, eyeing me balefully.

She still wasn't making much sense, but peevishness was at least normal.

"Grandma was just fine, last I heard. Or as fine as she's been in the last six months anyway," I said, sitting on the edge of the bed. "I thought that's what you meant with your 'family at times like this.' "

"Oh, for Heaven's sake, Grandma's been loony as long as we can all remember. It'll be a blessing when she finally goes." Junior rolled her eyes and sighed.

"Then I haven't the slightest idea what you're talking about," I said shortly. For some reason, even agreeing with Junior irritates me.

"I just meant that it's good to have family around when things are falling apart and you're not up to taking care of everything yourself." She winced a shaky little smile at me and continued. "Tres does a wonderful job with the little ones, but she's just a child. It's too much responsibility for her alone."

It was clear to me now—Junior wanted a family baby-sitter. A *free* family baby-sitter. Is this what Neil meant about giving her a break?

"You want me to sit with the kids a while?" I asked, sighing, amazed at my own magnanimous offer. "I can't stay long, though. I have to meet Del and Rhonda for Phollies rehearsal soon."

For the first time, I was happy about the backup singing gig.

"Not today, Clay will be home soon. But . . ." She trailed off, busy straightening sheets and covers.

"But what?" I asked, cursing Neil.

"Well"—she twisted the sheet around her finger— "I'm not supposed to be up and about until Sunday, which means I won't be able to take the kids to watch Clay play softball on Saturday, and they do want to see their daddy pitch . . ."

I doubted if three-year-olds had much interest in watching anyone do anything, and tried to say so, but Junior interrupted.

"They're really good kids, super easy to take care of. And I'd like for them to get to know you better."

"Why? So I can baby-sit more often?"

"Tory, that's not fair and you know it."

"Actually, Junior, it's a perfectly legitimate question. Besides, why were you ordered to bed in the first place? You don't seem that ill."

"It was a mild case of food poisoning—we all had the

cramps, nausea, and diarrhea for a day or so. Someone brought tainted chickens to the post office for Mother, and she gave us one and we ate it," she explained. "The doctor thinks, under the circumstances, that I should rest completely awhile before resuming my normal duties."

"Under what circumstances?" I asked, but Junior switched gears on me too quickly.

"Good"—she nodded—"we have that settled. Clay will drop all four off at your trailer early Saturday afternoon."

She beamed a genuine smile at me, catching me off guard and without a contradiction. "It'll be fun, you'll see." She sipped her 7Up and waited.

I'll get Neil for this. The real person inside Junior is the one I always suspected—the Master Manipulator.

"Now, tell me what you and Stuart McKee saw at the carnival yesterday." She was pale, but all business.

"Why don't *you* tell *me* what we were supposed to look for—we never did get that part straight." I was stalling, still not sure how much to repeat to Junior.

Besides, Stuart McKee hadn't seen anything at the carnival yesterday, though that was our little secret.

She narrowed her eyes at me. "Okay, but you have to keep it quiet until we're certain—we don't want a panic. This was faxed to me from Mobridge last week."

She reached into a bedstand drawer and handed me a folded piece of paper.

"You have a fax machine?" I was surprised.

"The church does," she said. "We've been getting things like this for quite a while now."

I opened the paper, expecting to read about petty theft, or perhaps illegal steroid use.

The paper was covered with crudely drawn symbols—circles and pentagrams and horns—with a caption underneath warning of the grave danger to our youth. "Beware," it read, "of vagrants, itinerants, and traveling businesses such as sideshows and carnivals. They spread their poison wherever they go! Watch for these UNHOLY danger symbols."

"So?" I asked. "What's this got to do with Hamilton Bogner? Or me, for that matter?"

"Don't you see, Tory? These are cult symbols. We may have brought Satanists to Delphi." She was genuinely upset; her voice trailed off in a wail.

"We? If I remember right, it was you who invited Satan's minions into our midst." I was having a hard time keeping a straight face.

I really cannot take this devil worship thing seriously.

"I know." Her eyes filled with tears. "I recommended them. And now it's too late. I've put the entire town in danger."

"Calm down, you're overreacting. First of all, I wandered all around that carnival yesterday and didn't see a single human sacrifice. No Black Masses, no one on broomsticks. All I saw were tired, dirty carnival workers spinning teenagers upside down for money."

"Think carefully," Junior said, pointing at the paper. "These people are clever and subtle; they work their symbols into everything. Did you see anything that looked like any of these?"

"I know a pentagram when I see one. And I didn't see one—or any clever or subtle people. If I had realized you wanted me to look for witches, I'd have stayed home and listened to James Taylor instead."

Though, of course, that's not true. I'd have braved real witches for an afternoon with Stu.

"Go ahead and make fun," Junior said seriously. "That doesn't change things."

"What could you do even if you were right and HBIE was a pack of flaming devil worshipers?" I asked.

"I'd make sure everyone knew, so they could stay away," she said positively.

"And get yourself sued in the process," I answered firmly, "for libel, or slander, or defamation of character or something. Even if they are Satanists, which I doubt, you have to remember that it's not illegal."

"It ought to be. It's dangerous," Junior said darkly.

What little good feeling I had for her would evaporate completely if I got into a debate.

"Well, you don't have to worry. I saw no indication that Hamilton Bogner's show was anything more than it seemed—a seedy little carnival. I guarantee your hardy Lutheran souls are safe there. In fact," I said, mouth running way ahead of my brain, "the only thing I might have seen was a little prostitution."

"What?" Her face crumpled. She pulled a Kleenex from the box and started crying uncontrollably. "Are you sure? What did you see?" She moaned, mumbling something about disease and contamination, and a lot of other things I didn't quite catch.

Flustered, I tried to calm her down. I'd never seen Junior cry, not even as a kid.

"Well, I'm not sure that's what was happening. It could have been something else."

Yeah, right. Like Lily was taking dictation in a motel room with Pete and Pat Jackson.

"It could have been worse," I continued bravely. "At least you didn't intentionally invite a prostitute to Delphi."

I was confused by her extreme reaction. I didn't think Junior felt personally threatened—in a million years, I couldn't picture Clay negotiating for Lily's services.

"Look at the bright side, I'll bet she's not a Satanist hooker."

Junior only renewed her wailing.

"Don't you see?" she cried. "It doesn't matter—how can I be trusted to bring more children into this world when I inadvertently invited evil into my own town?"

I know what they say about the paving on the road to Hell, but I thought Junior was being a little hard on herself. And Lily might be misguided, but she wasn't, I'm sure, evil.

And then I realized what Junior just said.

Now I understood the fainting in the cafe. The soda crackers. The borderline insanity.

I found myself, for the first time in my life, comforting Junior, patting her back awkwardly, and finally holding her as she cried herself out.

No wonder she was distraught, unsettled, and acting

strangely. No wonder Neil said there was a "real person" inside of Junior.

No wonder Clay was confused. He didn't know yet.

15

....

Mountain Oyster Feeding Frenzy

FRIDAY EVENING

There is a point during almost every Midwest summer evening, no matter how hot the day, no matter how high the humidity or fierce the wind, when the Weather Gods declare a truce with each other and give us mortals a break.

Not that the break is large or long, we're talking relative relief here: the difference between 92 and 98 degrees, for instance; or a drop in humidity by seven percent; or the wind's slowing to a regular breeze rather than a gale.

But for a while, at least, the air seems lighter and the eyes unsquint just a bit and the hair unglues from the forehead and the waistband isn't quite so sticky.

Unfortunately, we were a good hour away from even that brief respite. In the tropics, people actually schedule their lives around the heat, sleeping during the hottest part of the day and working during the early-morning or late-evening hours.

We Dakotans are too proud and stubborn to let an outside force like the weather dictate to us. We have things to do, people to see, and Rocky Mountain oysters to eat.

It's Delphi Daze, dammit, and we're going to have a good time even if we die of sunstroke.

Long ago, Aphrodite gave up trying to compete with the oyster bash—nothing she serves compares with all-you-can-eat testicles (thank goodness). These days, she good-naturedly closes the cafe and gives everyone the afternoon off to enjoy the festivities, though with Aphrodite, good nature sounds a whole lot like mumbled complaints.

And so there we were, milling around in the hot evening sun, squinting and straining to hear each other over the noise of the carnival, which was kitty-corner across the street.

The whole block in front of Jackson's had been cordoned off since early afternoon with sawhorses and pennants and balloons and signs proclaiming the opening of Delphi Daze. The few cars parked along either side of the street on Delphi's main drag had been moved (easy enough since everyone leaves the keys in their cars).

And there had been steady traffic into town for an hour or so already. Pickups and cars were parked along the side streets and beyond the sawhorses all the way down the block to the cafe. People from a fifty-mile radius came to drink, get laid, and pick fights. And maybe dance a little.

And eat a plate full of Rocky Mountain oysters, something quite a few were already doing, seated at picnic tables which had been placed in the street, large plastic cups of beer in hand, talking and laughing and generally having a good time.

Even more people waited in line in front of folding tables—borrowed from the school and now covered with butcher paper and vats of assorted food—to hand money to a dour Pat Jackson, a transaction that usually made her smile but this evening held no amusement.

"You'd think she'd be happy, raking in this much money," Del said in my ear. We'd just walked over from the trailer and hadn't worked up enough ambition to get in line yet.

"She's probably cranky because she doesn't get to keep it all," I said. "The profits of this shindig are supposed to go to the pool fund, remember?"

"*Profit*'s the operative word there," Del said, waving back at Rhonda, who already had a big plate of fried things and was eating with a group of her friends. "The pool won't get a hundred bucks from this."

"What do you mean? There's a couple hundred people here. They'll pull in a thousand tonight, minimum."

"Sure, they'll get that much, but I bet a week's tips there'll be a few unforeseen expenses along the way." Del ticked off on her fingers. "Extra help to cook and clean, rental of the deep-fat fryers, disposable plates and cups, reimbursement for closing the bar for the evening—"

"Wait a minute," I interrupted. "They offered to host this thing, and they're going to charge us anyway?"

"Just watch and see." Del nodded at someone. "She won't hand over a penny she doesn't absolutely have to. Pat Jackson is so tight she washes out Tampax."

"Yuck," I said. The air felt and smelled like hot grease, and my appetite had already vanished.

We were in line now, with ten or so people ahead of us, shuffling slowly in the street. Scattered among the locals I spotted a few black HBIE shirts, eating together here and there at the picnic tables.

I would happily have skipped this portion of the festivities, but the late-evening sun turns our trailer into an oven, and the carnival, set up right outside our door, was too noisy to allow rest, reading, or music.

Besides, I was hoping to see Stu in the throng, figuring this was one of the occasions when I could talk to him in public without arousing suspicion—as long as I made it a point to talk to everyone else I ever waited on. Much to my disappointment, he was nowhere in sight.

Nearly everyone else was out and about, though.

"Lovely crowd," Iva Hausvik, in line behind me, said.

"Oh, hi, Iva, I didn't see you back there." I peeked around her tightly sprayed hair. "How are you doing, Willard? Hot enough for you?"

"This ain't hot," he said, wiping his forehead with a blue hanky. "Back in '57 . . . now, that summer was a hot one. This don't hardly count."

Ask an old fart about the weather and you'll get a half century overview. At least he wasn't ragging about Fran Tarkenton.

"Say, I've been meaning to ask you," Iva said as she turned and blocked Willard's view. He had been gazing appreciatively at the back of Del's shorts. "How's your grandmother doing?"

"About the same, I guess. She's hanging on longer than anyone expected."

"Such a tragedy." Iva rummaged in her purse for a tablet and pen, and smiled brightly. "Also, I understand you visited our little carnival in Webster on Wednesday."

I tried a smile, but didn't answer. I wasn't going to volunteer any unnecessary information for Iva's newspaper column.

"You went along with the younger Mr. McKee, right?" Iva inquired brightly.

"That's right." I could see from the tilt of Del's head in front of me that she was listening intently. I didn't have to see her smile to know it was there.

"Now, whose idea was it for him to check out the carnival with you?" Iva's birdy eyes narrowed. She didn't know where it was, but she scented a worm somewhere.

I certainly didn't want to say that he volunteered to go; Iva would have been on that like a hawk.

"I believe Junior Deibert asked Mr. McKee to go as a

special favor to her," Del said, turning and grinning. "Just before she fainted in the cafe, remember, Tory?"

"Yes, absolutely," I said, "that's exactly what happened."

That threw Iva off the trail. "Oh, my, dear, and do either of you know what's wrong with Junior? And is she any better?"

I knew and was aching to tell someone, but had been sworn to secrecy by Junior herself.

"She probably choked on her fucking Bible," Del mumbled.

"I'm sorry, I didn't catch that, Delphine. Could you repeat?" Iva was still grinning, so she must not have heard Del.

"I think Junior mentioned something about bad chicken and food poisoning," I said. "Salmonella."

Iva's brows knit into a little frown as she wrote on the tablet.

I turned back to Del and whispered in her ear, "Thanks. I thought I was going to have to create a distraction by asking Willard about Fran."

Del laughed, dug into her pocket for a handful of dollar bills. "You owe me."

We were finally at the head of the line, standing in front of a still-unsmiling Pat Jackson, this time wearing a pink terry cloth tube top. Her permed hair fluffed around an orange plastic Grain Belt visor.

Del paid and waited for change, picked up a Styrofoam plate, and moved down the line.

"Got quite a crowd tonight, Pat," I said. "Should make enough money to get that pool built sometime this decade after all."

I think she sensed I was needling her. Pat's shaded eyes glassed over, and if possible, she smiled even less. "We'll see." She dismissed me and focused on Willard and Iva.

I followed Del along the trestle table as assorted squinting helpers ladled potato salad and pork 'n' beans onto my plate. I was allowed to choose for myself from the finger foods: dill pickles, potato chips, buns, and homemade deer sausage.

Ahead of me, Del laughed loudly and said something to the male Pat Jackson about preferring fresh balls. He wiped sweat from his clean upper lip with the back of his hand and then shook a basketful of sizzling fried oysters into a serving dish lined with paper towels.

"All you can eat." He leered at her. "Anytime."

Del filled her plate, smiled flirtatiously, and moved on.

He lowered a newly refilled basket into the bubbling grease. "How about you, Tory, how many balls can you take?"

This was pretty racy talk coming from a man whose large unsmiling wife was less than ten feet away.

"None for me, Pat, I'm not very hungry," I said with a small shudder. "I took some of your deer sausage, though."

"Now I'm insulted," he said, holding a hand over his heart in a wounded fashion.

"Hey, I've never liked Rocky Mountain oysters, even before I knew what they were. It's not your cooking, believe me." I was slightly embarrassed at having to defend myself.

He laughed. "Between you and me, you couldn't get me to eat these things if I was starving." He winked. "I'm just hurt you don't recognize me—after we rode all the way back from Webster together. Really, I'm disappointed in you."

"Huh?" I wasn't tracking very well. Pat Jackson, with no mustache and short hair, was berating me because I didn't recognize him, though Stu and I had ridden home with Pete?

Del chuckled and pointed at the card table, set back a little from the long food line. "That's Pat over there, pouring beer. I know they look alike, but you're talking to Pete. I can tell them apart in the dark." She waggled her eyebrows and continued on.

With hair and mustache differences, the brothers had

looked similar. Now the Jackson filling cups with keg beer looked exactly like the Jackson who stood over the deep-fat fryer—both were pale and dark-eyed, had short dark hair, and were clean shaven.

"I'm sorry, Pete," I said to the one closest to me, flustered. "You've been gone so long, I forgot how alike you two are. You'll have to start wearing name tags."

"And spoil all the fun?"

That sort of fun should have lost its allure right around the fourth grade. But since I didn't have much to do with either one of them it probably wouldn't complicate my life any if the Jackson twins started impersonating each other.

Still, it was absolutely amazing that two grown men could look so much alike.

"That's what the word *identical* means," Del said when I mentioned it to her on the way to Rhonda's picnic table.

The night would be a long one, and I was on early shift at the cafe in the morning, so I had already decided to go easy on the alcohol. But the sun and wind had dried my throat, and I wanted a closer peek at Mr. Pat, so I figured an early beer wouldn't hurt.

"Jeez, I thought you guys'd never get through the line," Rhonda complained as we sat down next to her.

I don't like picnic tables—they're built for long-legged skinny coordinated people. I can't seem to thread my legs inside without spilling plate or cup, or both. Luckily, there was room at the end and I was able to scoot into place without contortions.

"You got someplace to go tonight?" Del asked. "That you're in such a hurry?" She popped an oyster into her mouth whole and crunched. "Mmmm," she said with her mouth full.

"Well, I thought if we got done eating early, we could get in a little extra rehearsal over at your trailer." Rhonda's plate was empty, and she easily swung her legs out from under the table and around on the bench to face the street. "Before the dance, and all."

"Nope," I said before Del could say anything. "I'm as ready as I'm ever going to be to sing that stupid song. I know the words; I know the moves. More rehearsal would just take the polish off." I took a bite of potato salad and raised my cup in a toast. "Shoop shoop." I smiled sweetly and drank.

Del busied herself with her supper, and Rhonda, who was too young to dwell on future humiliations when the night had so much promise, patted me on the shoulder and said, "Of course we're gonna kick butt. Don't worry about it."

She tucked her hair behind her ears, searching the crowd for familiar faces. Spotting one, she said, "If we're not going to practice, I think I'll wander over to the carnival for a while and check out the hunk running the ferris wheel."

She sauntered off, waving over her shoulder. Slim and young and blond, off to check out cute guys. A woman with a purpose.

We finished eating, sat gabbing, and killed another forty-five minutes or so. The sun was close to the horizon now, but it'd lost none of its searing power.

We left our table to other diners and walked among the rest, carrying beer cups. Del laughed and flirted. I kept an unobtrusive eye out for Stu, but didn't see him in the crowd. Neil was nowhere to be seen either, which was odd. He rarely missed a community event.

I groaned a little when I realized that I, neither young nor blond nor slim, was on the lookout for cute guys myself.

Of course, that was Del's mission too, but since Delphi is notoriously short on cute guys, she settled for Ron Adler, who motioned her over, blinking furiously.

"See you later," she said. "I'll grab a good table and you bring the stuff from the trailer."

We already had a cooler packed for the dance, heavy with ice, beer, a small flask of whiskey, and cans of diet Coke. We also had a paper sack filled with cups, napkins, bug spray, and sweaters, on the unlikely chance it cooled off after sundown.

After the oyster feed closed down, all of the picnic tables would be moved to either side of the street, where they would be immediately claimed by groups attending the street dance. There were never enough tables to go around, and the penalty for being too late to get one was standing until the wee hours with nowhere to put your butt or cooler except on the hard ground.

In fact, many of the tables were occupied already by groups of out-of-towners who drove in early and were now playing cards and bullshitting until the dance started.

I ducked under the bunting at the end of the block and stood by the carnival ticket booth, scanning faces for Presley and his friends, hoping to coerce them into carrying the cooler back up the street for me.

The rides whirled and the riders screamed and the music blared, a blur of frenzied activity in which it was impossible to identify individual faces.

Pres wasn't among those standing in line for tickets or waiting at the nearby rides. I reluctantly decided it'd be too much effort to go and search for him, when he popped out from behind the fun house, out of breath and plainly upset, pulling a furious Lily with him.

"Let me go, you little twerp!" Lily shouted at Pres, trying to pull her arm away.

Presley was small but strong, and he held on, though he was obviously confused and unsure of what to do next. Pres was mostly a commonsense kind of kid; he would not try to restrain someone a good ten years older than himself without good reason.

No one else seemed to be paying attention to them, so it was up to me to be the token adult and interfere.

"Hi, guys," I said. "Got a problem?"

"Tory, God, I'm glad you showed up." The relief was evident on Pres's young face. "You gotta stop her. Talk to her, she's gonna get hurt."

Lily had stopped struggling and looked from Presley to me and back again.

"That your mother or something?" she asked Pres.

"No, she lives with my mom and me," he said. "But she's smart. Listen to her, she'll help."

While the vote of confidence was gratifying, I wasn't certain I could be either smart or helpful.

"What's up?" I asked Lily directly. "You want to talk about it?"

"Not really," Lily said, tight-lipped.

"She's going to fight him, Tory. You gotta stop her," Pres said insistently.

"Who? Why?"

Lily sniffed deeply, crossed her arms, and looked at the ground but was silent.

"The guy in the ticket booth," Pres said.

"Doc? You want to fight Doc?"

She tapped her toe and then looked at me fiercely. "The little creep got me fired. He ran tattling to Bogner and the idiot believed him and fired me."

"What happened?"

"I don't know," she said, not as angry now, sounding more like a lost child. "Things were going really well. I'm feeling really good, in control. They didn't want me to do this, to travel with the carnival, you know."

"Who didn't, Mr. Bogner?" I wasn't following her train of thought.

"No," she said plaintively. "My family. They didn't think I could deal with this." She swung her arms wide. "With being on my own, coming to Delphi."

She looked up and smiled. "But I was doing fine. Me and Marko were getting along great, and I was doing my job. Until *he* called me into his office."

Pres was silent, standing closer to me, now, than Lily.

"What happened?" I asked again.

"Doc went to Bogner and told him I was turning tricks," she spat. "Big Bog read me the riot act and threw me out. Do not pass go, do not collect two hundred dollars."

I glanced over at Pres, wondering if he understood the terminology. His face tightened.

I didn't know what to say, though of course that didn't stop me. "Well, it's illegal, you know. It would get him in trouble too, if you got caught."

Her face crumpled. "But that's just it." She began to cry. "I wasn't. I didn't." Lily put her head on my shoulder and cried harder—a frail skinny kid, lying and crying her heart out.

I was surprised Good Old Father Figure Ham hadn't given in. If I hadn't known better, I'd have believed her myself.

And it looked like Doc was cutting off his nose to spite his own face, since he seemed to be involved in Lily's extracurricular activities.

"Hamilton Bogner told you that Doc accused you of prostitution?" I asked. Beside me, Presley suppressed a small gasp.

"No." Lily was still crying. "Bogner just said I was to clear out and that I was disgracing his precious carnival."

Not knowing what else to do, I patted her shoulder. Pres patted her shoulder. We both tried to comfort Lily.

"Why do you think Doc was the one who told him, then?"

"Right away I told Marko. Midge said that Doc had been spreading rumors about me."

Lily wiped her nose on the back of a hand. Pres dug a wad of Kleenex out of his pocket and handed it to her.

"Thanks, kid." She gave him a wan smile and ruffled his hair. Pres blushed.

"Anyway"—she sniffed again, straightening—"it's not the end of the world, I guess. People have thought a lot worse things about me." She shook her hair back from her forehead. "Delphi looks promising. I think I'll just stick around for a little while. That okay with you?"

"Sure," Pres said.

I had no answer for her—Delphi had exceeded its quota of unstable and unreliable residents a long time ago. I avoided the question by asking one of my own. "Where are you going to stay? We don't have any motels or B&Bs here."

Lily smiled. It was a small but confident smile. "I'm

pretty sure I have a place to stay. But I'm gonna need a job. I think I'll stop in tomorrow morning and ask that redheaded cook of yours if she's hiring."

16

....

Do You Wanna Dance?

As a social event, our modern version of the street dance evolved from the horse-and-buggy days, when isolated and work-worn pioneers would travel miles for company and conversation, a little bit of music, and as much alcohol as the community standards would allow.

It's not so different these days, though our pioneers are just as apt to be accountants, nurses, or insurance salesmen as farmers. And they often travel the dusty miles in pickup trucks with gun racks in the back window, or on motorcycles.

The purpose of the gathering, then as now, was to see and be seen, to talk and perhaps to fight, to dance and to drink—with sex, or the possibility of it, wafting a heady promise through the entire proceedings.

Unfortunately, nothing much was wafting through the air at the moment except the smell from the popcorn machine set in the doorway of the bar and that Avon stuff that everyone slathers on to keep bugs from biting.

Mosquitoes, which are not such a problem during the day, come out in full force at sundown, in the hour or so of calm before the evening breeze picks up. Believe me, whoever invents a truly effective mosquito repellent that smells good will be crowned King of South Dakota.

In the meantime, we slather and we slap and we bitch and moan. And we scratch.

"Spray my back, will you?" Del asked, handing me a can and turning around. "I'm being eaten alive."

Del was dressed to kill, or at least seduce, in a knit top so low cut that I thought she had it on backward until I saw the back.

"If you'd cover up, you wouldn't get bit so much," I said, spraying.

"I know." She laughed. "Unfortunately, that would defeat the purpose." She rummaged in the cooler and popped the top on a beer. "I'm going to mingle, see you later."

I was dressed neither to kill nor to seduce. But wearing a loose, light cotton outfit, and sitting on our picnic table with my feet comfortably on the bench, I sipped from an insulated mug of diet Coke and felt rather spiffy myself.

We had tagged a good table about three-quarters down on the bar side, far enough from the band to hear ourselves think, and with a good view of the whole layout.

The bandstand was set in the intersection between Neil's house and Jackson's, facing up the street toward the crowd. The Dakotah Stompers was a typical Midwest bar band. Male and female band members alike wore long ponytails, T-shirts, tight blue jeans, and cowboy hats.

The crowd studiously ignored the band's opener, "Your Cheatin' Heart." Groups of women gathered around tables with mixed drinks in flowered paper cups to compliment each other's hair and clothes and brag about their children and keep an eye on their spouses.

Men stood just out of their wives' hearing and compared scores on their first nine holes at Fishers Grove, drank beer from a can, and quietly pointed out the hooters over there.

It was a good half hour before anyone found the courage to dance, though the music worked its slow magic on everyone. People were still talking and drinking and gesturing, but they began to sway imperceptibly to the beat and tap their feet.

Then, like a signal had been given, the street filled with jostling couples. It would stay that way until about two A.M., when the whole thing shut down.

Of course, not everyone danced, and even the dancers took breaks, so there were always people standing in clumps around the street, sitting at tables talking and smoking. There were coolers and sacks of munchies stacked everywhere on tables and tailgates. The lines at the Porta Pottis were still short enough to encourage their use, a formality that would be dispensed with as the evening progressed.

I was content to sit on the table and watch as the shadows lengthened, idly slapping mosquitoes and enjoying the music even though the band played mostly country standards.

As the evening breeze rose, so did the noise level. People laughed louder, and the occasional drink sloshed over the edge of a cup as an enthusiastic talker waved his arms to make a point. A sort of benign hilarity overtook the crowd.

I danced a two-step with an uncharacteristically shy and awkward Willard Hausvik while Iva glared from the sidelines, then returned to the table to find Presley elbow-deep in the cooler.

"No, you may not have a beer," I pre-empted his request.

"Who me?" Pres asked in mock innocence, hand clasped firmly over his heart. "I wouldn't dream of doing something so blatantly"—he paused, searching for the right word, grinning when he found it—"illegal."

"Yeah, right," I said. He stood, hands in pockets, watching the dancers. "Nice shirt," I complimented. He was wearing a black T-shirt with the words "Carpe

Wiener" printed in large white Gothic letters on the front.

"Cool, isn't it?" he asked, looking down at his chest. "We all got them at the carnival. They'll put anything you want on 'em. John and Chainlink got ones like the workers wear, with their names on the front."

"And you had to be literary?"

"Mardelle Jackson takes Latin and she told me to do it." He grinned. Mardelle, daughter of Pat and Pat, owned the bustline of Presley's dreams.

"Did she tell you what it means?"

"Of course, don't be a dork. I can't wait to wear it to school."

"Don't hold your breath," I said, "they speak Latin there too."

Pres shook the water off a can of Coke and opened it, scanning the dancers. "Where's Mom?"

I pointed. Del was dancing with a stiff, wide-eyed Ron Adler, who held her gingerly, like a porcelain figurine. Ron's wife, Gina, at the next table over, didn't obviously watch the couple, though she was plainly aware of them.

And Del was plainly aware of her. She leaned closer to Ron and said something in his ear as they danced past. Ron blinked and blushed and Gina's lips tightened.

Presley's lips tightened too, and he looked down and then back up at me and changed the subject. "You think Aphrodite will give Lily a job?"

"I don't try to predict what Aphrodite will or won't do," I said. "We're not shorthanded right now, but she might take Lily on. I don't know if it's a good idea for her to stick around Delphi, though."

"You mean because of the prostitute stuff?" His dark eyes blazed. "She said she didn't, and I believe her."

It was a challenge—twelve-year-old Presley Bauer defending the honor of a lady.

"She could be lying," I said gently. "And even if she isn't lying, I think she's a troubled kid who has a lot to work through." I remembered the scars on her wrists.

"Well, I think we should help her," he said defiantly, then abruptly about-faced and walked off.

"What's the matter with him?" Del appeared at the table, wiping sweat from her forehead.

Things had been tense between Del and Pres for a while. "He made friends with a girl from the carnival and she got fired and he's upset about it," I condensed carefully.

Del took a long drink and then answered, "He got that from you—wanting to take in strays and save the world. You'd do him a big favor by teaching him to mind his own business instead."

I surprised us both by agreeing with her, and poured myself another diet Coke, this time with a dollop of whiskey in the cup. "Anyone interesting here?" I asked.

"Everyone's here, but no one who's particularly interesting." She grinned slyly. "Your sweetie dropped in about a half hour ago."

"Oh?" I tried to be nonchalant, forgetting that I hadn't officially admitted that Stu was even a friend, much less a "sweetie." "Is he here with a group?"

"No," Del said pointedly, "his wife wasn't with him. I haven't seen the Minnesota Queen at all. I think you're safe tonight, though I can't figure out what you see in him."

Green eyes, I thought. Strong hands. Great smile. "The South Dakota Snail," I said finally.

She raised an eyebrow. "Whatever. I think the lead guitar is giving me the eye, I'd better investigate," Del said, patting me on the shoulder. "Good luck."

"You wanna dance, Tory?" Ron Adler blinked in my ear as the female lead launched a musical attack in full overwrought Whitney Houston mode.

"Sure," I said. No point in sitting on a table all night, though a slow dance with Ron was apt to be pure torture.

I set my mug down next to the cooler and let him lead me into the middle of the dancers.

Periodically, I was able to spot Gina, who didn't look

nearly as concerned about my dancing with Ron. Del whirled by and waved, held tightly by Marko, who winked broadly. In between making inane remarks to Ron and commiserating about his having to wear a tux for the Phollies, I kept an eagle eye out for Stu. I finally saw him standing with a group of guys not too far from my table.

He wore plain blue jeans, a white long-sleeved shirt with the cuffs rolled up, and a Seattle Mariners cap. Not a seed company logo in sight. My heart did a sad little flip-flop.

The music was too loud for real conversation, which was just as well. We moved to the beat, or at least Ron's interpretation of the beat, his damp hand on my back throughout the interminable song. By the time he led me back to the table, Stu had disappeared.

"Pretty laid-back crowd for a Delphi street dance," Neil commented as he plopped himself down on the picnic table next to me.

"Amazing," I agreed. "I haven't seen a single fight, no girls crying, and so far everyone seems to be holding their liquor well."

"Ah, but the night is young." He smiled and pointed at the crowd with his pop can. "They've many hours before they sleep."

He was right. As the evening wore on, tempers would flare and hearts would be broken.

We sat for a little while in companionable silence, something I had missed lately.

Neil waved at Rhonda, who was now trying to polka with another girl. Both were flushed and laughing and making a miserable mess of the dance.

"Oh, good," I said. "Rhonda's supposed to open with me in the morning. I bet she'll spend the whole time in the bathroom."

"As long as *you're* not hung over, you'll get by just fine," he said.

"I'm doing my best to avoid it," I said, emptying my mug on the ground. "Why weren't you at the oyster feed? I expected to see you there, especially since it was a fund-raiser for the pool." I was surreptitiously searching the crowd, hoping to see Stu, and was surprised to spot him dancing with a simpering Iva Hausvik.

"I was waiting for a phone call," Neil said. "I did a little checking up around Mobridge about those burglaries and the steroid thing."

That got my attention. "Anything interesting?"

"Not really, all we know so far is that the robberies took place and no one wants to say anything officially. But I think I can get some concrete information tomorrow."

"You have a mole in the Mobridge police department?"

He grinned. "Well, let's just say I have a friend who has a friend who likes to talk. A lot."

"And do you have a mole at the doctor's office too?" I asked.

"Huh?" Neil's eyebrows knit briefly as Del waltzed by—deliberately, I'm sure—with Stu, who smiled in a friendly but not overfamiliar fashion.

"Ah." I'd lost my train of thought momentarily. "How else could you know about Junior? The Psychic Network?"

Neil laughed. "No psychics or moles. It was pure"— he tapped his forehead—"deductive reasoning."

"Sure," I said. "You broke into her computer system and deduced she was pregnant."

The news had been driving me nuts all day. At least I could talk about it with Neil since he already knew. Somehow.

"Nope. I just figured it out. But believe me, you don't wanna know how."

"Of course I want to know," I said indignantly. "What did you do, sneak into her bathroom with a urine test stick?"

He licked his lips and grinned. "I just watched her. Junior's a slim woman; it was pretty obvious from the start, especially when she started fainting in public."

"It is not obvious," I said. "I was with her yesterday and her stomach is still flat as a board."

"Ah," he said, lips twitching, "but her chest isn't. And it used to be."

"*Neil.*" I was flabbergasted. "I thought you were above noticing things like that. I can't believe you spend time checking out Junior's tits."

"Tory"—he laughed—"every man in the world notices . . ." He paused.

"Bazongas, maracas, jugs, melons, garbanzos . . ." I filled in for him.

"Breasts," he said firmly. "If a guy tries to tell you he isn't acutely aware of every set within fifty yards, he's either blind or lying. I just happen to be uncommonly observant."

"So it seems," I said, resisting the urge to cross my arms over my own chest, and collapsed in laughter with Neil instead. "Is anyone else pregnant that I don't know about?"

"Not so far," he said, wiping his eyes. "But it's still early."

The noise level of the crowd had risen another notch. Del was now earnestly talking across the street with Pete Jackson.

Or Pat, who could tell?

The band switched gears with a lovely version of "Light My Fire," à la Jose Feliciano.

I sensed Neil staring at me gravely.

"What?" I asked, a little uncomfortable.

"Would you care to dance, Mrs. Bauer?"

"Why, Mr. Pascoe," I said, standing up, "I thought you'd never ask."

I had not danced with Neil before. He was medium height and solidly built, we fit together well, his arm around my back with just the right amount of pressure as we moved to the music.

A flushed and smiling Lily danced past with the other Jackson twin. Rhonda, this time with a young man I didn't recognize, gave me the "all right" signal over his shoulder.

I gradually forgot to watch the other couples and gave myself over to the rhythm of the song. Neil's arm tightened and I leaned into him, eyes closed, and it felt warm and comfortable and right.

A blur of images, Stu and Neil and Nicky danced in my head.

I pulled back, confused. Neil loosened his arm. The spell broken, we finished the dance awkwardly.

Returning to the table, he said without looking at me, "I'll let you know what I find out from Mobridge."

"Yes, please," I said. "I'd like that."

Rhonda skipped up and fished in the cooler for a beer.

"Go ahead, have a beer," I said as she popped the top, but she was too far gone for sarcasm.

"Thanks," she said. "Say, you and Neil Pascoe look pretty cute together." She elbowed me in the ribs. "I'd never noticed how handsome he was until tonight."

She took a long pull from the can and then wiped her mouth with the back of her hand and leaned over me unsteadily. "You know why he's so handsome?"

"Because he's intelligent, and kind and loyal, and has a nice smile?"

"No," she hooted. "Because he's so fucking rich."

"Rhonda!" I was shocked. "That's disgusting!"

"Well, geez," she said, pouting. "You don't have to take it like that. I was only teasing."

Tears welled up in her big blue eyes and threatened to spill over. She was seriously inebriated.

"Okay, okay, forget it," I said, trying to soothe her. "You didn't mean it."

"Damn right," she said, perking up and looking around. "Say, where's the bathroom? I need to pee."

"Over there." I pointed to the two Porta Pottis, each sporting a line of at least fifteen people.

"Shit, I'll never last that long, you got some napkins?" She rummaged in the paper sack by the cooler. "Aha! I knew good old Tory would have the stuff." She surfaced with a handful. "Come with me. I'm going to have to use the alley and I don't wanna go by myself."

I shrugged and followed her around the corner of the

bar, under the bunting, and into the darkness behind an out-of-county pickup.

"You keep an eye out for intruders," she commanded as she unzipped and squatted against the bumper. "Listen and see if anyone's coming."

Though the voices and laughter were muted somewhat in the alley, the band was as loud as ever. Still, I could hear the unmistakable sound of someone else using the alley between us and the street. For the same purpose.

I searched the shadows, not trying to spy, just assessing Rhonda's chances of finishing without being stumbled over.

"Aaah," she said, rezipping. "All done, thanks for guarding. You want me to watch out for you?"

"No thanks," I said. "Maybe later."

She waved and ran unsteadily back into the light.

I picked my way carefully between the cars, watching the ground for wadded Kleenexes and napkins, and nearly didn't stifle a scream as I realized the dark shadow next to me was actually a man.

A man wearing a white long-sleeved shirt and a Seattle Mariners cap.

"Stu, for Christ's sake, you scared the shit out of me." I was frightened and relieved and a little angry at the same time.

"Sorry," he said. "I didn't mean to startle you, but I saw you go into the alley and followed hoping we'd get a chance to dance." His words were a little slurry, but he was steady. "Or whatever." He grinned, and his green eyes sparkled, something I sensed more than saw in the dim light of the alley. He ran a gentle finger down my cheek.

"What if someone saw you? Us?" I asked, horrified. "This is dangerous."

And stupid. And wonderful.

He pulled me into his arms and whispered, "No one saw me, and if they did they'd think I was back here pissing a gallon."

"But Stu . . ."

He stopped my protest with a kiss. A long warm one. "Come on." He led me farther into the darkness. "Let's dance."

I looked over my shoulder at the brightly lit crowd and caught sight of Lily next to the bandstand. Her posture was stiffly erect, and she held a beer can in her hand.

Stu was softly kissing my neck, but I turned to keep Lily in sight. She was shouting at someone in a black HBIE T-shirt. Shouting and, apparently defiantly, drinking from the can.

The man's back was to me and I did not recognize him, though he was plainly furious, his neck bright red with emotion, the bows of his glasses dug deeply into the flesh above his ears. He shouted and then took an awkward swing at Lily which she didn't even bother to duck. His fist connected with the beer can, sending it flying, its contents spilling in an airborne arc.

Lily, face flushed deep red with anger, shouted something else, a parting shot that caused the man to take another step toward her. She spun on one heel and ran off through the crowd, and the man followed her.

I lost sight of both of them, and pulled away from Stu's arms as if to follow. No one in the crowd had seemed to notice. Fights at street dances are par for the course.

"Don't go," he said softly. "It'll be safe here. Come dance with me."

I watched the crowd for another long second, but neither Lily nor the man were anywhere to be seen.

I turned back to the man who held both of my hands and who wanted me, and let myself be pulled into his warmth.

And as I slowly forgot my surroundings, I tried not to worry about being caught, or feeling guilty, or why, for a brief moment, Neil's name repeated itself in my head.

17

....

Delphi Daze

What exactly is it about sex that causes normal, rational people to be so stupid?

The word *orgasm* pops into my head, but the answer isn't as simple as that. Relationships are far too complicated to be forged or broken, vows kept or ignored, just because the bone dance feels good.

Of course, the Big O is a powerful incentive, an excuse, if you will, for grappling in a litter-strewn alley with a married man while a bar band pounds out "Witchy Woman," a song that will now be forever entwined in my mind with gravel and beer breath and lost underwear.

It takes a special determination, let me tell you, to block out that kind of distraction and enjoy yourself.

It was not my proudest moment. And the residual guilt and embarrassment left me owly.

It had been an exceptionally busy morning, crowded early with mostly drunk and hungry dancers who had not yet been to bed. The midmorning rush was populated by hangovers in dire need of Aphrodite's strong coffee.

"Put hair on their chests with that stuff," she said around her cigarette, eyeing the subdued customers.

By noon, hung over or not, everyone was back, ready to rehash the dance.

"And where exactly did you disappear to last night?" Del, who still wasn't home when I left for work, asked me with a wink. "I lost track of you somewhere around midnight."

"I went home, which is more than you did," I said, hoping she'd get the hint to leave me alone.

Del is not that subtle.

"Funny thing, no one saw Stu McKee after you left, either." She took advantage of a small lull to sit at the counter and quietly needle me as I searched through the tape box for different music. Perversely, Del had played an old Eagles tape over and over during the noon rush.

I wasn't even sure James Taylor would help, but I plugged *Sweet Baby James* into the player anyway, hoping that sweet nasal voice would work its usual magic.

"You know," Del said softly, "for a woman who's getting it on a regular basis, you're sure crabby."

"If sex made for good moods, you'd be the happiest woman on earth," I snapped.

Aphrodite set a couple of full plates on the counter for Del, who stood up smiling. "My point exactly," she said over her shoulder.

Earlier over his cheeseburger, Presley had asked anxiously if I had that "premenstrual fever stuff."

I decided it was time to smile, whether I felt like it or not.

"You want to go to the ball game with me this afternoon?" asked Rhonda, who looked like she should go home and sleep instead.

"Can't," I said, "already got a date. Four of 'em."

"This sounds interesting," Del said, sitting down at the counter again. The cafe had cleared out almost completely.

"Oh, yeah, real interesting. I'm taking Junior's kids."

"All of them?" Del asked me, incredulous. "By yourself?"

She knows that I don't find small children particularly enchanting. And she knows I'm even less enchanted with these particular children's mother.

"Yup." I poured myself a diet Coke and leaned both elbows on the counter. I remembered to smile.

"That should be fun," Rhonda said earnestly. "Those are the cutest kids in the world."

"What did Junior do, put a spell on you?" Del asked.

I thought over the past few days—all the things I'd done that were out of character, from helping Junior, to agreeing to sing with Del and Rhonda, to having sex in the alley behind the bar.

"The whole town put a spell on me, I think. I'm in a real Delphi Daze."

"You're in something, honey," Del said. "And I hope you snap out of it pretty soon."

"That makes two of us," I said.

The screen door creaked and we all looked up as Marko and Midge stepped in, squinting, out of the bright sunshine.

"I'll get this one," Rhonda said, with more of a smile than we'd seen all morning.

That was fine by me, though Del would have taken them too.

"Oh, shit," Rhonda said under her breath. "You'll have to do it, Del, my mom's out there." Rhonda's mother had pulled up in front of the cafe in their old farm pickup. "I'd better see what she wants."

She grinned at Marko on her way out. He sat at the counter. Midge arranged herself on a stool, pulled her tight black T-shirt down, and lit a cigarette.

"What can I get you?" Del asked, the sweetest, most polite waitress anyone ever had.

Seeing the pair reminded me of Lily. Pres had made me promise to ask Aphrodite to give her a job, but the shift had been so busy, I hadn't had a chance to talk to her.

I pushed through the swinging gate that divided the cafe from the kitchen as Aphrodite slapped a couple of patties on the grill and lowered a basket of fries into the bubbling oil.

I sat on the tall stool beside the dishwasher and watched her put together two burger platters with a minimum of motion and no wasted energy.

"What?" she asked, not looking up.

"Did anyone come in and ask you for a job this morning?"

I hadn't seen her, but Lily could have cornered Aphrodite before the cafe opened.

"Nope," she said, lighting another cigarette. "Why?"

Short and stocky, with impossibly tall red hair, Aphrodite Ferguson is an impressive figure, one not given to unnecessary conversation.

"Well, there's a girl named Lily who was with the carnival . . ."

"Was?"

"She got fired yesterday, and needs a job, and she wants to see if you're hiring."

"Why'd she get fired?"

I wondered if Aphrodite ever used words with more than one syllable.

"That's kind of complicated," I said lamely.

Aphrodite turned from the grill and looked at me and said nothing.

"Well, the carnival owner thinks she's been making money on the side as a . . . you know . . ." I hesitated. This wasn't exactly a glowing reference for Lily.

Aphrodite nodded. "Is she?"

"Yeah, I think so," I said. "But she seems like a nice kid and she needs a break. I thought she might be able to work with us for a while until she figures out where to go next."

That seemed like a pretty weak argument, even to me.

"I won't have any of that shit here," Aphrodite said as she poured herself a cup of coffee. "You know that."

Aphrodite looks and acts tough, but inside she's a marshmallow. She'd just agreed to hire on a former prostitute she hadn't even met, though she'd terrify Lily into good behavior if anyone could.

"Thanks," I said, relieved, and left the kitchen. I didn't bother to tell Aphrodite that she'd never regret it. We knew we'd both probably regret it.

That's what comes of being marshmallows.

"How're you doing today, gorgeous?" Marko asked me with his mouth full. He was handsome, but a lug. I didn't see what Del or Rhonda—or Lily and Midge, for that matter—saw in him.

"I'm fine," I said, watching Rhonda through the big front window. She was still leaning on the pickup talking animatedly with her mother. "How's business?"

I wasn't really looking for conversation, just making small talk. Aphrodite had put me in a better mood than I'd been in all day.

"You people sure love your T-shirts," Midge said, tapping the ash off her cigarette and blowing smoke directly in my face. "They're selling like hotcakes, and not just to the kids either."

It occurred to me that Lily might be afraid to come in and ask for a job. I hadn't been too encouraging last night.

"Say," I said, "you two are friends with Lily, aren't you?"

Midge's stenciled eyebrows arched, and Marko's burger stopped midway to his mouth.

"Lily?" Midge asked.

"Yeah, Lily." My bad mood was returning fast. "The one who worked with you until yesterday, when she got fired. You know, Lily."

"Oh, Lily." Marko laughed. "Of course we know Lily."

"Well, if you see her, tell her that Aphrodite is willing

to give her a job here," I said. "All she has to do is come in and ask."

Marko and Midge exchanged glances and then looked down at their plates.

"Sure, we'll tell her," Marko mumbled.

"If we see her," Midge added.

Rhonda's mom drove off, and she loped back into the cafe carrying a large paper sack, smiling widely.

"You got 'em?" Del asked, excited too.

"Yep. Tory, come here when you get a minute," Rhonda said across the counter, Marko and his muscles forgotten. "Got something to show you."

Since Marko and Midge were Del's customers, and no one else was in the cafe, I had all the minutes Rhonda needed.

She stood at the first booth by the door and shook out a pile of pink and yellow satin onto the table, oohing and aahing.

"Mom just finished sewing them. Aren't they great?"

Del held up a pair of pink satin shorts. Short pink satin shorts with yellow cuffs. "Fantastic," she cooed.

"What are these?" I asked with a sinking heart.

"Our costumes for the Phollies, dummy," Del said. "They're beautiful," she said to Rhonda, who was admiring a matching satin blouse, perfect fifties carhop attire—yellow satin with pink cuffs and her name embroidered over a breast pocket.

"Here's yours." Rhonda handed me a wad of cloth.

I held the fabric up gingerly. "These aren't going to fit. You should have said your mom was going to sew costumes."

Nothing homemade has fit me ever. Not even in high school home ec class. I'm lumpy in the wrong places and flat where I shouldn't be. Trying on clothes is a misery I avoid whenever possible.

"Of course they're going to fit you," Rhonda assured me happily. "My mom's a genius with a needle. She sewed all of me and my sisters' clothes."

"Go," Del said with a small push. "Try them on in

the bathroom, so we'll know for sure. That way Rhonda can take them back if they need alteration."

"Great idea," Rhonda agreed.

Marko and Midge were intent on their meals, and the cafe was empty. I had no reason to refuse, except that I didn't want to.

"Do I hafta?"

"Yes," they said. "Go."

So I shut myself in the bathroom and tried on the pink-and-yellow satin shorts set, which, to my absolute horror, fit perfectly.

"How are they?" Rhonda asked through the door.

"Fine," I said flatly, looking at the dirty mirror.

"Good, come out and let us see," Del said.

"No."

"Oh, come on, you gotta. You're going onstage in them tomorrow night. You might as well let us see now."

"Maybe I'll have a heart attack first," I said. It was an encouraging thought. Maybe a comet will hit the Earth tonight.

Maybe I'll break a leg.

"Oops, no time for modeling now," Del said.

"Why?" I asked, more than happy to put my own clothes back on.

"Got us some customers," Del said, laughing. "Come out and see."

I rolled the outfit into a ball, quickly rebuttoned, and opened the door, expecting to see a busload of clowns. Or maybe Stu McKee, since my discomfort often amuses Del.

Rhonda was on her knees, her hangover forgotten, listening seriously to three toddlers all talking rapidly at once.

The Deibert triplets, my charges for the afternoon, and their older sister, stood beaming in the middle of the cafe while Del grinned at their father, who wore a baseball uniform.

"Well, Clay," jolly Del said, "you're looking good these days."

"Hello, Delphine," Clay said carefully. He holds Del at a respectful distance, like a sack full of rattlesnakes. "Oh, Tory." He turned to me with evident relief. "I know it's a change in plans, but I thought it might be fun for you and the children to go to the carnival before the baseball game. I have some work to do at the church and would really appreciate if you could take them early."

The chorus of small excited voices was deafening.

Clay pressed a couple of twenties into my hand. I gaped, waiting for some sort of protest to come out of my mouth.

Before that could happen, studiously avoiding eye contact, Clay thanked me. "Junior and I appreciate this so much, Tory. You're a lifesaver."

And then he was gone. And I was left, alone with four children, for an afternoon in Hell. Over the noise of the very noisy children, I could hear Del's laughter.

18

....

The Hall of Mirrors

I've always been leery of perfect children, the paragons of politeness and good behavior. It seems to me that kids learn by being messy, rude, noisy, and disobedient because that's exactly the kind of behavior that they need to survive among the grown-ups.

The louder and more obnoxious they are, the better satisfied I am because I know that inside the irritating shell, a real human being resides.

The quiet ones who sit still and say "Yes, ma'am" give me the willies. There can be no conversation, no real interaction, with one who does not speak until spoken to, one who never interrupts, regardless of age.

I sometimes amuse myself by searching their eyes, looking for future mass murderers, expecting the glint of the upraised ax.

That is, until I'm left in charge of four of them for an afternoon. Then I'm grateful for whatever Nazi routine produced children who will actually do what they're told.

For perhaps the first time in my life, I appreciated Junior's iron will and her absolute control over her life and children, who at the moment, at least, were wide-eyed at the carnival spectacle but docile as we stood in line at the ticket booth.

"How about if we just walk around the grounds first?" I said with a totally false enthusiasm, pocketing a couple of full ticket books. "And then we can decide what rides to go on."

I wanted to kill as much time as possible. Stretching forty dollars over two hours among four children was going to be a challenge.

"Okay." Tres shrugged, holding Joshua and Jeremy by a hand on either side.

At least I assume she had the boys, since the one who clung to my hand had a small yellow bow nestled among the red curls. Without the ribbon, all three would have been entirely interchangeable.

We wandered among the rides. The little ones did not try to escape, and Tres rode herd better than I ever could have. I slowly started to relax.

That was, perhaps, a mistake.

The crowd was thick with people even I didn't recognize, and the noise was a deafening mix of Sousa and screams. The kids stared with openmouthed wonder at everything, babbling to each other incomprehensibly.

We strolled beyond the kiddie rides, taking time to step over cables and to examine the ground for dropped popcorn and candy bar wrappers.

"Can we have some cotton candy, Tory?" Tres asked, eyeing pastel fluffs hanging in the window of a concession cart. "Mom lets us have cotton candy."

I saw no harm in letting the kids have what was essentially sweetened air. They oohed in amazement as Daisy in the booth expertly twirled a paper cone around the tub, magically manufacturing blue spun sugar.

Tres separated short pastel strips and handed them to the little ones while I held the cone. They munched carefully, surprised that the candy disappeared before they could chew.

We stood for a little while, doling out cotton candy to each other, eating neatly and staying together. Then Tres pointed.

"Oh, look, it's Presley!" she said, her big brown eyes lighting up. "Let's go say hi to him."

She grabbed the hand of the triplet nearest to her and took off, leaving me with a cotton candy cone and a couple of toddlers intent on getting more of the sweet stuff.

"Wait for us, Tres," I said, juggling sticky hands and candy and purse, following her through the crowd.

By the time I caught up to her, she was in front of the ferris wheel, studiously ignoring Presley, who stood about ten feet away, laughing with Chainlink Harris.

Marko was at his post, lazily stopping the gondolas, adding passengers and letting others off. He spotted us and tipped his hat.

Pres saw us too and sauntered over, grinning.

"You look just like a mama duck"—he chuckled— "with all your little ones quacking right behind you."

Right then, the little ones were behind me. They'd clustered around my legs, peeking through at Pres, who, like all Bauer men, was irresistible to children.

He squatted down and talked to them in some sort of language they obviously understood, because they loosened their death grips and gathered around him gabbling.

Tres, who was too old to qualify as a kid and not yet old enough to be interesting to Presley, stood off to the side forlornly.

"I wanna ride on the ferris wheel, Tory," she said plaintively.

"I don't think so, kiddo," I said. "The little ones are too small for it and you're too young to go by yourself."

"I'll watch the kids while you take her on the ride," Pres said from the middle of his adoring crowd. His eyes lit up with pure evil. He knows I hate heights.

Tres clapped her hands, excited.

"That won't work, Tres," I said. "First, I can't leave the little ones with anyone but another grown-up. And second, I'm scared to death of these things." I craned my neck to look at the top of the wheel. Even that made me dizzy.

Tres's face fell, and I had an equally evil idea.

"How about if Pres rides with you?" I said sweetly. I hoped he wouldn't bolt.

"No way," he said.

"Come on, Pres," I said. Be nice, I thought. "Please, just this once."

He glared at me and mumbled something I'm glad I didn't hear clearly. "I'll never live it down if anyone sees me with her, you know that," he said quietly. "She's just a kid."

Tres was about to explode with delight. She preened, hoping, I imagine, that someone, anyone, would see her ride the ferris wheel with handsome Presley Bauer.

"You brought this on yourself," I said. "But thank you from the bottom of my heart. I really appreciate it."

"Yeah, yeah, yeah. Gimme some tickets."

I tore out a page apiece and handed them over as they stood in line. I could hear Pres setting down the rules.

"And no matter how scared you are, there will be absolutely no hand-holding."

Tres nodded happily, and Marko, who had been listening in, laughed out loud.

The triplets were bereft at Tres's desertion. They stood mournfully at the foot of the ride, watching the cars swing up and around and back down again.

When the ride was finally over, Marko sent smiling Tres and scowling Presley down the ramp with a salute. Pres disappeared before we could thank him.

All three triplets had consoled themselves by stuffing handfuls of blue cotton candy into their mouths during the ride. They were now a sticky mess, with blue lips and teeth and wisps of spun sugar in their hair.

They were also getting restless, probably the beginnings of the sugar rush I had just treated them to. They started to chatter and pull at our hands instead of letting themselves be led around quietly.

I decided to aim for the kiddie rides and plop all three on the carousel and take a small break.

At least that was the plan, but Joshua or Jeremy, I couldn't tell, refused to go on the merry-go-round, wailing at full volume when I tried to settle him on a horse. The other two chose to sit on opposite sides of the platform, so that Tres could only stand by one, while I tried to keep track of the other, with another sobbing child in my arms.

I was beginning to have a glimmer of respect for Junior.

We tried some popcorn, which had the advantage of being nonsticky but also had the tendency to spill from the torn sack as three children, who suddenly could not remember to take turns, lunged at once.

We stood in line for the Kiddie Plane, which they'd all assured me they really wanted to ride.

A small hand tugged at my shirt. Jessica, I think, said something very quietly. I squatted down to hear her better, my knees protesting loudly.

She repeated a sentence that vaguely sounded like it had to do with Josh eating bugs.

"Josh eats buggies?" I repeated. Jessica nodded. I turned to Tres. "Do you know what she means?"

"Not buggies." Tres laughed. "Boogies."

I was still confused.

"Josh is eating boogers!" she howled.

Sure enough, Josh (I assume it was Josh) was knuckle-deep up a nostril, digging for all he was worth.

"Jesus Christ," I muttered under my breath. "What next?"

That was a silly question.

I let go of Jeremy's hand to find a hanky, and he took off like a shot.

"Let's go, Tres," I shouted. "We gotta catch him."

She grabbed Josh, finger still up his nose, and I swung

Jessica up into my arms, and we ran through the crowd, but we'd already lost track of him.

"Jeremy," I hollered, searching knee-high in the crowd for a small, red-haired, blue-lipped boy. "Come back, Jeremy!"

Tres was calmly calling and scanning the crowd, but I was starting to panic. All those stories about kidnappers, and even Junior's mythical Satanic cultists, surfaced in my mind as I frantically searched.

"You lose something?" an amused voice asked behind me.

I whirled around to find Stu McKee holding a smiling Jeremy in his arms.

"Oh, thank God, Stu." I was so grateful, I nearly cried. Junior would never forgive me if I only brought back three of her children. "He just took off and we couldn't find him anywhere."

I violated my own prime directive and gave Stu a quick public hug in thanks.

"Stuart?" a woman's voice said from behind him. "Did you find the child's mother?"

Renee McKee stepped out from behind her husband. Stylish and pretty, she held the hand of a small boy who was a five-year-old carbon copy of Stu himself.

Their son, the one I consistently managed to forget.

For one long second we stood, three points on a triangle, my heart pounding in my ears, face flushed.

"Well, actually," Stu said, his voice sounding normal, unaffected, "I believe she's their aunt." He looked to me for confirmation, public face well arranged, eyes clear.

I licked my lips. "Cousin," I said. "They're my cousin's kids. I'm just helping out for the afternoon."

"How nice of you," Renee said noncommittally.

There was another pause, a breath and three heartbeats long.

Then Stu did the unforgivable. "Renee, have you met Tory Bauer? She works at the cafe here in town." He turned to me, actually met my eyes. At that moment, I hated him.

Or maybe I hated myself.

"I believe we've met already," Renee said, extending a hand.

I have no idea where I found the strength to reach out and shake Renee McKee's hand, but I did.

Stu went on, compounding my misery. "And Tory, this is our son, Walton. Walton, say hi to Tory."

I made myself smile at Walton, who squinted up suspiciously.

"I wanna go in the fun house," Tres interrupted from behind us. The triplets were subdued, staring at Walton, who returned their stares.

"No," I said without turning. "The fun house is no place for the little ones, and your mother would kill me if I let you go alone."

"We'll watch them for you," Renee said, "while you take the little girl through. Won't we, Stuart?" She laid a proprietary hand on his arm.

"Sure," Stu mumbled, this time not meeting my eyes.

"Thank you, but I couldn't let you do that. Tres will have to come back later with her parents. These three are too much of a handful."

"Nonsense," Renee declared, taking Josh's and Jessica's hands. Stu still held Jeremy. "We'll be fine."

"I really wanna go in the fun house, Tory," Tres whined. "You said you could leave the trips with another adult. These guys are adults."

I tried the Mother Look on Tres, hoping she would realize the terrible timing of her descent into normal rotten kid behavior.

No dice.

"Come on, Tory," she wheedled.

"Yes, take her through. We'll wait for you on the other side," Renee said.

Thoroughly rattled, shaking, and furious at being manipulated, I nodded.

"All right, but after this we go home, agreed?" I said to Tres.

She nodded seriously, belatedly picking up on some of the adult tension that surrounded her.

Tres skipped ahead of me to get in line. I walked steadily, not turning back, toward the semitrailer that held the fun house and tore off the proper number of tickets.

Tres and I climbed the steps and went inside; the darkness was cool at first. Tres clung to me as we wound our way between the Walking Dead, though even she could see that they were just painted dummies dressed in rags.

She added her shrieks to the canned screams that filled the interior of the maze, jumping and grabbing me, enjoying herself thoroughly as we fumbled our way through.

Cobwebs draped across the doorway in the Lair of the Giant Spider, which was a large, furry, mechanical thing that dropped out of a ceiling trapdoor. Strings of stuff stuck to our hair, and tinny maniacal laughter echoed from a speaker just at my ear level.

I was numb, unable to feel anything. I worked my way around some obstacles in the dark and rounded a corner into a brightly lit room with mirrors angled all around.

Tres gasped at the receding images of herself, all taller, fatter, or distorted somehow from the original. Then she laughed out loud, enjoying the sensation of being in the middle of a crowd of herself.

I felt oppressed. Each of my images looked back at me accusingly. He is married, they said. He has a child, they said. She touched his arm and you touched her hand.

Nothing will ever be the same again, they said.

I knew the voices were right. Sighing and exhausted, and sick of seeing my own sad, weary face staring back at me, I looked up.

19

....

Real Dead

Sometimes you know the Real Thing when you see i
Real power, real talent, and real diamonds all have
depth and a sparkle that assistant vice presidents i
charge of advertising, and cubic zirconium, simpl
cannot muster.

Real butter may not actually be better than marga
rine, but it is appreciably different. Like silk and polye
ter. Asphalt and cedar. Ivanna and Marla.

Unfortunately, the same goes for dead bodies.

In the middle of a sweltering amusement park attra
tion, with faux fatalities lying around everywher
where random limbs were scattered in the corners ar
assorted internal organs decorated the doorways, it w;
still impossible not to recognize the Real Thing.

So when I looked up into the girder-crossed ceiling
the Evil Hall of Mirrors and saw open-eyed Lily Mitc
ell peeking over the edge of a bank of mirrors, I did n
mistake her for an artfully posed prop.

She looked dead.

I stood, stunned, for a full thirty seconds as my chest tightened and my heart hammered. I had no urge to scream or run, though I had to fight for enough air to breathe.

I honestly didn't know whether to continue on through the maze or to double back to keep anyone else from entering the mirrored room.

I couldn't send Tres ahead alone without an explanation, and those behind me would likely ignore any warning. It seemed less likely to cause panic if we continued on.

Tres had not yet looked up, or she did so without realizing what was up there. I took her hand and shouted over the noise, neutrally, casually, "We'd better hurry through, hon. The little ones are probably raising a ruckus."

There were several people behind us, bumbling through the obstacles. I could hear real screams and laughter behind us.

I hurried Tres as quickly as I could through the final dark passages, conflicting emotions warring inside.

Sadness for Lily was paramount—Lily who'd looked forward to seeing Delphi, not knowing she would die here.

I was angry at whoever put Lily's body in the mirror room, where children might have seen her first.

And then there was fear, barely repressed, because I knew immediately that Lily had not crawled up into the rafters to die. She was put there deliberately.

And through it all ran a thread of self-pity, a whining, wailing "Why me?"

Finding dead bodies was Miss Marple's job, not mine. I am a waitress and a reader and a small-town widow with a life already complicated enough, thank you.

I considered saying nothing, letting someone else deal with it. But I knew even as the thought formed what I had to do.

Tres, eager and excited, let go of my hand and burst through the exit door ahead of me, laughing. Momentarily blinded by the sunlight, I followed her, squinting, through the crowd.

Stu and Renee stood on either side of the triplets, who sat cross-legged on the dusty ground licking multicolored Sno-Kones. Calmly sitting, neatly and quietly eating, making no mess at all.

Renee talked quietly with Tres, who babbled enthusiastically. Stu held his son's hand and did not look my way.

I had little time for conversation and none for subtlety, the previous awkwardness irrelevant. With one ear cocked toward the exit, listening for a change in the timbre of the screams, I touched Stu's arm lightly.

"Listen," I said quietly, panting, "I'm going to need you to watch all of the kids for a little while."

"Huh?" Stu asked. His eyes darted quickly to Renee who was bent over talking seriously with Tres. "What Tory, what's going on?" His voice was low, but something in the tone caused Renee to straighten and look our way.

"There's a . . ." I said, still listening behind me "dead body in the fun house. Junior can't come for the kids right now, but Clay might still be at the church and he can take them. Or he can be pulled from the game if it's already started. But the police will want me to stay here. I won't be able to take care of the kids."

"A body? Dead? What do you mean?"

"A body," I said impatiently, voice still low. "There's a dead girl inside, one of the carnival workers. I have to tell the guy to stop running people through before someone else sees her and panics. I need you to keep these kids for a while, or find Clay to take them. It's going to get busy here real quick."

"Are you sure? I mean, this *is* a fun house. It's their job to make you think you're seeing bodies." He actually sounded condescending.

"Of course she's sure, Stuart," Renee said, now standing next to her husband. "Look at her face. There's obviously something out of order inside."

"Yes," I said to her gratefully, fighting a rising sense of urgency and panic. "And they have to close the maze down until the police get here. Will you watch the kids?"

"But how do we know what she actually—" Stu asked.

"Shut up," Renee interrupted, voice hard. Stu blanched. To me she said, "They'll be fine; go do what you have to."

"Thanks," I said, filing away the last exchange between husband and wife for later consideration.

There was a small knot of children waiting to enter the fun house. I pushed through them to the front of the line amid complaints about crowding.

"Listen," I said quietly to Larry, who automatically took tickets without looking up. His greasy hair was tucked behind his ears; body odor rose from him like a cloud.

"Wait your turn like a nice lady," he said. "These kids were here first."

"I don't want to go inside," I said, out of breath. "And you can't let anyone else in either."

He raised an eyebrow, still tearing off tickets and shooing kids through.

"Get in line or go away," he said.

"No, you don't understand," I said, positioning myself between the line and the entrance, trying to speak quietly so no one else would hear. "There's a dead body inside. Lily Mitchell is in the mirror room and she's dead. You're going to have to shut down until the police come."

"Yeah, right," he snorted. "I don't care if the Queen of England's inside. The bottom fucking line in this enterprise is money." He rubbed dirty fingers together in my face. "I have to run a certain number of units through per day or I'm out on my ass. The boss has been especially testy lately, and I'm not about to close a moneymaker without his say-so."

"But she's dead," I said, thinking he'd misunderstood

the main message. "You're going to have to stop anyway, and it'd be better to do it before anyone else sees
her."

The kids in line were getting restless, tired of waiting.

"Listen yourself," he said snottily. "I been doing this
a long time now, and you'd be surprised how many
loonies think they see real bodies in there. It's hot and
it's dark and they see things that scare them. That's
what they pay for. You go get Bogner—if he says shut
down, I'll shut down. Not before."

Larry locked eyes with me for a moment, then he
flashed a fuzzy-toothed smile and pushed the next kid
pointedly towards the entrance stairs.

"She's dead," I said, sort of a pre–I told you so, and
shrugged, backing out of the line.

Kids exited the fun house screaming, faces flushed
with mock terror as they ran in search of other manufac-
tured thrills. No one seemed genuinely frightened yet.

Except me, as I ran through the crowd to Hamilton
Bogner's trailer. Dimly, I realized that the McKee
entourage was not grouped where I'd left them.

Taking the metal stairs two at a time, a sure indicator
of my agitation, I pounded on Ham's door.

Doc, in the ticket booth adjacent, craned his head out
to watch.

"Well, if it isn't the freelance writer," Ham said
jovially, though he stood in the doorway, blocking my
access. He held a newspaper in one hand, and there
were others scattered on the desk and floor behind him.

"Sir," I said. Some people are loud and commanding
in an emergency. I just get polite. "You've got to come
with me right now. Lily Mitchell is dead, she's up in the
fun house ceiling, and Larry won't close down. There's
little kids going through there, someone else is going to
spot her pretty quick, and then you'll have a real mess."

He stood, peering through half glasses perched down
on his nose, bald head shining, face impassive.

I thought maybe he didn't hear me, or worse yet
didn't believe me either.

"I know it sounds weird," I said, heart still hammering. "But Lily Mitchell has been killed. Her body's been stuffed in the rafters of the fun house. She's there now, I just saw her. You have to come, and we have to call the sheriff. Now. Please."

I work with the general public too, so I know just how flaky the Great Unwashed can be, but I'd never discount reports of dead bodies on the premises the way these guys did.

I decided to give them about fifteen seconds more before I sprinted across to the bar to call it in myself.

My obvious determination, more than any confidence in there actually being anyone dead, moved Ham to action.

He folded his glasses and slid them into the breast pocket of his polo shirt. "All right," he said slowly. "Fun house, huh? Let me get a flashlight first."

He disappeared back into the trailer, closing the door but not latching it. I heard desk drawers opening and the shuffle of papers. He reappeared carrying a yellow nine-volt and loped down the stairs so quickly I had to run to catch up with him.

He beat me to Larry, who frantically reminded Ham that he needed Ham's permission to close up shop and that they didn't have any extras to cover for him so he could check out the maze himself to see if the nutcase lady was telling the truth.

"Which," he said as he glared over his shoulder at me, "is probably all bullshit anyway."

"Keep everyone else out until I say otherwise," Ham said to Larry. "Come on," he said to me over his shoulder. "Show me."

"She's in the Hall of Mirrors," I said as I followed surefooted Hamilton Bogner through his own fun house maze.

He entered the mirror room in front of me and stopped dead in his tracks, neck arched, shoulders sagging, and flashlight shining uselessly on the floor beside him.

There was nothing for me to say. Lily was there, and she was dead, and Ham Bogner was now, by default, in charge.

And he knew it.

Without turning around, he said quietly, "Go call the sheriff. I'll wait here and see to it that no one touches anything. You know they'll want to talk to you too."

"Yeah," I said glumly.

"Here, take this." He handed me the flashlight. "Go back out front and tell Larry to shut off the damn speakers, wouldya?"

"Sure," I mumbled.

Larry's jaw dropped open in astonishment when I gave him Ham's message.

"You mean she's really in there? Dead?" His voice rose an octave.

"Just don't let anyone in until the sheriff comes," I said. "And try to keep this as quiet as you can."

The crowd itself wasn't paying attention to us. A few grade school girls booed when Larry told them that the fun house would be closed indefinitely. The rest milled and laughed and ate and sweated in the hot sun, oblivious.

But the carny workers knew something was up. Marko, who had a good view of the fun house from the ferris wheel, stared intently our way. Midge and a couple of others from the midway booths stepped out and shaded their eyes toward us.

It had already occurred to me, as it probably had to Ham Bogner, that no one was quite so familiar with a carnival fun house as a carnival worker.

And it occurred to me now that probably no one had a better reason to murder one carnival employee than another.

I felt vulnerable and exposed crossing the dusty street. Men and women in black shirts slowly grouped around the fun house, talking mostly among themselves. But some of them, I knew, were watching my back as I stepped into the darkness of Jackson's Hole.

20

Typhoid Tory

The planners of Delphi Daze thought they had a pretty good lineup of events, a combination of attractions that would draw not only residents but also people from the neighboring communities for three days of good ole pioneer-style fun.

And they were right—we had respectable crowds for the oyster feed and dance, the baseball game was sold out, and tickets were rapidly disappearing for tomorrow night's Phollies. Fifty miles was not too far to drive for entertainment on a midsummer Saturday, especially since the small grain harvest hadn't yet started.

But let me tell you, nothing packs them in like a dead body.

I'd pretty well known what to expect after I made the call from the relative calm of Jackson's Hole. The twins had been working behind the bar, keeping the patrons well sluiced. Faint strains of piano music drifted down from the upstairs living quarters, as Mardelle Jackson rehearsed Bach pieces for her performance at the Phollies.

"Can I get you a cold one, Tory?" a twin had asked.

"Better not," I said, though it was mightily tempting. "I have to use the phone. Got change for a five?"

"Sure." He rang open the cash drawer. "But if it's a local call, you can use the house phone and skip the quarters."

"Long-distance," I said over my shoulder, jingling quarters in my hand. "Thanks anyway."

I hadn't played fair by Delphi rules—I should have told the twins, in strict confidence, of course, who I was calling and why, not only to establish myself as the sole arbiter of the big news but also to give them the chance to be primary spreaders.

I could have used the house phone anyway. The Jacksons would have been thrilled to pick up the long-distance tab in exchange for eavesdropping on my end of the conversation.

But Lily's death was too new, too raw, to consider its gossip value. I wanted to give her fifteen more minutes of peace.

If lying dead among the girders of a fun house was peace.

It might not have been peace, but it was surely more peaceful than what happened after. I made the call, catching all three Jackson adults hovering as close as propriety would allow, and then hurried back across the street to wait in front of the fun house as I'd been officially requested to do.

My phone call to the sheriff might have been private, but the radio call for patrol cars, ambulance, coroner, and Department of Criminal Investigation agent went out over the police band, meaning everyone with a scanner knew there was a dead body in Delphi.

Pickups and cars loaded with strangers and friends, eyes peeled for excitement, drove in even before the squad cars arrived. The TV news crews set up shortly thereafter.

The commotion caused by the scanner report was

nothing compared to what happened as the sirens roared into Delphi. People poured out of houses and businesses, suspecting, at first, a fire or serious accident. Then as the news spread, the speculation became a buzz, and the buzz became a roar.

"A carnival worker, I heard."

"I thought for sure they said there was more than one body."

"Hacked to bits, inside the fun house, some sort of ritual, I bet. Satanic."

"Three dead and one injured—someone from Delphi dead too."

"Well, that's not what I heard."

"Who found 'em?"

This time there were no errors in reporting.

"Tory Bauer."

"*Our* Tory Bauer?"

"How many Tory Bauers do you think there are?"

"What was she doing in there anyway? She's kinda old for the fun house, dontcha think?"

"Weird how she's the one who found the body."

"Maybe people just wanta die around her."

This was followed by laughter.

"Maybe it's her new calling, finding dead bodies. I think I'll just keep outta her way."

"Like Typhoid Mary, dead bodies wherever she goes."

"Yeah, Typhoid Tory."

More laughter.

I did my best to blend into the crowd, trying not to hear the disjointed conversations and hoping to avoid any undue recognition from the TV people, while the officers cordoned off the perimeter of the fun house with yellow crime scene streamers.

DCI Agent John Ingstad, a tall, bald man dressed in shirtsleeves and a boring tie, stood inside the cordon, directing the operation. After a consultation with Hamilton Bogner on how to turn on the interior lights of the maze, paramedics were allowed in to ascertain that Lily was, indeed, dead, and not in need of resuscitation.

If it hadn't been totally inappropriate, I might have smiled at the notion of these serious officials making their way through the Lair of the Giant Spider.

Before going inside with Agent Ingstad, Ham Bogner held a hurried conference with Larry, who then disappeared into the crowd. His mission was soon apparent.

The ferris wheel, Octopus, and carousel ground to a halt, lights blinked out, and the music died. All of the rides stopped; faint protests from people with tickets at the ready could be heard in the unexpected silence.

All of the booths closed down, except for the refreshment carts. Ham Bogner was no fool—this crowd was certain to want pop and Sno-Kones after standing around gawking in the hot sun.

Black-shirted employees congregated in little groups around the outer edge of the Delphi crowd. Most of them were pale and tight-lipped, though Midge, whom I spotted with an arm around a miserable-looking Marko, whispered animatedly to the woman next to her.

"Tory, there you are," Clay Deibert, surrounded by his children, said. "Are you all right? How terrible for you."

It was pretty terrible for Lily too, but as a fellow Delphi resident and relative-by-marriage, his first duty was to minister to me.

"I'm as okay as I can be, considering," I said, squinting. "I see you found your children."

"Yes, the McKees sent a messenger to the ball diamond and waited until I arrived before going home."

So Stu and Renee were gone already. I was surprised to feel relief. I didn't want to see either one of them.

"How's Tres? Is she going to have nightmares about this?"

"She might. Though as far as I can tell, she didn't see, uh, anything."

"Good. I tried to get her out of there without causing any panic."

Clay leaned closer and said quietly, "I want to thank you for keeping your wits about you. A lot of these people"—he gestured toward the gossiping throng—"would not have been able to do that."

That was, perhaps, the nastiest thing I'd ever heard him say.

"Yeah, well, it's gonna cost me regardless," I said, remembering the crowd's comments.

"No, you're a strong person, and Junior and I are grateful," he said.

"Junior is going to be furious with me for taking Tres into the fun house to begin with."

"No, she'll just be glad you kept your head," he said, squeezing my shoulder. Then he straightened. "Oops, they're bringing her, it, out now. I want to get the kids home before the real circus starts." He gathered his children around him. "Thanks, Tory, I really mean that."

I nodded but had already turned to watch the paramedics back out of the entrance carrying a bulky zippered gray-vinyl body bag. There were too many twists and turns, and the passageways were too narrow, to fit a gurney into the maze.

I pushed to the front of the crowd, knowing that the officers would want me soon, surprised that the body had been moved before talking to me. Hamilton Bogner's version must have been enough for the discovery site statements.

The opaque bag was laid carefully on a gurney and then wheeled into the back of the ambulance, which drove off without lights or sirens.

No need to hurry now.

I stared after the roostertail of dust, lost in my own thoughts, and did not see the young uniformed officer approach.

"Mrs. Bauer?" He waited for my acknowledgment. "Could you come with me, please? Agent Ingstad would like to talk to you now."

Like the Red Sea, people parted for us as I followed him under the yellow ribbon and over to the metal stairs leading to the entrance of the fun house.

Agent Ingstad was speaking quietly with the man I recognized as the county coroner.

Trying to appear as though I was not eavesdropping, I strained to hear the conversation, though I caught only bits and pieces.

"Pretty unusual circumstances, but . . ." the coroner said.

"Any indication of violence?" Agent Ingstad asked.

"No gunshot wounds, bruises, or any injuries that I could see in the preliminary . . ."

". . . so it seems as though we've got nothing more than . . ."

". . . been twelve or fifteen hours . . . autopsy and test results back in about four weeks, but I'll be willing to say now that . . ."

". . . awfully young, isn't . . . ?"

". . . no real age limit. Stroke or heart, that's my . . ."

". . . makes my job easier if that's the case . . ."

". . . will know for sure after testing in Sioux Falls . . ."

My mind reeled with what I thought I'd just heard these two officials decide about Lily Mitchell's death.

"Thanks," Agent Ingstad said to the coroner, and then turned to me. "Mrs. Bauer, I understand you were the first person to see the body in place."

"Well, first except for whoever put her there," I said.

"Yes, well, we'll be looking into that during our investigation."

"And how thorough will your investigation be?" I asked, surprised by my own temerity.

"We investigate every case thoroughly, I can assure you, Mrs. Bauer," he said shortly.

"But didn't I just hear you and the coroner decide that Lily Mitchell died of natural causes rather than murder?"

"Mrs. Bauer, I'm surprised. I thought you were better behaved than that. If I'd known you were going to listen in on conversations that weren't meant for you, I'd have had you wait in a car."

"Finding dead bodies messes up my equilibrium,"

said. "I didn't mean to overhear." Which was a lie but a permissible one. "But since I did, can you answer my questions?"

He pursed his lips for a minute and then said, "This is a brand-new investigation, and as such, we have no official opinion of what has or has not happened here."

"Well, opinion or no, you had a dead girl stuffed into the rafters, and I doubt she got there by herself." I was adamant.

"What we *have,* Mrs. Bauer," he said firmly, "is an unusual circumstance. The world is full of unusual circumstances. Until the normal, routine tests are run and analyzed, we will not know for certain what caused this unfortunate young woman's death. But our esteemed coroner has given me a preliminary opinion and I'm inclined to accept his assessment."

"That she had a stroke?" I was flabbergasted. "Up in the rafters?"

"I didn't say that," he said sternly. "No one here has said anything as to the cause or location of death. You would do well to remember that, especially if you intend to talk to the media today."

"I have no intention of talking to the TV people anytime," I said, unwilling to let him or the subject go. "But—"

"But nothing." He took my arm. "After the test results have been analyzed, they will be made public. Until then, I'd appreciate it if you'd curtail any wild speculation. Now, you can help us most if you'd please tell Officer Larson over there exactly what you saw."

Agent Ingstad pointed to my escort. He did not look old enough to be out of high school, or to drive, much less be charged to protect and serve.

"If you'd come this way, ma'am," he said, unsmiling.

21

....

Censorship Anyone?

I am a First Amendment maniac—freedom of speech is what really separates us from the French (or Canadians or Israelis). The right of individuals and the press to say and print what they please cannot be overemphasized.

Not that I carry picket signs or generally get worked up enough to write letters to editors, except when fringe groups incite the mainstream populace (and our ever-excitable legislature) into considering laws that forbid certain kinds of music and books, or worse yet, amendments to enforce respect for the flag.

When some current outrage transforms the passive masses into engines of prohibition, I try to remember what whoosit said about defending to the death your right to speak, even if I don't agree with what you say.

I was prepared to man the battle line if necessary, to fight the good fight for my country and constitution. Of course, that was before I realized just how interested the media was going to be in the person who discovered Lily Mitchell's body.

The three local television stations had already staked out territories of their own around the fun house as close as possible to the police barricade. Lights and tripods and microphones were set up in the dust, while young men and women with cameras balanced on their shoulders jockeyed for position in the crowd as the officials conducted their interviews.

I stood with Officer Larson near the fun house exit, painfully aware of the cameras pointed my way, as he dutifully took my statement down, word for word. Most of what was being filmed would be cut into snips for background color while a seated anchor droned on about the body discovered in Delphi. But I knew competing stations would vie for the juiciest interview bits to liven up the footage. Out of the corner of my eye, I'd already seen Ron Adler and Willard Hausvik happily talking to cameras.

And over the crowd noise, I'd heard my name mentioned more than once to interested newspeople.

"Is that everything, Mrs. Bauer?" Officer Larson asked without looking up. We'd already dissected the fact that I knew the deceased and had recognized her immediately.

"I think so," I said. "I can call you if I remember anything else."

"That probably won't be necessary; it looks like you've given us a pretty complete statement," he said, flipping his notebook to a new page before sliding it back into a breast pocket. "Thank you for your help."

He turned and walked away, leaving me alone behind the flapping yellow banner as several people, some I knew and some I didn't, called my name.

"Tory!" Ron Adler blinked. "Hey, Tory, come here for a sec." He was talking to some cafe regulars, all of whom, I knew, would be dying for insider details.

I would probably not have been anxious to rehash the afternoon with Ron even if he hadn't had a camera pointed directly at him.

"Can't now, Ron," I said. "Gotta run."

"Mrs. Bauer, Eyewitness News, can you talk to us for

a minute about what you saw in the fun house?" A handsome young man tried to stick a microphone in my face as another shouldered a camera toward me.

"Sorry," I mumbled. I'd hoped to make a run for our trailer, but the crowd was too thick in that direction and the sea of faces was dotted by entirely too many television cameras.

"Tory Bauer!" another shouted. "Did you have any idea, this morning, that you'd be finding a dead body in the maze of this carnival fun house?"

The stupidity of that question stopped me, and I turned to stare at the man in disbelief.

"How does it feel? Are you upset? Do you think she was murdered? What do you think happened?" He fired questions in rapid succession.

A dozen equally stupid responses bubbled in my brain; most of them would not have been suitable for an early-evening newscast. I settled for a withering look and searched the crowd fruitlessly for a friendly face.

"What did the body look like?" a woman shouted. She actually pushed the first young man out of the way, then asked the sixty-four-dollar question. "How did you happen to be in the maze at that particular time?"

Never any repression around when you need it, I thought grimly.

"Excuse me," I said, ducking under the ribbon. "I have to leave now."

"But, Mrs. Bauer, don't you want to make a statement for us?"

They were genuinely confused. TV types are always surprised by people who'd rather not perform for the cameras.

I just wanted to get out of the sun, to go home and sit for a while and try to figure out for myself what had happened—how, as the reporter wanted to know, I ended up in that maze at exactly the wrong time.

But the crowd around the fun house blocked the street entirely. Several serious-looking people with flash cameras popped shots at the crowd and the carnival in general, taking notes and conducting interviews.

The newspapers were here too.

Some were camped out on the sidewalk in front of Neil's house, across from the carnival, leaving me no way to get past them.

I edged my way carefully toward the ticket booth, away from the crowd, necks craned now to hear a prepared statement being read by Agent Ingstad.

I waited for the cameras to swing in his direction and then quickly slipped out of the carnival grounds past a grim-faced Doc, who leaned against the ticket booth talking to a visibly pale Marko.

Risking a quick glance back over my shoulder to make sure I wasn't being followed, I ducked across the street into Jackson's, whose cool dark interior felt like a sanctuary.

"Pretty exciting, huh?" young Mardelle Jackson asked from behind the bar. "I mean, how often does anything exciting happen in Delphi?" She stood and put her thick book facedown on the counter.

"Every day is exciting around here," I said wearily, sitting on a bar stool.

"If you say so," she said with a shrug. Dark-haired Mardelle was pretty in a way that resembled neither of her parents, and she was built like no sixteen-year-olds were built when I was sixteen.

It's no wonder Presley was intrigued.

I hadn't formulated an escape plan any further than getting away from the reporters and out of the heat. Now that I was in the nearly empty bar, I had a little time to think before making another move.

"Who's bartending?" I asked. "I'd like a beer."

"Mom and Uncle Pete are across the street, watching everything," Mardelle said, pointing out the door. "Dad went to his class."

"On Saturday?" I asked. Pat Jackson was taking an accounting class three afternoons a week at the college in Aberdeen. At his wife's insistence. We all knew that.

"They're getting ready for finals, so they decided to hold a special study session. He's working really hard for this class."

"Good for him," I said, looking around for whoever was waiting tables. "So who's bartending?"

"Honor bar till Mom and Uncle Pete get back," Mardelle said, indicating a mug with a few bills and some change in the bottom. "I can't sell anything officially since I'm underage, but you can pay for your beer and pull the tap yourself if you want."

"Sounds good to me." I dug in my pocket for a couple of loose bills, mentally thanking Clay for the beer. I didn't think he'd mind. I stood on the railing and leaned over the bar and pulled on the handle while Mardelle held the mug underneath.

"Be sure to give yourself a good tip." Mardelle laughed, handing the full mug back to me.

I sprinkled salt on top of the foam and drank. It was wonderful.

"You need anything else?" Mardelle asked, reaching for her book again. *The Stand,* 1,153 pages of light reading for a summer afternoon.

I had an idea.

"Yeah, do me a favor, would you? Go peek and see if there are people standing around the front door of my trailer."

"If you want," she said, probably thinking that adults were alien beings.

She opened the screen door and peered around it and then hollered back. "Some guy holding a video camera, and another standing with a microphone right on your front steps."

"Shit," I said. Now what? I didn't want to be stuck there all afternoon. And how long before it occurred to them to check out the bar?

"TV people?" she asked.

"Yeah," I said glumly, "and I'd like to avoid them."

"Why? Being on TV would be cool."

"I'd just as soon not, if I can help it," I said.

Mardelle shrugged and started reading again.

I had another idea.

"All right if I use the phone? It's a local call."

Mardelle nodded, not looking up.

I dialed and drank another gulp waiting for an answer.

"Hi," I said. "Just me. Listen, can I camp out at your place for a while? I'm in the bar and the paparazzi are everywhere so I can't go out on the street or get home without being seen. They've staked your house out too, but I could sneak out the back door and across the alley to your side entrance. If you'll have me."

I realized, with a small shudder, that I would have to walk past the exact spot where Stu and I were last night.

I firmly squashed that thought.

"Sure, come on over," Neil said over the phone. "I've been watching the proceedings. You certainly know how to liven up a lazy afternoon."

"Tell me about it."

"I'll keep watch just in case the minions of the press spot you," he said with a laugh. "Oh, and hurry. I've got something to show you."

22

....

Neil's Mole

I'm a predictable crier. For instance, I cry every time Tiny Tim dies: whether he's surrounded by Muppets, George C. Scott, or Mr. Magoo; read from a book or performed by high schoolers onstage; big screen or little.

It matters not that I have known the ending to that particular story since childhood.

I still cry.

Though I've read it over and over, I cry whenever Glen, Ralph, and Larry leave Stu Redman behind with his broken leg in Utah, on their doomed pilgrimage to Las Vegas.

Disney movies do it too—from *Pollyanna* to *Beauty and the Beast*. And I refuse to go within a block of any VCR playing *Old Yeller*.

I cry at weddings, graduations, overdue bills, and often after stepping on the bathroom scale.

But I don't cry when I find dead bodies.

I am upset, sad, confused, frightened, weary, and self-pitying.

And angry.

"What do they think? That she crawled up into the rafters by herself to die?" I demanded indignantly. "That she felt a heart attack coming on and thought the fun house would be a cozy place to check out?"

I'd been fuming like that for ten minutes or so up in Neil's unfinished tower. We were taking turns with the binoculars, keeping track of the confusion below on the carnival grounds.

Neil was benignly neutral. He let me rant until I ran out of steam on my own.

"Natural causes, bah," I said, disgusted.

"Humbug," Neil agreed.

"I mean, it's obvious that she was murdered. She was tucked up in the rafters to hide the body, and there would be no need to hide a death from natural causes, right?"

"Doesn't seem likely," he said, leaning over to switch CDs from Prince's *Greatest Hits* to Queen. "Fat-Bottomed Girls" blared from the speakers.

"What are the physical indications of a death from stroke or heart failure anyway?"

Neil put the binoculars down to think. "I'm not really sure there are any, at least ones you can see in a superficial examination. Unless the person died clutching his chest with one hand and a note reading 'I'm having a heart attack' in the other."

"That's what I mean. They're probably saying 'natural causes' just because her throat wasn't slit."

"On the other hand, Tory," he said gently, "they might be right. We don't get many murders in South Dakota. But we have plenty of heart attacks and strokes. The coroner might well be able to recognize one."

"That just doesn't make any sense," I said stubbornly. "Even if it was natural for a healthy young girl to die that way, how did she get in the fun house?"

Neil raised the binoculars again. "You got me there."

"And anyway, there are poisons that make those symptoms. I know; they use them all the time in mystery books. And the medical officials are always fooled."

"This isn't Saint Mary Mead or Isola. We don't have access to exotic potions, and I don't know anyone with the expertise to use them."

"Us flatland dumbshits might not," I said, pointing out the window at the carnival, where the police were wrapping up their interviews with workers and getting ready to leave. "But *they* might. Where do they come from, where have they been, what do they know? Those are important questions."

"You know, you just might have a point there. I could get on the horn and ask around a little. Maybe I can find out a little about Hamilton Bogner's International Extravaganza," Neil said. "And I'll check the medical books for poisons that mimic strokes."

"Oh, would you? That'd be wonderful. Bogner International is supposed to be traveling with a Harvard doctor who just might know an exotic poison. And how to use it."

"Aker, right?"

"Yup, Dr. William, according to Ham Bogner himself. And Lily told me that the one they call Doc is the one who got her fired."

"Curiouser and curiouser," said Neil, taking notes. "What about the guy who got in the fight with her last night?"

"God, I forgot about that," I said, suddenly remembering who I was with when I saw the beer can go flying out of Lily's hand. I faltered a little. "I know I've seen the guy around, but his back was to me so I couldn't read his T-shirt. He was tall, and he wore glasses."

Neil handed me the binoculars. "Do you see him down there anywhere?"

I scanned the whole block. "Nope, but the workers are pretty well scattered. The rides are shut down and the news crews are packing it in, so there's no reason for them to stick together now. Ah," I said, leaning forward.

"What, the mystery man?"

"No, but Doc, Midge, and Marko are all heading for

the bar. I haven't seen Del all afternoon, but I'm sure she'll stop there after work, so we can get a full report from her if they do anything interesting besides drinking."

"Yeah, like discussing in loud voices how they killed Lily and stuffed her in the rafters?" Neil said, raising an eyebrow.

"Of course not. But none of them strikes me as especially intelligent. Maybe they'll say or do something odd. Del will notice; she watches Marko like a hawk."

"That reminds me," Neil said, hitting his forehead with the flat of his hand. "There was info on our less-than-brilliant Muscle Boy waiting for me last night after I got home from the dance. That's what I wanted to show you."

He dug in his back jeans pocket and pulled out a folded sheet of paper and handed it to me.

"Remember, you didn't see this here, or anywhere else, for that matter."

It looked like an official form of some kind, covered with single-spaced, sloppy typing. The paper was smooth and shiny. Probably a fax.

"Read it," Neil encouraged.

I skimmed the first few paragraphs without understanding much of what was written until it dawned on me that this was a police statement. Made by some juvenile boys in Mobridge who had been charged with possession of steroids.

I looked up at Neil. He grinned. "Keep going, it gets better."

The boys claimed to have bought the drugs from a guy who worked with a carnival. A young, dark-haired, muscley guy whose name they couldn't quite remember.

And this group of young men were also found in possession of several of the items listed as stolen during recent burglaries in Mobridge. In fact, they were found in possession of almost all of the stolen goods, except for a turquoise cross necklace, which was still listed as missing.

The statement went on to say that the juveniles swore

they purchased that particular batch of items from the same unidentified carnival worker some two weeks ago.

"Holy shit," I said, something of an understatement. "Why didn't you show me this right away? And how did you get it?"

Neil laughed. "You were too upset at first. I figured I'd let you get it all out of your system before going on to other subjects. And I already told you, I have a friend on the Mobridge police force who likes to talk."

"And fax, apparently. What do you mean, 'other subjects'? Don't you think it's just a little too coincidental that the same Marko, it's gotta be Marko they're talking about, who gave Lily a turquoise cross, is implicated in all these Mobridge robberies and just happened to be very friendly with the dead girl? And the turquoise cross, which was still missing, was wound around the dead girl's hand?"

"It's certainly interesting, though we shouldn't jump to conclusions. Robbery and friendship don't necessarily add up to murder, if it was murder. Besides, Lily had lots of 'friends,'" Neil finished.

"Oh yeah, who?"

"Well, you for instance. Weren't you the one who felt sorry for the poor reformed prostitute and went to great lengths to get her a job at your own place of employment?"

"What does that have to do with anything?" I demanded.

"Probably nothing. It just means that Lily had more connections here than the carnival. We shouldn't get so bogged down by the obvious that we forget to see that.

"Lily consorted, on at least two occasions, with Pete and/or Pat Jackson. And young Presley Bauer was willing to brave a black eye to save Lily from herself. Remember?"

"Yeah." I sighed, deflated and sad again. "It's all so complicated. It's amazingly easy to forget that a real person is dead. And that a twelve-year-old boy had a crush on her. Was Presley in the crowd this afternoon?"

"He was there most of the time," Neil said quietly,

"watching everything. He looked pretty miserable. I lost track of him just before you called."

"I'd better get home and see if he's there. It won't occur to his mother to check on him. If we're by ourselves, he might let me give him a hug. Not that hugs are much of a buffer against anything."

"Oh, I don't know about that," Neil said, planting a soft kiss on my forehead and a strong arm around my shoulder. "Works for me."

23

....

Sex Rules

Sigmund Freud said that the workings of the human brain are a mystery that can never be completely understood.

Or at least, I think he said that. And if he didn't, he should have, because it's certainly true.

Take the case of my human brain, for example. With last night's agitating and jumbled experiences followed by the extremely disturbing course of events today, you'd think that I would be wired beyond relaxation. One would expect the combination of sadness, fear, and anxiety to produce a wakefulness, an inability to sit still or let go.

That's what I thought when I got back to the empty trailer. Neither Del nor Presley were home yet. I prowled through the quiet rooms, restless and unable to focus or concentrate. I picked up the new Sue Grafton and read the first page three times without understanding a word.

Even James Taylor didn't help. The eerie quiet of the

carnival grounds, deserted after the police and TV crews left, seemed louder than the noisy rides and screaming crowds had earlier.

I spread the crocheted afghan on the vinyl couch and stretched out on it, prepared to lie there until either Del or Presley came home, hoping I could talk to Pres before his mother did.

I knew he'd be upset.

I lay there on the couch, listening to a fly buzzing over my head, wide awake, tense and unhappy.

Upset and unhappy and wide awake and waiting.

"Hey." Someone was shaking my shoulder. "Hey, wake up."

"I am," I said slowly, mouth dry and eyes unfocused.

"Yeah, you look like you're awake." Del laughed. "You sound awake too. Funny, I never pictured you as a snorer."

I sat up. "I don't snore," I said, rubbing my eyes. "Besides, I wasn't asleep."

"Coulda fooled me," she said. "I've been home for five minutes and you didn't break rhythm once."

"Musta dozed off," I mumbled. "I only lay down a couple of minutes ago."

"Couple hours ago, you mean," Del said. "It's after seven."

"You're shitting me." I rolled my neck, wincing at the cracks and pops. "I was wide awake. Not sleepy at all. Just waiting for you and Pres to come home. Did he sneak in while I was sleeping too?"

"I don't think so. I haven't seen him since before the excitement."

That was one way of putting it.

"Some excitement," I said, lying back down.

"Who says nothing ever happens in small towns, anyway?"

"Not me. Where were you during the media circus?"

Del went into the kitchen and poured herself a beer in a frozen mug. "Let's see," she said sarcastically, "my shift doesn't get over until six o'clock, so I guess I was at work all afternoon. Which, by the way, was a bitch.

Every third person who stood around hoping for more
bodies decided to celebrate with a hamburger and fries
afterwards."

"Bet Aphrodite was happy."

"She even smiled. I think she's going to schedule a
murder every month. It's great for business."

"It's a little hard on me, though," I said. "Tell you
what, you find the next one."

"Nope, honey, that's your job from now on. People
think you might have some sort of psychic talent for
finding bodies. Like a water witch."

"Oh, good, just what my reputation needs." I stood
up and stretched, still amazed that I'd fallen asleep.

"Everyone's really interested in what you saw."

I grimaced.

"But personally"—Del grinned—"I wanna know
what sent you into the fun house to begin with. I know
you. You hate those things, wouldn't go into one if you
were paid to."

Del's beer looked good and so I fixed one for myself
while I worked out an answer.

"I *was* paid to. Clay gave me money to take his kids to
the carnival, and Tres wanted to see the fun house, so I
took her through."

"That line might fool the masses, sweetie, but it won't
wash with me," she said. "I already know that Mr. and
Mrs. Stuart McKee watched the little shits while you
ventured forth. Iva Hausvik was especially interested in
that point."

"Oh, Jesus," I said, sinking back down on the couch.
"What a mess."

"No shit," Del agreed. "I think I have the scenario
figured out—it was either take Tres through the fun
house or stand outside making small talk and compar-
ing dick stories with Mrs. Philanderer, right?"

"Something like that," I said, pressing the cold mug
against my hot forehead. "How did I get into this
anyway? How do I get out of it?" That last was to
myself.

"You can't." Del laughed. "Unfortunately, you forgot the most important rule of sex."

"Just say no?"

"That's drugs, dipshit. Nope, the first rule of sex is: You can't unfuck 'em. The horizontal tango is forever, babe. So consider carefully *before* you undress. Just think of all the complications you'd have avoided."

I groaned and Del continued. "Now, in my case, I just don't give a shit. If it stays quiet, fine. If everyone knows, fine.

"But for some reason, it matters to you—you don't want anyone to know about you and Stu. And I got news for you. The second rule of sex is: It never stays secret for long."

"I think I'll just hibernate. Become a recluse, stay inside for a year or two," I said, eyes closed.

"Won't work. If you stay away they'll *know* something is up. Right now, I don't think anyone suspects a thing. Stu is discreet, and you're not over your dead husband yet. No one thinks of sex when they look at you."

"Fat ladies don't fuck, is that your point?"

"Of course not. But good girls don't, at least not with married men. And you're a good girl—or so they think. Besides, you can't hibernate. You have work to do and bills to pay and places to go tonight."

"Tonight? I don't want to go anywhere. I want to stay home, and I need to talk to Presley."

"Why?"

"He had sort of a crush on the dead girl. On Lily. He's probably going to have a hard time with her death, and maybe I can help a little."

"You plan to make her undead or something?"

"No, I just think he'll need a hug or want to talk, and I'd like to be here when he gets home. You go to the bar alone; I don't feel like going out or having a drink, or whatever you've got planned."

"Don't worry about Pres," Del said, patting my shoulder. "The kid is a brick—he'll get through this better than you will, believe me. Anyway, you can see how he is for yourself. He'll be there."

"Pres will be at the bar?"

"No, idiot, Pres will be at the Phollies dress rehearsal tonight. It's required for all the participants, including us. You can see him in"—she consulted her watch—"fifteen minutes. That's why I woke you up. We're nearly late."

She tossed a handful of pink and yellow satin at me. "Put on your short shorts. We're going to boogie."

24

....

Who Wears Short Shorts?

It doesn't matter if it's a one-room country school (yes, they still exist) or a multiplex campus with twelve buildings and a TV broadcast studio, all schools smell the same—a combination of moldy paper, chalk dust, and old sweat socks.

And anxiety. It's been a long time since I had to worry about locker combinations and tardy slips, yet every time I walk into the building, I have the gnawing suspicion there'll be a history test next period on three chapters I haven't even read. Or that I've lost my physics book and have to explain again to Mr. Walker, who tolerated no fools gladly, why my homework isn't done.

I'm not the only one who feels it; every adult I passed in the hallways backstage had that same strained smile, the Don't Send Me to the Principal's Office Cringe, as though we'd all just been caught shooting spit-wads in study hall.

"Have you noticed?" Rhonda asked as she expertly

twisted her blond hair into a perfect Barbie Doll ponytail. "Everyone's sorta whispering. And I haven't heard
a single swear word all night. Why do you suppose that
is?"

"Beats the shit outta me," Del said with a wink. She
was inspecting her backside in the girl's locker room
mirror. "It's not like Old Lady Beiber is waiting outside
to make us roll our skirts back down below the
knee."

I was desperately avoiding the mirror altogether, self-
conscious in front of Del and Rhonda, who looked just
fine in pink and yellow satin. My only consolation was
that Del had vetoed the roller skates—her balance was
even worse than mine.

"Here, Tory"—Rhonda stood in front of me with a
hair brush—"let's see if we can do something with your
hair."

I'd already spent a half hour trying to manage a
vaguely fifties do, before giving up in disgust.

She brushed and pulled a couple of bobby pins out of
her mouth and placed them at random in my hair,
squinted and rearranged some more, then choked me
with a cloud of hair spray. "There, much better." She
turned me around to face the mirror. "See?"

I winced at the reflection of a middle-aged bobby-
soxer carhop backup singer.

"Just have to finish with your makeup," Rhonda said,
eyeing me critically.

Del handed her a small tube. "Here, try this one."

"You know, I am capable of putting on my own
lipstick," I said as Rhonda lunged for my face.

"Shush, you're going to smear," she said.

"Does it have to be such a bright red?"

Rhonda ignored me. "There," she said to Del, "what
do you think?"

"Perfect. Let's move it." She took one last glance in
the mirror. "I want to see some of the other acts before
we go on."

"Sounds good to me," Rhonda agreed. "Come on,
Tory."

"You guys go ahead," I said, suddenly feeling sick. "I'll catch up backstage."

"Not on your life," Del said, grabbing my arm. "You'll disappear if we let you out of our sight. You have that rabbit-in-the-headlights look."

"Relax," Rhonda said, taking my other arm as they pulled me through the locker room door into the hall. "This is gonna be great."

That's probably what they said to Custer, I thought, trying to scrunch down behind Del, wishing I'd had the foresight to go on a diet last year.

Not that anyone noticed me anyway. The hallway was packed with people who would have been right at home in a Fellini flick.

The Boogie Woogie Singers filed past, patriotic in blue hair, white blouses, and impossibly red cheeks.

Against the lockers leaned a troupe of incredibly sweet little girls in frothy tutus, rhinestone tiaras, and tap shoes, holding a burping contest.

"'Scuse us"—a man touched my shoulder—"we need to get through." I stood aside as five Belly Whistlers, navels painted with big red lips and nipples overdrawn with wide, surprised eyes, squeezed by. One young farmer looked even more miserable than me.

I felt slightly less conspicuous as we worked our way through the crowd, past the backstage area, and in through the auditorium side door.

The bleachers were spotted with other oddities in costume and a smattering of ordinarily dressed folks intently watching the dress rehearsal.

"I think we're just in time," Del whispered, nodding at the stage. Ron Adler, looking almost handsome in black tie and tails, stood with a microphone in hand in front of the heavy red and gold curtains.

"Very few people know," he intoned, hardly blinking at all, "that the King of Rock and Roll visited Delphi about thirteen years ago, making the acquaintance of several of our local ladies. I present to you now John Presley, Chainlink Presley, and Presley Presley"—he paused for effect—"the Sons of Elvis."

"He isn't really going to introduce them that way, is he?" I whispered to Del. "I mean, he's talking about his own son up there. I don't suppose Chainlink's dad will appreciate the suggestion either."

"If Chainlink was your kid, would you want to claim him?" Del asked.

She had a point.

"They wrote the intro themselves. I don't imagine anyone is going to take it too seriously."

Del was right, the audience and other performers watching all laughed as the curtain opened on three boys arranged in a tableau of Elvis's life.

Pudgy Chainlink represented the latter years, with a black pompadour wig and a white flare-leg jumpsuit covered with spangles. John Adler wore someone's old army uniform cut down. Presley would probably get the rumor mill going again with his heartthrob outfit— slicked-back hair with one rogue curl looped down on the forehead, black jeans· and shirt, and guitar slung carelessly over one shoulder.

He looked so much like the young Elvis that if I hadn't known better, I would have wondered about his lineage too.

In perfect character, he and the other Sons sneered in unison, then launched into a five-minute lip-synch set of Elvis's greatest hits.

The small audience cheered and clapped as each kid gyrated to a solo dance from his own particular period.

"I helped them with the music," Del said smugly.

"They'll bring the house down tomorrow night," Rhonda said glumly.

"Why didn't we think of lip-synching?" I asked.

The boys finished their performance and bowed as the curtains closed.

"We'd better get lined up," Rhonda said, leading the way back through the hallway. "We're on pretty quick."

"He looked good," I said to Del's back. "But do you think he's okay?"

"Why wouldn't he be?"

"Because he knew Lily and she's dead and no matter how he looks, he's still only twelve."

"See for yourself," Del said, pointing.

Pres and the others were laughing and high-fiving each other, loud enough to get stern glances from some of the other performers.

On the other side of the curtain, Ron Adler complained about wearing the "monkey suit," then segued clumsily into the next intro, which happened to be for Mardelle Jackson's Bach piano solo.

Lovely lacy piano music floated backstage as I quietly congratulated Pres.

"Good job, kiddo. I think you're gonna win."

"You bet," he said, wiping sweat from his face with the back of a hand.

"Listen, we don't have time to talk right now, but are you all right?"

His smile died and his eyes clouded over. "Sure, why wouldn't I be?" He sounded just like his mother.

"You don't have to pretend with me," I said quietly. "I know you liked Lily."

"She was just a carnival worker," he said harshly, looking anywhere but at me. "I didn't even know her. Even her boyfriend says she was a prostitute."

"What do you mean?"

"Well, that Marko guy, the one on the ferris wheel, I heard him talking to the old ugly broad from the T-shirt booth this afternoon, before the police came. They were saying how she's been sleeping with everyone and taking money and it's a good thing she's gone."

"You sure they said this *before* the police came?" I asked, suddenly excited.

"Yeah, they knew something was up, though. The owner, that Bogner guy, was standing on the steps of the fun house and I was watching, over by the ferris wheel, so I could hear them talking pretty clear."

"Is that all they said?" I asked, hoping for a murder confession, I guess.

Presley squinted in concentration. "I think so; he went into the fun house right after that."

"What? Who?"

"Marko went inside, through the back door, while those other two guys were talking up front. He was in there for a couple of minutes and then came back out the same door really pale. I think he was gonna throw up. Was she really awful?"

"Dead is always awful," I said absently. "You're absolutely certain that Marko went in before it was roped off?"

"Absolutely," he said. "Is that important?"

"I guess it depends on whether or not he told the police that he went inside," I said, thinking quickly. "I might be able to find that out. Listen, don't be telling anyone else about this until after I talk to Neil Pascoe."

Maybe Neil has a mole in the DCI too.

"If you say so," Presley said doubtfully. He opened his mouth to say something else, then clamped it shut in a disapproving line.

"You were great, just like your dad." Del clubbed Pres's shoulder gently.

"Yeah, thanks," he said tonelessly, wheeled on one foot, and stalked off.

"What's that all about?" I asked, watching a stiffly erect Presley disappear through the throng.

"He's got a hair up his butt about something. If he doesn't snap out of it pretty soon, I'm going to bean him with a frypan."

"The child psychologists will love that," I said.

"It'll get his attention, that's for damn sure," Del said thinly, then brightened at something over my shoulder. "Your daughter is certainly talented. She plays beautifully, Pat."

"She is good, isn't she?" Pat Jackson asked. At least I assumed he was Pat, since he didn't contradict Del. "I don't know where she got it. Her mother and I wouldn't know real music if it bit us on the ass."

He slipped past and gave Mardelle, who had just finished playing, a big hug.

"How can you tell them apart?" I asked Del.

She shrugged. "I don't know. I've always known which was which—even when we were kids."

The Belly Whistlers filed toward the stage, arms, heads, and upper torsos stuffed into large top hats perched just above painted eyes. Bellies undulating in and out to the opening bars of "The Colonel Bogey March," stuffed dangling arms tucked into waistbands, they marched resolutely onstage to the raucous cries of the audience.

"And you think *you're* going to be humiliated," Del whispered.

"At least their faces aren't showing," I said, my own anxiety reaching a higher level. I could barely breathe. We were on soon.

"Aphrodite's in the audience," Del said, grinning at the guys onstage.

"Don't tell me things like that," I said.

"Why? I thought it'd help if you knew there were people rooting for you. Neil's out there too."

"I'd just as soon imagine that the audience is all strangers. I can't function as it is, and I'll never be able to go through with this if I know I have to see those people tomorrow."

"Buck up, kid, too late to worry now."

"Come on, guys," Rhonda said breathlessly. "It's time. Got your hankies, got your lipstick, got your mojo rising?"

"Huh?" I said.

"Never mind, it's a joke," she said, shaking her head at Del, who shrugged in reply.

"Don't make me do this, guys," I pleaded as we arranged ourselves onstage behind the closed curtain. "Please."

"Delphi's own Waitresse," Ron said as the curtains opened.

"Smile," Del commanded through clenched jaws.

In the doorway, Neil flashed a grin and a quick A-OK signal. Aphrodite, front row center, concentrated on us seriously.

We began to shoop.

25

....

TGIS

The prevailing wisdom holds that a terrible dress rehearsal precedes a stellar performance. If that's really true, then Waitresse is gonna kill 'em at the Phollies tonight.

Optimistically speaking, we weren't all that bad. Unless you define *bad* as sloppy choreography, off-key singing, and a Willie Nelson approach to timing.

And that was just me.

Rhonda's unnervingly cheerful stage presence wore thin as she fought an erratic sound system which picked up and broadcast approximately every third word. Like a beat poet in satin shorts, she wailed an arrhythmic lyric that ran something like ". . . face, oh, charm, warm, oh no, arms, wanna, love . . ." while Del and I did our best not to shoop into each other behind her.

Even though the rehearsal audience mostly consisted of the other Phollies acts, whose there-but-for-the-graceof sympathy was genuine, nothing but a dead body in town would have kept us from being the hot topic this morning at the cafe.

Lucky for us, we had a fairly recent dead body.

"Lookee here," said Ron Adler, whose own rehearsal performance should have kept him under cover. He pointed to an article in the Aberdeen Sunday paper, blinking furiously.

"I can't right now, Ron," I said, blowing bangs back off my forehead and carrying a tray to a table full of churchies.

The Methodists got out early and hungry. Clay was obviously long-winded, because the Lutherans were still inside their church across the street. We were always thankful for Saturday-night masses, which insured a trickle of bleary-eyed Catholics all morning rather than a crowd of them all at once.

Which commandment is it, exactly, that states "Thou shalt not cook breakfast for your own family on Sunday morning"?

Just because I was too busy to look at the paper didn't mean that everyone else wasn't devouring the latest on Lily's discovery in the fun house maze.

"Jeez, you'd think the headline would at least mention Delphi, instead of just the carnival," groused Willard over his third refill. He smiled up at me. "They spelled your name right, though."

"Now, there's a relief," I said. "It'd be a real shame if everyone thought someone else found her."

"Ah, come on, admit it," Ron said, folding the paper open and pointing at a grainy picture of me talking to Officer Larson. "Isn't it just a little fun to be the center of all this attention?"

"Of course not," Rhonda said. "And shame on you for even thinking like that. It must have been terrible for Tory." She picked up a couple of number 4 scrambled egg platters and a Children's Blueberry Pancake Surprise from the counter and deposited them at the booth behind Ron. "That kind of thing can scar a person for life. It makes them suffer from posttraumatic stress stuff so they can't carry on a normal life or anything. I read about it."

"From what I can see, Tory hasn't ever led a normal life." Ron snorted. Blink, blink.

"You're right," I said, "and I'm too traumatized to go back onstage again tonight. Can you find a replacement for me on such short notice, Rhonda?"

There was not much chance of being taken seriously on that point, but it was worth a shot.

"Good for you," Rhonda said, nodding seriously. "Humor has been medically proven to help people deal with horror like what you've experienced."

"Proven, huh?" I asked. "Take two Dave Barrys and call me in the morning?"

"That's exactly what you need." She grinned over her shoulder.

"No room for Dave Barry goofy shit today." Willard had absolutely no sense of humor. "Paper's full of dead carnival worker articles. Have you read any of this yet?"

"Nope, everyone and their cousin has been in for breakfast this morning, and we forgot to have the union negotiate for newspaper-reading time in the last contract." I ferried dirty plates to the trolley. "Why don't you read it out loud while we work?"

Everyone in the cafe was listening to us anyway; Willard could just as well perform a public service.

Willard settled reading glasses on his nose and began. I didn't listen too closely except when my name came up (which was a good deal more often than I liked), and the cafe was still busy enough that his voice faded to a low background drone. I remembered to nod at him reassuringly once in a while, and he continued to read.

"'. . . the body of the young woman was discovered by . . .'"

"You want to take this one?" Rhonda leaned over and whispered as I cleared another table. Stu McKee had just ambled in to sit alone at one of the few empty booths.

"'. . . wearing a uniform T-shirt and jeans, with no

other identifying articles or possessions either on or
near the body . . .'"

Nonplussed, I froze and whispered back. "What
makes you think I want him?"

Rhonda tilted her head and looked at me for a
minute. "Nothing, I guess. You just usually do Stu. I
thought you were friends or something."

"'. . . no immediate evidence of injury or assault to
lead suspicions . . .'"

"Of course we're friends. I'm friendly with nearly
everyone in town. I'm a friendly person," I said sharply.
I had not realized that I was expected to "do" Stu. How
long would it be before someone jumped to the correct
conclusion about us?

"'. . . until further testing is done, no conclusive
statements about the cause of death can be made . . .'"

I squeezed my eyes shut and rubbed them with a free
hand, sighing. "Sorry, Rhonda. I'm tired. Good thing
it's my last day. I can use some time off."

She patted my shoulder absently. "Of course. I understand. You want me to take him?"

"'. . . but preliminary indications point toward natural causes and at this time we aren't . . .'"

I considered Rhonda's offer. After yesterday, I wasn't
anxious to see Stu at all. It would be easier just to let her
take over. And let him wonder what was wrong.

But if people already expected me to wait on him,
then antennae would also wag if I broke the pattern.

"Nah," I said finally. "I got it."

"'. . . contact the parents of the dead girl, Harold and
Virginia Waltman of Cody, Wyoming, for . . .'"

"Hi," Stu said softly. "How're you doing?"

"I'm okay." I shrugged, arranging a paper placemat
and silverware on the table in front of him. Even with
Willard reading, Rhonda giggling, and Aphrodite clanking dishes in the kitchen, there wasn't enough noise to
cover up a real conversation with him.

Only generalities were safe, and I didn't have enough
energy for them either.

"You want a menu?" I asked neutrally.

"Just coffee," he said, looking down at his hands, clasped on the table. "I'm sorry, you know," he said without looking up.

"For what?" I asked. For introducing me to your wife? I wanted to ask. For letting her take over? For putting me in that situation to begin with?

"For not believing you. You know, when you said there was a dead body inside. I mean, it just sounded so crazy that I didn't want to believe it . . ." His voice trailed off.

I didn't want to look at him, afraid I wouldn't have the heart or courage to stay mad. Afraid I would be mad at him forever. Afraid that no matter how I felt, he was still going to be married. Afraid to remember that I knew that going in and could blame no one but myself. I tightened my jaw and poured a cup of coffee. Stu placed his hands around the cup as though hoarding the warmth.

"'. . . a bizarre situation, for now the authorities are not admitting that foul play could have been part . . .'"

A table full of Methodists burst into noisy laughter and got up to leave. Stu took advantage of the camouflage to lean over and say, "You're off tomorrow, right?"

I nodded, digging in my pocket for tickets to sort as an excuse not to look at him.

"That's all they had to say," Willard said. "Pretty damn spooky if you ask me."

"Can't disagree with you there, Willard," I turned and said. "Thanks." Willard beamed.

Stu touched my arm and said quietly from behind me, "I'll call; we need to talk."

I nodded numbly and went behind the till to ring up assorted breakfasts.

The cafe cleared out a little after that. Stu waited until Rhonda was cashiering to leave, and I picked up Willard's discarded newspaper during the brief lull.

The pay phone in the corner rang. Rhonda answered it and talked animatedly while I sipped a diet Coke and read about poor Lily.

I'd refused to give an interview to either the newspapers or the TV crews, so there were no first person accounts from "Tory Bauer, Delphi waitress who first discovered the body."

I thought reading about it would keep me at a safe remove, and hoped to replace my memories with Agent Ingstad's dispassionate description of Lily peering over the edge of the mirrored walls, pitiful and alone, empty hand beseeching.

But the account left me unsettled and uncomfortable. I folded the paper and closed my eyes, trying to figure out what was wrong. I mean, besides the obvious.

The newspaper had padded the meager details about Lily and her death with conjecture and hypothesis, enjoying the juicily bizarre circumstances, but did not question the official version of a death naturally caused.

"Hey, Tory, wake up," Rhonda called. "It's for you." She held out the phone, smiling. "It's Neil."

Wearily, I took the phone. "What's up?" I asked without a preamble.

"Saw you in the papers, kiddo," Neil said. I could hear him rattling and folding pages in the background. "But I'm not sure they caught your good side."

"I don't have a good side," I said, leaning back against the wall.

"You sound beat."

"Plumb tuckered. Say," I said as if I just had a brainstorm, "you're rich; you got a condo in the Bahamas or somewhere nice I can go and hide for a while? Never come back?"

"Sorry." I could hear his smile. "Fresh out of secluded tropical hideaways. But I do have something that might perk you up."

"New James Taylor?" I asked, feeling better already. Or at least hopeful. "Or Lawrence Block? Another movie version of *Pride and Prejudice*?"

"Nope, even better."

"There is nothing better than James Taylor," I said severely.

"Well, maybe not better, exactly. But certainly interesting."

"I'm all ears."

"He's for real," Neil said excitedly. "He really does exist."

I generally find nonsequiturs amusing, but not this morning. "You haven't gone and found Jesus Christ on me, have you, Neil?"

"Huh?" he asked, and then laughed. "No, the doctor is real. Harvard, Johns Hopkins, and everything."

More nonsequiturs. "Huh?"

"Dr. William H. Aker," he said patiently. "Not only is he for real, his partner says he's traveling with a carnival this summer!"

"You're shitting me," I said, standing up straight. "How'd you find this out?"

"Come over after work and I'll tell you all about it."

"No fair," I said. "Tell me now."

"Shit," I heard Rhonda mumble as she cleaned a dirty booth by the big front window and pocketed the tip.

I covered the receiver and mouthed "What?"

She pointed across the street, waggled two fingers in the air, and moaned. "Both of 'em. We're having some fun now."

"Well, you're off the hook for the time being," I said to Neil. Car doors slammed and more pulled up in front of the cafe. "But I'll be over right after work."

"What's going on?" he asked.

"Looks like the Lutherans and Baptists got out at the same time."

I picked up a handful of clean mugs and placemats, and went back to work.

26

....

Who Parks His Car in Harvard Yard?

This time it was root beer Popsicles, but it was always some kind of food. In the winter there might be hot chocolate and fudge. Or beef stew, steaming with tender chunks of carrots and potato.

In the fall it could be freshly baked bread (made from scratch, not frozen dough), thick with butter and wild plum jelly.

The list goes on, but it boils down to the same thing—there was always food.

Food and books and music.

Three of the four main comfort groups. Things I had always shared with Neil, at least until my affair with Stu turned our relationship tense. The things I was beginning to share with him again, and was just now realizing how much I had missed.

Though Stu was seeing adequately to the fourth comfort, and I'd never thought of Neil in that way, I found myself noticing things about him that I never had before.

How his eyes lit up when something caught his interest. The way he laughed with his whole body. His strong, capable, builder's hands.

I've always been a sucker for strong hands.

The way he balanced on the sawhorse, keeping an eye on the quiet carnival grounds below, and read from the computer printout about Dr. Aker.

I shook my head and forced myself to pay attention, surprised and even a little annoyed. My life was already complicated enough.

"Graduated from Harvard Med School in 1971, completed residency, subsequently set up private practice treating depressed rich women in the D.C. area. A real prescription cowboy, looks like," Neil said, scanning the page. "An actual Okie from Muskogee, attended Harvard on a full scholarship. His partners like him, his patients send in referrals, and he seems to have fit in with the Beltway crowd, except for his eccentric notions about summer vacationing."

"No cottage on Martha's Vineyard and backyard barbecues with Carly Simon, huh?" I asked. "Or frolicking along the Riviera with the other Beautiful People?"

"Nope." Neil laughed. "A couple of years ago, he spent the summer as a cook-slash-doctor in northwest Washington at a logging camp. Last year he traveled with a rodeo on the lower Texas loop. Collects workingman's wages, builds up his muscles, and returns to work in the fall, ready to treat suicidal lobbyists again."

"And this year, he's renewing himself spiritually by seeing the upper Midwest with a seedy carnival." I chewed on a root beer–flavored stick, thinking. "Is he deliberately choosing low-rent activities, or is he demonstrating a connection with the common man—Harvard sheepskin notwithstanding?"

"Hard to say," Neil answered, handing the sheets to me. "He was pretty easy to track down, once I found out Dr. William H. Aker really did exist. You know," he said conversationally, "there is really nothing you can't find out about anyone, if you know where to look and are plugged into a good computer network."

"So how'd you know where to look?"

Neil fished in the small cooler at his feet, came up with another Popsicle, snapped it on the windowsill, and handed half to me. Orange this time.

"Actually, I had no idea where to start, so I decided to take Hamilton Bogner at his word—that, as unlikely as it sounded, Bogner International really had a highly educated doctor traveling along with them for the summer. I didn't expect to hit pay dirt right out of the chute."

He bit off half of the Popsicle and grinned. "I just got lucky."

"And Harvard happily supplied you with all this info?" There were at least six pages of computer print-out on the good Dr. Aker.

Neil shrugged. "Graduation records are available to the public, and Harvard is proud of its alumni. And a doctor who succeeds is very often a doctor who publishes, and if he's published, you can find him."

"What'd he publish?"

"A couple of articles on antidepressants, very technical. I got copies if you want to read 'em."

"No thanks, I'll stick to Dick Francis. That all?"

"Nope." He leaned forward, pointing at the stack of papers with the remainder of his Popsicle. "A while back, he wrote an article about illegal steroid use among high school athletes, and how to recognize the symptoms, for a general practitioner's magazine. Seems he spent a summer in his home state working with young football hopefuls. He made friends with the kids and even got to know the suppliers. For the article, of course."

"Oh really," I said, thinking that one over. "So the guy is sort of an expert on steroids, and knows enough about how they're distributed illegally to write an article on the subject."

"Pretty fascinating, huh?" Neil asked. "Especially since we seem to be surrounded by steroid-using muscle boys and wannabees."

"Did the information superhighway happen to have

any pictures of this guy? It'd help if we knew what he looked like."

"Unfortunately, no one had any photos to send, except for a very fuzzy pic from the yearbook. They faxed it to me, but it's not much help."

He handed me an extremely blurry picture that could have been anyone with glasses and shoulder-length hair, male or female.

"So, which one is he?" I asked, looking down on the carnival. No workers were in sight.

"Since simplicity worked for me before, I'll put money that our Doc is Doc," Neil said.

"This doesn't look much like our Doc," I said, frowning.

"But *our* Doc wears glasses," Neil pointed out.

"Okay, but I still can't picture, him at Harvard," I said. "Or treating the rich and powerful. But I can sure see him at home with the ranchers, with his mustache and the cowboy boots. And the aw-shucks bedside manner."

"We'll just have to wait and see if anything more comes in tonight. I have a couple people still searching archives and maybe there'll be more tomorrow. In the meantime, what do we do with all this?"

"Is there any point in calling Agent Ingstad?" I was reluctant. Tattling always makes me feel like a nerdy third grader. Or a Gestapo informer.

"You could," he said slowly. "But what do we have here really? Confirmation that a doctor with intimate knowledge of steroids is working with the carnival."

"Sorta makes me think of Jimmy Stewart in *The Greatest Show on Earth*. Makes me wonder if he has anything to hide."

"Except in the movie, Jimmy Stewart masqueraded as a clown and never told anyone his real identity. This guy travels as a doctor, and at the end of every summer goes back to being a real live practitioner. It's eccentric, not suspicious."

"I suppose you're right." I leaned back against the bare studs. "As interesting as all this is, I doubt if it actually ties in with Lily's death. No one in his right mind would suspect her of taking steroids—she was skinny as a rail. And while I'm pretty certain that Marko *was* taking them, that still doesn't tie him to her death. As much as I would like it to," I finished, muttering.

"No one else thinks it was murder, you know," Neil said quietly.

"I know, that's what makes me sure it was," I answered. "They all act like finding the body in the rafters is some kind of glitch that has nothing to do with her death. I just can't buy that. She was up there for a reason," I said stubbornly. "And she died for a reason."

"Well then"—Neil stood up and brushed the dust off his jeans—"I guess we'll just have to figure it out. Won't we?"

I could have hugged him.

27

....

The Empty Hand

I don't remember summers on my grandmother's farm as being particularly hot, though a South Dakota summer on the endless windswept prairie could not be otherwise.

What I mean is, I don't remember noticing the heat. I don't remember hating the heat. I don't remember when Heat banded with its good buddy Humidity to become The Enemy.

Of course, around here, everyone loves summer. They stand outside, faces tipped up in the fierce sunlight, storing warmth against the long winter.

I'd hate them if I had the energy to do anything that strenuous in the waning hours of a July afternoon. As it was, it took all of my effort just to reassemble the scattered sections of the Aberdeen Sunday paper strewn around the living room floor.

I should have been happy that Presley was interested enough in what was going on in the world even to look at the paper, though at that moment I'd have been more pleased if he'd been an obsessive-compulsive with a clean floor fetish.

I would have left the papers where they were for Pres (who was taking a long noisy shower) to pick up for himself, but I wanted to reread everything that had been written about Lily and her death. To see if the sinking feeling in the pit of my stomach, the notion that something was not quite right, had a basis in fact. Or was just an undercurrent of stage fright before tonight's debut performance of Waitresse.

I heard Pres yodeling over the noise of the shower. Singing both parts of the James Taylor/Carly Simon version of "Mockingbird," effectively pumping even more humidity into the air, and using up most of the hot water at the same time.

Humming the counterpoint along with Pres under my breath, I folded the front page over and began to read, again, the official description of the scene.

Even though I'd only listened to Willard with half an ear at the cafe, the official version sounded pretty much like the statement I'd given to Officer Larson.

Everything gibed. Lily in the rafters, eyes open, hand reaching out over the mirrors.

And then I stopped and reread the paragraph that Willard had already read out loud. And read it once again. The one where Lily was found without identification or possessions, with her hand hanging out over the mirrors.

Her empty hand hanging over the mirrors.

I sat up straight, a wild sort of elation surging through me, stage fright forgotten, heat and humidity forgotten. Seeing again Lily's greasy blond hair and wide surprised eyes. Seeing her outstretched hand, with the chain of a cheap turquoise cross wound around and around her closed fist.

A turquoise cross swaying gently overhead. A turquoise cross that had been stolen from Mobridge. That had been given to Lily by Marko.

A turquoise cross that was nowhere mentioned in the newspaper accounts of the scene.

I read them again to be sure and then sat back on the couch, sweat trickling down the small of my back, chewed my lip, and considered what it might mean.

The cross was not a figment of my imagination. It had been there, wrapped around Lily's fist, when I first saw her.

It was still there when I followed Ham Bogner back through the maze.

But it wasn't there when the police came.

Marko, I realized. It always came back to Marko. Marko with his muscles. Marko with his rages.

"Pres." I tapped on the bathroom door. He was still singing. "Presley!"

The water was still running. I couldn't imagine what he was doing in the shower for that amount of time.

Well, I could imagine; twelve was old enough, as Neil had reminded me. But I couldn't imagine even the most versatile male being able to do that and sing double harmony at the same time.

I opened the door a crack. Steam billowed into the hallway. "Presley!" I shouted into the bathroom.

The shadowy form scrubbing his armpits behind the plastic shower curtain started visibly and stopped singing.

"Hey, I thought we respected each other's privacy in this house," he said sharply, quoting one of my own cardinal rules.

"I knocked," I said, leaning back into the hallway again for a breath of relatively fresh air. "Several times, in fact. You just didn't hear me."

"Okay." The shadow shrugged. "Did you want something. Or are you just letting all the cold air in?"

"You should thank me for the cold air; it's awful in here," I said. "Be sure to open a window when you're done or you'll steam up the whole house."

"Is that all?"

"No, I have to ask you something." The shadow stood still as water splashed off the top of his head. "Last night at rehearsal, you said you heard Marko talking to Midge about Lily being gone *before* the police came, right?"

"Marko, he's the ferris wheel guy, right?" Pres didn't wait for my assent. "Yeah, he was talking to the lady with the tight T-shirt, big hair, and fake eyebrows. That was before the police came."

"You're absolutely certain they used the word *gone?*" I guess I was hoping they'd used the word *dead*.

"Of course I'm certain," he said testily. "It musta been after you found her, because they'd already turned off the screams and stuff inside the fun house. No one else knew there was anyone dead yet, but Marko and the old broad knew something was up."

I made a mental note to coach him, later, on some proper terms of respect for older women.

"They stood talking to each other for a minute or two, then Marko trotted over to the fun house and went in the back. He came out the same way after five minutes or so."

Five minutes. More than long enough to find Lily, unwrap a necklace, pocket it, and get back out.

The steam in the bathroom was so thick I could hardly see. I tried to keep the excitement out of my voice. "And Mr. Bogner, the owner, did you see him?"

"Yeah, he was on the front steps of the fun house talking with that other guy, the slimo who ran the ride."

"Did Mr. Bogner go back inside the maze?"

"Nope. He was out front the whole time until the police came."

"Did he see Marko go in or out?"

"I don't think so. I mean, he didn't point at him and holler or anything. This stuff matters, huh?"

"I think so, but I have to check a couple other things first," I said. "Thanks. Oh, and hurry up. I want to take a shower too."

I sat on the cracked vinyl couch again, sweating and considering, and then dialed the phone.

"Delphi Cafe. We're busy, talk fast," Del answered. Dishes clanked in the background.

"Are you really busy, or you just being rude to callers?" I asked.

"Half and half." Del laughed. "You need something?"

"Yeah, a couple of answers. Friday night after the dance you didn't come home," I said, remembering that Del had flirted outrageously with the lead singer of the band.

"That's a statement of fact, not a question," Del said.

"You didn't let me finish," I said. "Friday night you didn't come home after the dance—now, I don't want any of the particulars, but I need to know if you were within view of the carnival grounds."

"Sure, we were in a pickup truck right on the outskirts. It was kind of cramped, but—"

"No details, please," I interrupted. Del was talking on the pay phone in the cafe, in full earshot of the whole place. Unfortunately, she was perfectly capable of entertaining everyone with the story of her evening. In clinical detail.

"Yes, we could see the carnival grounds. Very well, in fact. Though he had a slightly better view than me," she said with a laugh. "Some of the time, anyway."

"I don't need to know that," I said. "Were there many carnival workers out on the grounds that time of night?"

"It was pretty late, but yeah, there were workers here and there, out walking and smoking. Or fooling around."

"And you knew they were carny people because . . . ?" I was testing her.

"Because they were wearing those dorky black T-shirts, dummy," she said. "In fact, we talked about that, in between rounds, if you know what I mean."

"Were they near the fun house?"

"Yes. They were also near the merry-go-round. They were everywhere."

"Could you recognize any of them?"

"It wasn't my top priority at the time," Del said. I heard the cash register open; she was ringing up tickets while talking on the phone.

"I suppose not. But think back. You've noticed Marko, the guy who runs the ferris wheel. Would you have recognized him if you'd seen him out walking around?"

She laughed. "I would have recognized Marko anywhere. Sure you don't want to know more about my evening?"

Del was infuriatingly unable to stay on the subject.

"No, that's not important." And besides, I could guess: she spent a comfy night snuggled in the arms of the Dakotah Stompers' lead singer. "It only matters if you saw Marko anywhere near the fun house."

"Have it your way, then." I heard the soft snick of a lighter and a quick inrush of air as Del lit a cigarette. She exhaled. "But you're missing the best part."

"I'll survive. Was he near there?"

"As far as I could tell, Marko was nowhere near the fun house."

"Did you see anything suspicious at all?"

"You mean like someone carting a dead body around, looking for some place to stash it?"

"Anything at all that looked odd."

"Believe me, Tory, the whole place is odd. But no, I didn't see anything any more out of the ordinary than usual. Now, can I tell you about my multiple orgasms?"

"No," I said. "Go back to work."

"I live to serve," she said wryly, and hung up.

28

....

Nerdy Third Graders

Informants give me the creeps. I am too much a child of the sixties to feel comfortable gathering information for the authorities. All that spying, snooping, confessing, and scrabbling reminds me of the Nazis in the forties. Or the McCarthyites of the fifties. Or Butchie Pendergast in the third grade.

I wasn't much for running to the grown-ups even before flower power, and I would have been happy to leave Butchie Pendergast alone to pick his nose and eat boogers in class, or make faces behind Mrs. Hochalter's back as she executed perfect Palmer penmanship on the blackboard.

I might even have looked the other way when I stumbled across him pocketing milk money from frightened first graders if he hadn't run to the principal first with a wild story about me copying from Donna Waldner's arithmetic test.

Of course I stoutly denied the accusation—and foolishly retaliated with a long list of Butchie's infractions.

Which netted Butchie an official spanking with the board of education, an oak paddle reverently hung in a place of honor on the principal's door.

And it got me a black eye, a torn dress, and a mouthful of boogers. Butchie's. He hid in a clump of cottonwoods, let me get past, then jumped out and grabbed my hair, screaming, "You had to tell! You had to tell!"

It left me with a lasting reluctance to tattle. Even when I know it's the right thing to do.

I learned early on that you pay a price for everything, even for being right. And I learned to examine my conscience whenever I had the urge to tell, since I really did copy from that damn arithmetic test.

This time, the price had already been paid. By Lily. Though I wasn't foolish enough to think that it wouldn't cost me, too, somewhere down the line.

I tried calling Neil repeatedly, but he rang busy for a whole half hour—he was probably on-line. The speed with which the carnival was packing up its remaining equipment convinced me not to wait until I cleared this decision with him.

Already, most of the concession stands were sealed down and some of the rides were in pieces on the ground, being loaded on semitrailers.

Pres was in his room, still humming and dressing for the Phollies.

Feeling mildly ill, but morally certain, I dialed the local DCI number, said I was Tory Bauer from Delphi, and asked to speak to Agent Ingstad about the dead girl they found yesterday.

"Mrs. Bauer," he said neutrally. "How can I help you?"

I took a deep breath. "It's about the necklace, the turquoise cross. It was wrapped around her hand when I found her, but no one mentioned it in the newspaper." An explanation suddenly occurred to me. "Unless you're not releasing that information to the public, keeping some of the clues to yourself."

That was it. They knew about the cross. It was a

classic ploy. They were setting someone up by leaving
crucial points from the public record. I felt like an idiot.

"Of course, that's what you're doing. I'm sorry for
bothering you," I said, embarrassed, ready to hang up.

"Mrs. Bauer, I'm afraid I don't know what you're
talking about. Do you want to start again and tell me
from the beginning, what's bothering you? You mentioned a necklace, I believe."

"Lily Mitchell had a necklace, a cross inlaid with
turquoise." He said to start from the beginning. "She
told me it was given to her by Marko, the guy who runs
the ferris wheel in the carnival."

Agent Ingstad rattled some papers; I could hear other
phones ringing in the background. "Let's see, yes," he
said. "Marko Parker, age twenty-one, been with Bogner
International for three years. Good steady worker from
all accounts." He paused. "You say he gave the deceased
a necklace."

"That's what she said. He gave her a necklace and she
wasn't supposed to show it around. That necklace is
stolen property. It was taken from Mobridge a couple of
weeks ago. I saw the cross in a newspaper picture with
some of the other stolen items. It's a distinctive piece
and I'm absolutely certain that Lily's cross is the same
one."

"That's very interesting, Mrs. Bauer," he said, though
the tone of his voice said exactly the opposite. "Thank
you for calling."

"No, you don't understand," I said quickly, before he
could hang up. "I saw the necklace yesterday. It was
wrapped around Lily's hand. In the fun house. It was
there when I first saw the body. But it's not mentioned
in any of the newspaper accounts. In fact"—I found the
article again—"the paper specifically said she was
found without 'possessions or identifications.'"

"I see," he said.

"No, I don't think you do," I said sharply. "That
necklace was stolen twice. Marko Parker stole it from
Mobridge and gave it to Lily, then he stole it back
yesterday. From her dead body."

"What makes you think Mr. Parker was involved with the theft of the necklace in Mobridge?" he asked quietly.

"He's already been implicated in that burglary. He's been named as a source for illegal steroids, and he's been accused of selling other items known to have been stolen at the same time as the necklace," I said triumphantly.

"And how, exactly, do you know that Mr. Parker has been implicated in those crimes?" Agent Ingstad asked. I could see him raising an eyebrow.

Oops. My brain did a quick backpedal. I knew because I had seen the police reports at Neil's. Police reports weren't released to the public. I would get myself—and worse yet, Neil—in big trouble if I wasn't careful.

"I, um," I stalled, thinking furiously. "I read it in the Mobridge paper."

"Really, Mrs. Bauer," he said, plainly not believing me.

I held my breath, waiting but not speaking.

The pause lengthened. Finally he continued. "All right. We'll stay with the necklace for the time being. You say that you saw it yesterday."

Relieved, I answered, "Yes, it was wrapped around her hand, dangling over the mirrors."

"And did you mention this to Officer Larson when he took your statement?"

I thought back. "I'm pretty sure that I did. I mean, I saw it immediately, and he asked me to describe everything I saw. But things were already in an uproar, and I was pretty upset and I can't remember for sure if I told him or not. Can't you check the statement?"

"I have to say, offhand, Mrs. Bauer, that I don't remember any mention of necklaces in any statements. Including yours."

"Honestly, if I overlooked it yesterday, I'm sorry. But you gotta believe me, that necklace was there and I'm certain that Marko took it back."

"And when did he do that? We don't have any

information putting him on the scene with the body. He didn't work in the fun house and the medical examiner allowed the body to be moved soon after we arrived."

"That's just it," I said quickly. "Marko went into the fun house yesterday. A witness saw him enter through the back door, before you arrived. He was inside for about five minutes. That's more than enough time to unwrap a chain."

"Why, exactly, would Mr. Parker be so worried about removing a necklace that he would compromise a crime scene?"

There were lots of answers to that one. Because he didn't want the necklace traced back to him. Because he didn't think. Because he's stupid.

But there was only one answer that made sense to me.

I swallowed. "Because he killed Lily Mitchell and wanted to remove evidence that would link him to her."

"Now, Mrs. Bauer, are you back to that again? Final tests on the body have not been completed, but the preliminary indications do not point to foul play. You know that."

"I know that nothing obvious has shown up yet. But that doesn't mean that someone hasn't missed something."

"Are you casting aspersions on our medical examiner?" There was a hint of humor in his voice. "We have every confidence in his expertise, you know."

"I'm not casting aspersions on anyone," I said, exasperated. "Except maybe Marko. I just think everyone is jumping too quickly to the wrong conclusion, that's all."

"You're entitled to your opinion. But we don't work with opinions, we work with facts. Can you give us the name of the witness who saw Mr. Parker entering the fun house?"

Turn Pres over to the Feds?

"I'll have to think about that," I said. "I can't just give you a name without talking it over with . . . ah . . . the witness . . . first."

"That's entirely up to you, Mrs. Bauer, but corrobora

tion is essential. In any case, I'm sure we'll want to talk to you further. Someone will be contacting you soon to ask about your acquaintance with the deceased. Apparently you knew her better than we had realized."

Oh, great, now they suspect me.

"You will follow up on this, won't you?" I asked, trying not to sound desperate. Agent Ingstad would probably prefer to forget I called.

"We follow up on every lead, Mrs. Bauer," he said formally. "Thank you for calling."

A while later an unmarked dark car drove onto the carnival grounds. The man in the car talked to various carnival workers, taking notes, keeping some workers only minutes and others for much longer.

He detained Marko so long that the ferris wheel was the only ride left standing when I walked past on my way to the auditorium for the Phollies.

It might have been a guilty conscience, or an overactive imagination, or perhaps the ghost of Butchie Pendergast, but I felt I was being watched the whole way.

29

....

If It Ain't Baroque

It seems to me that there are two kinds of audiences. There's the Broadway play kind, who've paid big bucks for tickets and now expect to be entertained god-dammit.

An audience with an attitude.

And then there are mommies and daddies, who pray for nothing more than the survival of the relative onstage. If little Ashley and Michael, Jr., get through the whole thing without throwing up, the evening is called a success.

And if everyone remembers their lines and no one falls down, it's standing O time. Moms and dads are anxious to be pleased, and delighted by sheer effort.

The parents packed together in the Phollies audience were having a wonderful time, oohing and aahing or cue, breaking into spontaneous applause, and laughing at Ron Adler's jokes, though why his running lament about wearing a monkey suit was funny is beyond me.

We performers milled quietly backstage, listening to

214

the other acts, amazed at how well everyone was doing. The Belly Whistlers, each fortified with several cans of Schmidt's courage, outdid themselves, undulating navels to thunderous approval.

A sort of Andy Hardy fever took over, and we found ourselves determined to give the town a good show. Even my own fear eased a little.

No one was laughing *at* anyone, we were all laughing *with* ourselves. And it felt great.

"Isn't this great?" Rhonda whispered, peeking into the auditorium from a side door. "Look at 'em all. There's not an empty seat in the whole place."

"Yep," said Del, who stretched over Rhonda's back, searching the crowd. "Everyone in the county is here, including some of the carnival people. A couple of them are over there."

Rhonda craned her neck to see as they continued to dissect the audience.

My reluctant goodwill toward singing only included going onstage, it did not extend to the outfit I had to wear. I still felt like a fool with my hair crimped in a pseudo-poodle cut, bandana tied around my neck, hot and sweaty in yellow and pink satin. Worse yet, the waistband button of the shorts was perilously loose.

A dandy image of my shorts falling down midperformance blinded me momentarily.

"Anyone got a needle and thread?" I asked the crowd standing around. "I better do a quick repair before I go onstage."

"Here." Mardelle Jackson fumbled in her pocket and handed me a safety pin. "Will this do?"

"Yeah, thanks," I whispered, slipping the pin into my pocket, then remembered she was due to go on next. "Your piano piece is wonderful. I love Bach; you'll kill 'em out there."

"Well, I made a couple of changes. I hope you still like it." She smiled, eyes dancing with mischief as she straightened her shoulders and marched backstage.

Del placed a heavy hand on my shoulder. "You are coming back, aren't you?" she asked suspiciously.

"Of course. I wouldn't leave you in the lurch. The show must go on." I saluted.

She searched my eyes carefully, looking for treachery. "Don't pull a Houdini on me," she warned.

"It's David Copperfield who makes big things disappear, not Houdini," I said, turning to leave.

"But Houdini did impossible escapes," she said darkly.

"No problem," I said as I pushed through toward the bathroom. "I'll be back in plenty of time."

"Hey, Tory," someone whispered from the other side of a group of hippies who might just that minute have wandered in from Woodstock. The first one.

"Tory, come here, quick. You gotta see this." It was Neil, dressed in a floor-length brown cotton robe tied at the waist with twine. In costume as Brother Pascoe, the Mesmerizing Monk. Though I doubt real monks wear fake plastic bald spots. Or Birkenstocks.

"You look really goofy," I said seriously. "I don't feel so bad now."

He motioned me to follow with a finger to his lips.

We tiptoed backstage, directly opposite the piano but out of sight of the audience.

"Watch and listen," he said very quietly as Ron introduced Mardelle and her Bach. "This is going to be great. Keep an eye over there."

He pointed at Mardelle's piano teacher, who was beaming at her star pupil.

Mardelle stood beside the piano and said in a clear voice, "I've decided to play something a little different tonight. I've been working on a piece of old music called 'Video Eam Stantem Ibi,' by Scarabaei. I hope you like it."

With a smile and a wink in Neil's direction, she sat down.

I don't pretend to be an expert on classical music, but I am familiar with the names, and I'd never heard of that particular composer.

"Scarabaei?" I asked Neil. "Who's he? What century?"

Neil didn't answer, he just nodded and smiled as Mardelle began to play. The piece was pretty in that lacy overdecorated baroque style. The melody was vaguely familiar.

"Do I know that piece?"

"Of course," Neil whispered back, grinning widely now.

Mardelle's piano teacher looked slightly dismayed and confused. The rest of the audience, most of whom would not know Bach if he bit them on the big toe, were quietly enjoying the selection, though I could see that several people were beginning to grin, just like Neil.

The melody danced in and out of my mind. I frowned in concentration, trying to remember where I'd heard it before. It was very familiar. I caught myself humming it as Mardelle played arpeggios around the tune.

There were more and more people smiling in the audience, and I heard a faint echo of chuckles.

That sort of rudeness is practically unheard of in Delphi—we never laugh at people to their faces.

Beside me, Neil shook and finally laughed out loud. A booming laugh that Mardelle surely heard onstage.

I was outraged. Behavior like that was totally unacceptable from anyone, much less Neil, who was the kindest and most considerate person I know.

I jabbed a swift elbow into his ribs.

He oofed. "No, you don't get it," he said, rubbing his side. "She wants us to laugh. It's a joke."

Sure enough, Mardelle was grinning hugely herself.

Neil raised an expectant eyebrow. "Listen to the melody. Can't you tell?"

I tried. I tried really hard, but for some reason, the words to "I Saw Her Standing There" kept getting in the way.

"Are you hearing lyrics?" he asked.

I nodded. Odd lines to remember while listening to classical music.

Neil sang quietly under his breath; I joined in. It was rude, but impossible to resist the lure of the lines.

I stopped dead just as Mardelle finished and took a

bow to great applause. "No," I said. "She didn't. It's not."

"It sure is." Neil laughed. "She's so good that she worked out the arrangement in the Bach style all by herself. Then she came to me for help with the Latin translation of the title."

"You speak Latin?" I was surprised.

"Well, I did a long time ago, and I still had a textbook and a dictionary on hand. We worked it out together."

"And 'Scarabaei'?" I asked.

"The Beatles, of course." He laughed. I laughed. Everyone laughed.

Mardelle walked past, enormously pleased with herself.

"Good job, kiddo." Neil patted her shoulder. "It went great."

She was flushed and smiling. "They got it, didn't they?"

"Everyone was way ahead of me," I said. "But I finally figured out what I was hearing."

She nodded. "Well, I better go find Mom and Dad. See what they thought." She turned to leave. "Oh, and Tory," she said with a thumbs-up signal, "break a leg."

Onstage, Ron said, "We're almost done, folks, and you know what that means—pretty soon I get outta this monkey suit." I swear I could hear him blinking.

"Are you still here?" Del whispered fiercely in my ear.

"Oops," I said sheepishly. "I waited to hear Mardelle play."

She pointedly looked at her watch and tapped her foot.

"I know, I know," I said, then turned and bumped smack into Aphrodite, who had been, apparently, standing directly behind me.

Carrying a cup of coffee.

"Shit," I muttered under my breath, checking for spilled coffee on my costume. It wasn't hot, but it was wet. And brown. "God damn."

"You okay?" Aphrodite asked.

I bent over to inspect my shoes and the waistband

button from my shorts popped off and rolled merrily under the curtain. Onstage, out of reach.

"Fuck," I said this time. And not particularly quietly either. A group of little girls in frothy pink tutus gasped. And then giggled.

"Just go to the bathroom and swab yourself off," Del said tiredly.

"Be quick," Aphrodite said unnecessarily.

Mumbling under my breath, I hurried through the assorted acts, lined up more or less in order of appearance beyond the backstage area. The high school cast of *Hair* was at the end of the line. They whispered conspiratorially with each other, ignoring me, and everyone else, completely.

No doubt planning their nude encore.

The earlier acts were watching from the auditorium aisles and the hall was now deserted.

And dark, though the light had burned brightly earlier.

I fumbled along, almost blind, running my fingertips along the row of lockers to the right, heading toward the thin strip of light shining under the girls' bathroom door.

I reached into my pocket for Mardelle's safety pin, anxious to put myself back together, worried that the coffee stains would make it look as though I had wet my pants.

Crabby and no longer enjoying myself at all, preoccupied with hurrying back to Del and Rhonda before they got really mad, I leaned against the door with my shoulder, to push it open.

A hand shot out of the dark from just beyond the door and grabbed my hair.

I squealed involuntarily, and another hand, from behind this time, clamped itself painfully over my mouth.

"You had to talk, didn't you?" Butchie Pendergast whispered furiously in my ear.

Applause broke out. Ron was probably complaining about his fucking tuxedo again.

Laughter now, even louder than before. Loud enough that no one heard me struggle.

Loud enough that no one heard them drag me through the side door and out onto the playground.

30

....

Round and Round She Goes

Of course, I knew it wasn't Butchie Pendergast almost immediately. The call to Agent Ingstad had put him in my mind, where he'd been lurking all evening.

Butchie Pendergast couldn't have a fistful of my hair and another hand clamped over my mouth. First because there were two people, adults, men, dragging me through the school yard and down the alley. I could hear them both shuffling and panting.

I am no small woman. It would take at least two grown-ups to move me anywhere without my cooperation.

I was not cooperating.

Second, Butchie Pendergast had drowned in the Jim River after a Homecoming kegger in 1969, the only fall on record where the oxbow east of town was deep enough to be dangerous.

Though I don't believe in ghosts, for a horrible second I thought Butchie had come back from the dead to exact revenge on me for tattling again. But spirits probably don't have bad breath and rock-hard muscles. My captors were reassuringly corporeal.

In fact, though I knew I was struggling and could hear my own muffled cries, inside I was strangely calm. Almost curiously, I cataloged my surroundings—the deepening dusk, the eerily quiet street, the dark houses except for a light burning upstairs at Jackson's, the faint echoes of the Phollies still going strong inside the auditorium a few blocks back.

"Damn, she's heavy," one of them said.

"Shut the fuck up and hurry," said the other.

They had my arms pinned to my sides as they pulled and dragged me from the alley behind Jackson's and across the street.

I was still not frightened. At least not on the inside. Sometimes people function normally, controlling their panic, doing all the right things during fires and earthquakes and bank robberies.

Shock, I thought to myself wonderingly. I'm in shock. That's why I'm so calm.

The one on my right stumbled, and for a split second his grip loosened on my hair. Enough for me to turn and catch a glimpse of droopy mustache, cowboy hat, beads of sweat, grim determination, and my own terrified face reflected by glasses lenses.

I had just enough time to register that I knew his face when the hand tightened again and yanked my head in the other direction. This time I clearly saw shoulder-length dark hair, an HBIE cap, and unmistakable fury.

I knew them.

Marko. Marko and Doc, I thought. Marko and Dr. William H. Aker. Marko and Doc have me. Why?

And the answer came instantly: Lily, the necklace, burglary, steroids, investigation, Agent Ingstad.

Murder.

Now I was frightened. Incoherent, terrified. My legs gave out completely, but I was hauled roughly up again.

"Walk, goddammit," Marko ordered. "We're not going to carry you."

"I didn't ask to go for a walk with you," I said, or at least tried to. But with Marko's hand firmly closing my mouth, only "Mmfph humpah roumh" came out.

"We couldn't carry her anyway." Doc chuckled nastily. "She's too damn fat."

I couldn't believe it. Not only was I being kidnapped by thieving, drug-pushing murderers, dragged off against my will into the night, but I also had to suffer the additional humiliation of fat jokes. From a professional man, no less.

Harvard, my ass.

I aimed a kick toward Doc's kneecap. He wasn't much taller than me, and the kick would have hurt if it had connected, but he jumped out of the way easily. "Careful, honey, or someone's gonna get hurt," he said.

We stopped. I'd dimly processed the fact that we were on the dismantled carnival grounds. We stood, all three panting, in front of the ferris wheel—the only ride left upright. It was running, the motor a low-pitched rumble, the wheel still.

Marko nodded at Doc. While keeping my arms firmly clamped to my sides, they both let go of my head. I snapped at Marko's hand as soon as it loosened, trying to bite him, though it's not wise to antagonize your kidnappers.

Unfortunately, I missed, but he recognized the intent and cuffed me roughly on the ear.

Head ringing and dizzy from the blow, I realized they were no longer muffling me and I screamed. It wasn't a great scream, like in the old horror flicks, but it was loud enough to catch the attention of anyone in earshot.

"Go ahead, holler." Doc shrugged. "There's no one around anyway."

He was right. The grounds were deserted, and we stood on the far edge of town, without any houses nearby except for Neil's and our trailer.

No one was home anyway. Everyone was at the Phollies. The campers and trailers around the perimeter of the carnival grounds were all dark, too, except one not too far from Hamilton Bogner's trailer.

I did not expect help from other carny employees, even if they heard me. I closed my mouth and relaxed my shoulders as much as I could, hoping that would lull them into loosening their grips.

"Why are you doing this?" I asked, keeping my voice as calm as possible.

"Now, why do you think?" Marko said directly in my face, wild-eyed.

I decided that was a rhetorical question and kept quiet. Marko's rage did not seem to be lessening.

"You like to figure things out, you like to talk," Marko said, punctuating each word with a painful squeeze and a shake. "I thought we might have a little talk. Just the three of us, and get some things straightened out."

"Okay," I said carefully, amazed to remember the safety pin clenched in one of my immobilized hands.

Though the damage quotient was low, I figured I could divert at least one of them with a fast jab. The nice thing about sharp objects is that aim isn't real important. It hurts no matter where you get poked.

As unobtrusively as I could, I opened the pin in my pocket and bent it wide with one hand. I performed a little halfhearted struggle for camouflage and waited for an opportunity.

"Can you let go of me a little? You're bruising my arms," I said, whining, hoping I sounded sufficiently subdued. "I won't run away."

Sometimes it's all right to lie.

"Fat chance," Marko snorted.

"Yeah, fat chance," Doc repeated, snickering.

A sudden gust of wind blew Marko's hat off. He loosened his grip and grabbed for it.

With that arm free, I twisted, lunged, and sunk the safety pin all the way into Doc's shoulder.

He let go. "Aagh!" he screamed. "Ow, shit. Goddammit. That fucking hurt! She stabbed me with something. Get her!"

I spun to escape, but Marko, hat now forgotten, was faster. And even more furious than before.

"We were just going to talk nice," he said, drops of

spit flying with each word, dragging me by my hair, all by himself, toward the ferris wheel ramp. "But you want to be nasty, we'll be nasty.

"Can you still run this thing?" he hollered over his shoulder at Doc.

"Sure," Doc said, rubbing his arm. "Hurts like a pisser and it'll probably get infected. But I'm here. Do what you gotta do."

Now I did struggle. I'd dropped the pin after I stabbed Doc, and was completely weaponless. Marko dragged me up the ramp with one hand, unlatched the safety bar on the lowest gondola, and flung it open.

And if I was calm before, with my fear nicely compartmentalized, I certainly wasn't when I saw that Marko meant for me to get on the ferris wheel with him. With a nutcase in the throes of that steroid-induced 'roid rage.

"We're going for a ride." He laughed.

"Nooo!" I wailed. "Don't make me do this!"

"Heights bother you a little?" Marko asked with mock solicitude as he pushed me down on the seat and then sat beside me.

He nodded at Doc while holding me in place. Doc engaged the gears and with both hands slowly released the lever. The wheel creaked and the car rose up and away from the ground.

I struggled helplessly, not believing this was happening.

"You'd better sit still," Marko said in my ear, with one arm wrapped around my shoulder. "Against the rules to rock the car, you know."

The wheel turned almost silently in the dark, music and lights off, picking up speed as we rounded the upper curve and descended. Marko grimaced in an approximation of a smile and leaned forward a little.

The gondola rocked alarmingly. We tilted forward, and I realized, for the first time, that the safety bar wasn't latched. That Marko had purposely left it unlatched.

I might have been frightened before, but until that

moment I had not known what the word really meant. The blood drained from my head in a flash. I was instantly covered with a clammy sweat. White lights danced in front of my eyes.

I swayed a little.

"Oh, no you don't," Marko said. "You don't wanna pass out while we're on this thing—you'll fall right out of the car and I won't be able to catch you."

That fact kept me conscious. With no safety bar to hold, I clutched the side of the car with one hand, and with the other, grabbed Marko's T-shirt in a death grip.

"That's better." He laughed. "Hang on tight." He signaled Doc below, and the wheel picked up speed.

We were whirling around faster than I'd ever seen a ferris wheel turn. The wind at the top roared in my ears and my hair whipped wildly around my head.

Marko laughed the whole time, tilting the car forward and back, rocking it maddeningly, dangerously.

"That's right," he shouted. "You don't like tall rides, do you? Especially ferris wheels."

How did he know that?

Because I'd said so, right in front of Marko, in fact. Shortly before I found Lily's body.

I groaned.

With my eyes clenched tightly shut, I tried to calm myself. But closing my eyes was even more dizzying. I opened them to see the ground and an evilly grinning Doc rushing at us. Then with a whoosh, we were up and rolling over the top again.

"Had enough for a while?" Marko asked.

"Yes," I whimpered. "Please." I would have begged. Anything to stop the turning of the wheel. Anything to stop the rocking of the gondola.

He raised a hand to Doc on the next downswing. Doc nodded.

We continued around.

"But," I said, panic rising, "you said we could stop."

"We are," he said just as the wheel ground to a jolting halt. With us at the very top.

Oh God, this was worse than moving. We swayed

wildly; my heart pounded so loudly in my ears that I didn't realize, at first, that Marko was talking.

He was still angry, but he seemed beyond his earlier fury. He wasn't looking at me anymore, he was just looking out over town, talking.

". . . stupid kid," he said, "more trouble than she was worth. We were just trying to take care of her. We were all trying to take care of her. It's bad enough she's dead, but you had to bring the Feds back on our cases." He glared at me accusingly.

I considered and rejected a denial. I don't know how he knew it was me, but he knew.

And this is how I pay for tattling, I thought. Sitting on top of Delphi with a madman in an open ferris wheel car.

He kept mumbling, but I was too frightened to pay close attention. Even sitting perfectly still, the car swayed alarmingly in the wind.

". . . loved her. We all did. At least we tried to." This last was to himself.

Suddenly I was angry. Angry for Lily, angry for myself. Angry at this idiot, a bully who thought he could terrify me for his own amusement.

"Bullshit," I said flatly.

"What?" He was surprised.

"You heard me," I spat. "Bullshit. Do not feed me that bullshit line." I was repeating myself, but I didn't care. "If you loved her, you wouldn't have killed her. And if you hadn't killed her, you wouldn't have stolen the necklace back."

It was a stupid thing to say, I know. The threat of being flung from the open car was more than implicit.

But Marko was already pissed. I was already in danger, and if I was going to die, I wanted to do it right—not cowering and cringing.

"What?" he asked, genuinely incredulous. "You think I killed her . . . necklace . . . I stole the necklace?"

He seemed to be focusing on the wrong accusation, but if he wanted to talk about the necklace, so be it.

"Yeah, necklace," I said, nodding for emphasis. "The

turquoise cross, remember? The one you stole in Mobridge and then gave to Lily. See, she showed it to me.
She told me you gave it to her and then told her not to
flash it around.

"Pretty stupid, I'd say, handing out stolen merchan-
dise where it can be spotted and identified. And then,"
like playing a trump card, I said, "you took the necklace
back after she was dead so no one could trace it back to
you."

Marko's mouth opened and closed but no sound came
out.

Take that, I thought. I may die in a minute, but at
least I got to have a dramatic accusation scene.

Unbridled fear brings out the theatrical in me.

"She told you I gave her the cross?" he asked. "She
told you I stole it to begin with?"

"Partly," I said. Marko didn't seem to be angry at all
now, just confused. "Lily told me specifically that you
gave her the necklace. But the boys in Mobridge are the
ones who said you stole it. They name you as the thief.
They said they bought a bunch of things from you, all of
which have been identified as having been stolen at the
same time in a series of thefts in Mobridge. Which just
happened to take place while your carnival was in
town."

I inhaled to continue, not even frightened myself
anymore. Marko didn't look like a guilty man being
confronted with evidence of his crime. He looked like a
little boy. He looked confused.

"She said I gave her the cross?"

"We've already gone over that part." A gust of wind
rocked the car again. I remembered to hold on.

"And those little shits said I sold *them* stolen goods?"

"Along with steroids. Illegal steroids supplied by your
friend Doc, I would assume."

"Doc?" he asked stupidly.

"Yeah, Dr. William H. Aker," I said sarcastically,
pointing at the ground. "As if you didn't know."

Marko did something astounding. He opened his
mouth and laughed.

"You all right up there?" Doc called.

Marko leaned over the side and hollered, "Fine, we're fine. Wait until you hear this."

"Huh?" Doc called back.

"Wait," Marko called over the side, and then said to me, "I never stole that necklace. I *bought* it from a couple of punks. In Mobridge. Along with the juice— the steroids. *They* were doing the selling. And then they turned me in," he said wonderingly to himself.

"That doesn't change things much," I said. "So you bought the necklace. *Then* you gave it to your girlfriend."

"Girlfriend?" Apparently this surprised him more than accusations of her murder. "Did you say girlfriend? She wasn't my girlfriend. She was just a mixed-up kid, and we all tried to take care of her.

"I treated her like a sister. It's not my fault she had a crush on me. It happens." He preened. "She stole the cross from me. I knew she had it because Midge saw her with it. I also knew she was telling everyone that I gave it to her, but since we all knew she lied a lot, I didn't care. What difference did it make if she told the locals too?"

He looked sincere. If I hadn't known better, I'd have said he was telling the truth.

Maybe I didn't know better.

I sat back in the car to concentrate, letting go of the side and Marko's T-shirt, flexing my poor cramped fingers and brushing off flecks of rust and blue paint.

"So you took the necklace after she was dead because it was yours and you wanted it back?" I asked, just trying to clarify.

"I didn't take it back at all," he insisted. "I haven't seen that stupid cross since Lily walked off with it. She sure didn't have it yesterday."

"You didn't take it back when you went into the fun house before the police arrived? There was a witness who saw you go in then."

"Yeah, I went in. We heard you talking to that stupid ass Larry. I didn't really figure you were making it up about her being dead in there and all. But I just wanted to check." He looked down, miserable. "You know, just to be sure."

"Well, if you don't have the cross," I said, mostly to myself, "then who does?"

"Hell if I know," he said amiably, leaning forward, tipping the car, to holler at Doc. "Bring us down," he shouted. "Wait until you hear. This broad"—he jerked a thumb in my direction—"actually thought you were a real—"

The car lurched into motion. Marko, off balance and already leaning forward, slid off the seat, wailing.

Without thinking, I jumped up to grab him and saw, just a fraction of a second too late, that though he was dangling in midair, he had a firm grip on the side of the car.

As I fell, I realized, with a growing sense of wonder, that Marko had told the truth.

My last thought was that Del was going to kill me for skipping out on the Phollies.

31

The Whole Picture

Jesus, I've had some goofy, jumbled dreams in my time, but this one took the cake.

I can't remember how it started, I don't even remember going to sleep, but I was flying over Delphi through the clear night air—it was quiet and restful, no mosquitoes, no voices. Not much going on at all, except for the flying, and the vague notion that I had to get away from someone. There was a low screech in the background which sounded sort of like a seagull.

Or someone screaming in the distance.

Or maybe even a little closer, I couldn't tell.

But this wasn't a nightmare. I wasn't frightened, even when I realized I wasn't flying anymore, but lying down. Outside, I think, because of the dirt in my mouth. The grit made me thirsty.

"I'd like a drink," I said, but I kinda forgot how to speak English.

"She's coming around a little," someone said from a mountaintop in Switzerland. "Can you hear me?" he asked faintly.

Of course, I thought, though I couldn't get my mouth to form the syllables. "Just wait a minute while I get my eyes open," I meant to say, but the dream scrambled the words and they didn't sound right.

With extreme effort, I pulled my eyelids open just enough to see a pink blur, divided by black glasses, bent over me. "Hi," I said. "I know you. Sorry for the trouble . . ."

What trouble? I couldn't remember. He wasn't in the picture and the picture was blurry.

Then the scene shifted, as happens sometimes in dreams. This time I was in a small white room that rocked and bounced along, and some damn dog howled up and down, up and down, just outside, and I was getting frightened a little. And I felt sick.

Not a good thing to feel in a dream.

"Relax, we're almost there," someone said, and I didn't care who.

And the picture changed again. This time on my back, I rode down a hallway with chipped acoustic ceiling tiles and a bad smell.

The smell alarmed me, and I struggled to get away, thinking I had a dagger in my pocket, but they had my arms pinned down. Painfully.

There were people in the hallway. A priest dressed for the Spanish Inquisition and a redhead. And then there was Elvis. A couple of Elvii.

It was all blurry, and everyone wasn't in the picture, but I could tell they were all worried.

How touching, Elvis was worried. I felt guilty for never having liked him in the first place.

Then they were gone and the dream turned nasty.

"Looks like a compound fracture of the right . . ."

"She's not completely out, we'll have to insert an airway before . . ."

There were more voices, but I couldn't open my eyes,

and I was terrified they were talking about me. I thought if I lay really still they wouldn't be able to find me. I wouldn't be in the picture.

But they killed me anyway, by forcing something down my throat. Something big that blocked it completely. I struggled and tried to protest, but I was too weak—and besides, you can't struggle for long when you're being smothered.

And of course I died, since you die when you can't breathe, though I was mildly surprised to feel my chest continue to rise and fall. Someone raised my arm, the right one, I think, and clamped things on my fingers and said, "Pretty bad, but we should be able to realign without surgery . . ."

"She's lucky that's all . . ."

Just before everything went peacefully black, I finally realized I was dreaming about a hospital, though I'd never been in one before, except to visit.

Like I said, one hell of a goofy dream.

"God, what a dream," I mumbled thickly.

"Oh, so you are with us," said a voice over in the corner. "You're a very lucky young woman, I hope you know that."

Though my eyes were open, I couldn't focus very well. I knew the voice's owner had to be heading toward retirement. Not so much because of the timbre of the voice as the fact that no one my age ever called me "young."

I'd had time to register that I wasn't in bed in my own room, if for no other reason than sixtyish women rarely sit in the corners there.

My eyesight cleared enough to see a TV mounted up on a wall at the foot of my bed, which was narrow with metal railings along the side, fastened in the up position.

"Shit," I mumbled, and closed my eyes again.

"You'd be surprised how many of them say that when they wake up, dearie," my gray-haired companion warbled. She wore green and had the earpieces of a stethoscope dangling down one side of her ample chest and the rest looped back around her neck and dangling down the other.

"Hospital," I said, heart sinking. "I'm in a hospital. And you're a nurse."

"Guilty as charged, dearie." She smiled, taking my pulse, looking into my eyes, adjusting the IV which drained into my left arm.

Oh shit, an IV. Needles.

I struggled to sit up, to see whatever there was to see, but an instant dizziness overwhelmed me. Besides, I seemed to be tied down.

"Lie still, hon, until you get your bearings. We don't want you to pass out."

Seems like someone else said something like that to me recently.

"What happened?" I asked. From my vantage, I couldn't manage a detailed damage assessment. I could, however, see that her name tag read "Charlotte Russell."

She adjusted the sheets and fiddled with the IV some more, and wrote something down on the chart that had been hanging in the slot on the wall. "Try and think back. It'll help clear your head," she said matter-of-factly.

I inhaled deeply through my nose, or as deeply as I could, until someone stabbed me in the side. "Angh," I said.

"Ribs," Charlotte said. "Gotta be careful of them for a while."

"Broken, huh?" I asked. It was starting to come back to me.

"Yup," she said cheerily. "Four of 'em, cracked nice as you please. But no lung punctures."

"That's good," I said, though I wondered if a lung puncture could possibly hurt any worse. "I fell. I remember now. What else is wrong?"

I was just beginning to realize that everything hurt. It was a frightening realization.

"Well, I'm not supposed to give out that kind of

information to patients, but the doctor is in the middle of his rounds and won't get back to you again for a while. Let's just say that you'll be okay."

"Okay" was too nebulous a term for comfort. I tried to sit up to see for myself, but a combination of broken ribs and arms weighted with cement blocks held me down.

I twisted my head gingerly to the left—that arm was securely strapped to the railing with a leather thong. A needle with a long tube running from it to the IV was stuck in the middle of an angry bruise on the back of my hand.

Charlotte shrugged. "Standard procedure to keep the patient from thrashing around and dislodging the IV needle."

It wasn't an apology, just a statement of fact.

I twisted painfully and slowly to the right and my heart sank. There, propped up on a couple of white pillows, was my arm, encased in a shiny new fiberglass cast that ran from between my thumb and forefingers to just above my elbow, now set in a permanent crook. The fingers were swollen and had that purply-greenish freshly fractured glow.

"Damn," I said.

"Patients say that a lot too," Charlotte chirped. "Can you wiggle them? Are you in pain?"

I waggled the fingers halfheartedly. They hurt, but not terribly. Not as bad as they would when the shock and painkillers wore off.

I closed my eyes. "What else is broken?" Or worse yet, what's gone? Or paralyzed? I didn't have the heart to take inventory.

"Actually, sweetie, you're a very lucky young lady," Charlotte said, again, severely. "Four cracked ribs, multiple contusions and abrasions, a mild concussion, and right radius and ulna snapped cleanly and set easily; a pretty small price to pay."

"Oh yeah?" I asked wearily.

"You could have died," she said shortly. "We rarely see injuries this minor from a fall like yours. And rarely does anyone have a prognosis for complete recovery like you do. Count yourself lucky."

"Just like winning the lottery." I sighed.

"No," said a voice from the doorway. "Winning the lottery is a heck of a lot more fun than this. And the food is better."

"Hi there," I said weakly to Neil, still wearing his Brother Pascoe outfit from the Phollies. "You were in my dream."

I sounded like Dorothy Gale just back from Oz, though I slowly realized that none of it had been a dream. Neil had been there, along with Del and Presley in his Elvis costume. Maybe even Chainlink. Everyone was in the picture.

Whatever that meant.

"Yeah." He grinned sheepishly. "I really gotta get out of this monk suit."

I would have laughed, but it hurt too much.

"Have you been here all night?" I asked. The morning sun shone through the window blinds.

"We all were," Neil said. "Me, Del, Pres, Rhonda, Aphrodite."

"Aphrodite too?" This was amazing. If Aphrodite was here, who was running the cafe?

Neil saw the question in my eyes. "Closed down for today. No one to work; we're all here in Aberdeen at the hospital. Some idiot fell off a ferris wheel, I heard."

I was truly amazed. And touched. And tired. Easy tears gathered in the corners of my eyes.

"Was Del furious? About me missing our song, I mean?"

"She wasn't happy, but it went off okay," he said.

"How? Did Del and Rhonda do it by themselves? That would have looked silly."

"No, you'll never believe what happened. Aphrodite sang your part!" He laughed out loud. "Danced and everything!"

"You're shitting me." That presented a truly unbelievable picture.

"Why not?" Neil grinned. "Most of the lyrics are one syllable, and Aphrodite watched rehearsals all along. She did great."

"Did they win?"

"Nope." Neil grinned.

"The *Hair* kids?" I ventured.

"Wrong again, though they wowed the house with their finale."

"Did they really take their clothes off?" I was sorry I'd missed it.

"Yep, right down to almost-invisible, flesh-colored bodysuits. It was great. I thought Iva Hausvik was going to have a heart attack when they started stripping."

"And how did those Delphi kids get their hands on flesh-colored bodysuits?"

"Beats me." He shrugged innocently.

"Well, who won, then?" I couldn't think of anyone else good enough to win the talent award.

"Mardelle, of course."

Of course. I smiled, then asked, "What happened?" Neil looked dead tired too. Body and spirit worn out. "I mean with me. Who found me? Where are Marko and Doc?"

Neil started with the last question. "In jail, for attempted murder."

"But they didn't kill Lily," I said anxiously, trying to reach for the phone with my left hand, forgetting that was impossible. "We've got to call Agent Ingstad and tell him. I know I started all of this, but I'm sure Marko didn't do it."

I remembered his genuine surprise at the accusation. I was certain he wasn't a good enough actor to fake that.

"No," Neil said seriously, pulling up a chair next to the bed. He lay a warm hand on my arm. "They weren't arrested for Lily's attempted murder."

"Did they try to kill someone else, then?" I asked, confused. Why hadn't I heard about it?

"They were arrested for *your* attempted murder."

"*Me?*" I asked; maybe I shouted. "No, no, no, no." I

was really agitated now, remembering Marko's bewildered face as I fell. How he let one hand go to reach for me. Too late, unfortunately. "Jeez, we really have to call now. Marko and Doc weren't trying to kill me."

"Then what in the hell were they trying to do?" Neil demanded. "You don't usually go on joyrides with psychos." He was angry. Tired and frazzled.

"I mean, it was an accident. They made me get on the ferris wheel, but they didn't mean for me to fall. They weren't trying to kill me."

"And it's just good luck they didn't," Del said, coming into the room, stirring coffee in a Styrofoam cup. She still had on her pink and yellow satin shorts and top. "Though I certainly considered doing it myself when we realized you were gone. You'll do anything to get out of going onstage, won't you?"

The rest of the past evening clicked back into place. I groaned. My forehead itched and I was thirsty. Charlotte had unobtrusively left the room, and my hand was still firmly secured to the railing.

"Unhook me, will you?" I asked Neil, wiggling my fingers. To Del, I said, "They were waiting by the bathroom. In the dark. I think they must have followed me. I didn't notice them backstage earlier. Did you see them? They were wearing their work shirts, you know, those black ones."

"There were carnival workers all over the place, in the audience and wandering the halls," Del said, sitting on the end of the bed. "In fact, I saw Marko in the audience before the show started."

"That doesn't explain the kidnapping. That charge should stick even if attempted murder doesn't," Neil said darkly.

I stretched my fingers and flexed my good elbow, enjoying even that limited range of motion. "Help me raise the bed up a little, will you?"

After a couple of tries, we got the head of the bed elevated. "Now can I have a drink of water?"

I was stalling for time. Embarrassed to tell them why

Marko was so angry at me in the first place. Angry enough to endanger both of us.

"She's stalling," Del said to Neil. "Tell us what happened."

I told them about the newspaper article and the missing necklace. Neil raised an eyebrow. "I tried to call you, but your line was busy," I explained.

Then I told them about calling Agent Ingstad, and my suspicion that Marko had killed Lily, and that he went back into the fun house. And the unmarked car that pulled up to the carnival not long after.

Neil frowned, but Del opened her mouth and laughed.

"I could have saved you all of this," she said with a sweeping gesture. "If only you had let me tell you."

"Saved me all what?" I asked, testy that she found my situation so amusing. "Told me what?"

Del was laughing and talking to the ceiling now. "I tried to tell her, didn't I? But did she want to hear what I had to say? Nooooo."

"What the hell are you talking about?" I demanded, though I had a feeling I wasn't going to be too thrilled with her reply.

"This," she said. "You, here, ferris wheel, fractures. Marko, murder. Lily." She sipped her coffee. "I could have told you he didn't kill Lily."

"Then why didn't you?" I snapped. I was too tired to play games with Del. My arm ached abominably.

"Because you wouldn't let me."

I closed my eyes and breathed as deeply as I dared, then looked to Neil for support. He shrugged. What could he do?

Then I knew. God damn, son of a bitch. I knew.

"He was with you, wasn't he?"

"Yup." Del grinned, smug, extremely pleased with herself.

"All night?" I asked, feeling more and more like an idiot.

"Whole night," she said nonchalantly. "Was a busy

one, too. Right there in his truck—never out of my sight." She waggled her eyebrows. "Didn't even get out to pee."

"You should have told me," I said wanly.

"Hey, I tried, You wouldn't listen." Del was enormously amused.

Neil was confused. "What's going on?"

"Lily died Friday night or early Saturday morning, and Marko was with Del that whole night. He couldn't have killed her. He didn't steal the necklace back, and thanks to Del, he now has an ironclad alibi."

I nodded grimly at smiling Del.

"She tried to tell me who she spent the night with, and I wouldn't let her," I explained to Neil. "I didn't think it was important. I only wanted to know if she saw Marko lurking about the fun house." I saw now the narrow stupidity of the question.

"You're the one who loves mysteries," Del said softly. "Don't you know that a good detective looks at the whole picture before drawing conclusions?"

That'd be easy, I thought, if I knew what the whole picture was.

32

....

Soft Landings

I would have been much more grateful to be alive if everyone hadn't made a special point to remind me, continually, just how lucky I was. And just how much they were enjoying the whole spectacle.

"This is the most amazing thing in my whole life," Rhonda said in between slurps around the edge of an ice-cream drumstick she'd picked up in the hospital cafeteria. "I mean, I actually know someone who was thrown from a moving ferris wheel and lived to tell about it. It's just too bad"—she paused for another lick—"that there wasn't someone with a video camera, like, right near there. You could have been on *Rescue 911*. Or *Code 3* or one of those shows."

Finally, something to be truly grateful for.

"That would have been cool," agreed Presley, still in his Elvis getup. He was happily chewing ice chips from the pitcher on my bedstand.

"Just what I'd want—my screams recorded for posterity," I said. "To be run during ratings sweeps week, or

picked up for Carnival Disaster Day on Sally Jessy
Raphael."

I was being sarcastic, though no one but Neil caught
on.

"You weren't screaming much when we got there," he
said, leaning back in the chair in the corner. "In fact,
would have felt much better if you had let loose with a
blood-curdler or two as they loaded you into the ambulance."

"You weren't there before the ambulance?" I asked.
was still trying to sort out what happened. "I though
for sure you were bending over me while I was on the
ground." I'd assumed the glasses were Neil's horn-rims

"How would *we* have known where you were?" De
asked. "As far as we were concerned, you were just
chickenshit no-show." She smiled as she said it, but he
real anger hadn't been totally displaced by my perfectl
valid reason for missing the performance.

"The whole talent show was pretty well over when w
heard the sirens," Pres said. "And we didn't go outsid
until we realized they were stopping in town."

"Well, who called me in, then?" I asked.

"Who knows?" Aphrodite paced back and forth at th
foot of my bed. The last fifteen cigaretteless hours ha
been a trial for her.

"They were anonymous," Pres said in an overl
theatrical voice.

"It was probably Marko and Doc," I said.

"I kinda doubt it was Doc," Del said, grinning.

"Why?"

"Because Marko wasn't likely to have reported him
self anonymously for an attempted murder he tried
commit," Neil said with a severe look at Del.

Something was up between them. Something abo
Doc.

"My, my, my," said a lilting voice from the doorwa
"And are you all coming from Delphi too?" A sho
dark man with his black curly hair slicked back, weari
a white çoat, stood in the doorway.

He surveyed Del and Rhonda in their satin, Neil

his gown, and Pres, still looking like a young Elvis, and said in a voice that reminded me of a bubbling brook, "I must make it a point to visit your charming town. You all dress so colorfully."

To me he said, "Hello, you might not be remembering me, Mrs. Tory Bauer. You were not fully conscious when they were bringing you in last night. I am Dr. Bangalor and I would like to examine you now again, if your good friends would be so kind as to leave the room for a moment."

He flashed a thousand-watt smile at them, and they all filed out docilely, though I caught Del checking out his naked ring finger with a contemplative look.

Shining a small penlight in my eyes, he asked, "And are you feeling very much pain right now, Mrs. Tory Bauer?"

South Dakota, for a state with almost no immigrant population, has a surprising percentage of foreign doctors.

"Yeah, I mean it's not horrible or anything, but I hurt all over and my arm aches a lot," I said. "The broken one. Though I suppose this is nothing, huh? Once the painkillers wear off, I imagine I'll find out how much I really hurt."

"Oh no, Mrs. Bauer," he said mournfully. "There have been no painkillers for your injuries. When you were coming in last night, we unfortunately did not know when you had been eating your last meal, and under those circumstances, we could not be prescribing the painkillers for you."

"Why not?" I asked, though I was relieved. I had been dreading how much worse the pain was going to get.

"Because . . ." He noted something on my chart and then walked to the other side of the bed and experimentally prodded the fingers poking out of the cast. "Can you wiggle your fingers for me now?" He smiled encouragingly.

I did my best.

He beamed. "Very good; the swelling has gone down too. You are a very lucky woman, Mrs. Tory Bauer."

"So they all tell me," I said. "Why couldn't I have any painkillers last night?"

"Because some drugs will be interacting badly with certain foods, and since we were not knowing when and what you ate yesterday, we could not be taking a chance that you would be reacting badly. It is a sad thing when that happens.

"But"—he brightened considerably—"since we know you have not been eating anything since last night we can be giving you some medications for your pain. Would you like some medications for your pain, Mrs. Tory Bauer?"

"Yes," I said gratefully. "Please." Soon, I thought. The ache in my broken arm was being replaced by a steadily rising howl.

"Okay. The nurse will be coming in soon with some medications for you, and also you should be eating something with this medication to keep from getting an upset stomach. You see," he said, "some drugs are also interacting well with foods, and you will not be feeling badly if you eat something when you swallow these pills. But remember, these pills will be making your pain go away, but they will also be making you very sleepy, so I think I will be telling your good friends that they should be coming back later to see you. Yes?"

"Yes, that's fine," I said. I was tired, and the notion of being whacked out on painkillers right then was pretty appealing.

Dr. Bangalor seemed satisfied with the examination and turned to leave.

"Oh, Doctor," I said. He stopped at the door. "When can I get out of here? I mean, how soon can I go home?"

I wasn't homesick. I had tried to forget that I was not only uninsured but also effectively unemployable for the time being. Unfortunately, my worry regulator was relentless. The sooner I went home, the smaller the bill would be. The sooner I could go crazy from wondering how I'd pay for all this.

No one leaves you tips when you're sitting at home.

"We will want to be watching the swelling in your

fingers, Mrs. Tory Bauer, but your other injuries seem to be nice indeed, and I think you might be able to be going home tomorrow afternoon."

Charlotte, who was still on duty and in high spirits, came in soon after to hand me a small plastic cup of pills and a couple of crackers.

"Doctor says to eat these so you won't have an empty stomach," she chirped, "and throw up all these expensive drugs."

She helped me, up on wobbly legs, to the bathroom. I gave up trying to protect my dignity. Neither arm was free to hold the back of my standard-issue nightgown together, and I had to be helped both on and off the toilet.

I did get a chance, however, to survey the bruises that dotted my whole body. They were everywhere, but especially concentrated on my right side. Including the right side of my face. I clucked at the shiner, though the pills were kicking in fast and I found I didn't care much about much of anything by the time I got back into bed.

Charlotte tucked me back in and carefully removed the IV needle from the back of my left hand. "Doctor says you don't need this anymore, as long as you promise to drink plenty of fluids."

"Okay," I said. "Sure, fine." With my eyes closed, I was beginning to remember just how wonderful it felt not to hurt anywhere.

"You could get a ton for this stuff on the street," I mumbled happily to Charlotte. "Make some drug pusher a very rich fella."

"Not a very good plan of action, Mrs. Bauer," said Agent Ingstad. "And certainly illegal. I hope you weren't thinking of a career change."

I was too groggy to be surprised that he was calmly sitting in the corner chair, but not far gone enough to ignore him.

"Oh, hi," I said, struggling to sit, but my ribs wouldn't let me. "What are you doing here?"

"We make it a point to talk to people who have been victims of near-homicidal violence. It's my job." He pulled his chair up close to the bed, crossed his long legs, and waited.

"Well, you better talk fast." I giggled. "I am currently under the influence and won't make sense for much longer."

He sighed. "Mrs. Bauer, if you'll forgive me for saying this, I didn't think you made much sense when you weren't under the influence. But you seem to be on to something. We thought it a good idea to come and talk to you."

"How come?" I wasn't tracking very well.

"Because," he said patiently, "you were attacked by the very young man you warned me about yesterday. That certainly warrants further investigation. Are you able to answer some questions? I'll try to be brief so you can get some rest."

"Sure." I could do anything. Anything at all.

"First, why did you contact Marko Parker and Stanley MacDochlan last night?"

"Stanley who?"

"Stanley MacDochlan," he repeated. "The carnival worker known as Doc."

"His name isn't William?" I asked, trying to figure out why I thought it would be.

"No. Did you meet to confront them with your theory about Lily Mitchell's death?"

"I didn't meet with them at all. They forced me to leave the school building. I didn't volunteer to get on that ferris wheel, believe me. I hate those things."

"They used force to make you accompany them, and they used force to get you on the ride?" he asked.

"I already said that." I was peevish. And sleepy.

"Why did they force you to go with them?"

"You'll have to ask them," I said. "Somehow they figured out I'd called you." I worked one eye open. "I'm pretty sure they weren't trying to kill me, though. It was their fault," I said, anxious to make that clear, "but it was an accident. Talk to them about it."

"We've already talked to Mr. Parker. He seems to confirm your story," he said.

"What about Stanley MacDochlan?" I giggled. What a stupid name.

"We haven't been able to talk to him yet."

"And why not?"

Agent Ingstad suppressed a small smile. He was probably a nice man in civilian life.

"Stanley MacDochlan is indisposed at the moment, though we expect to talk to him sometime today."

"Indisposed? I thought he was in jail."

"He's both."

"Why?" I was thoroughly confused.

"Mrs. Bauer, haven't you wondered how you fell more than twenty feet onto hard-packed ground with only relatively minor injuries?"

They didn't feel minor, but I had to concede the point.

"You weren't seriously injured because you landed on something," he said, grinning. "You landed on Stanley MacDochlan."

This struck me as pretty amusing. Though I supposed I'd be plenty embarrassed later on.

"Did I kill the little cocksucker?" I asked. Fat jokes, huh? Guess I showed him fat. If they'd called him Mac instead, none of this would have happened.

Agent Ingstad laughed. "Off the record, I'd agree with your assessment. On the record, no you did not kill Mr. MacDochlan. He, however, did suffer a broken leg and some other contusions. He's in the hospital right now, under guard."

"Good," I said. "Even if they didn't kill Lily, they did kidnap me. That wasn't nice, you know."

"Ah, so we're in agreement, finally. You realize now that Lily Mitchell wasn't murdered?"

Not exactly, I thought. We just agree Marko didn't do it. Someone still stuffed her in the rafters. I nodded foggily. "I don't like ferris wheels. Hate 'em, in fact."

"I only have one more question for you, then I'll leave you to your nap. You're absolutely sure you saw a necklace wrapped around the deceased's hand?"

"Yup."

"Give me your best far-fetched conjecture as to who might have taken it."

"You got me," I said, happily drifting. I really had no idea who took the necklace.

But on the way down, I was pleasantly surprised to know that the picture would tell me who was, or at least who was not, Dr. William Aker.

33

....

Baloney and Ham

I now have a profound respect for the left-handed. It had never occurred to me just how difficult it can be to survive in a right-handed world.

In the same vein, I'd never been particularly aware of how hard it is for the disabled, the paralyzed, the amputees to get through their daily grind with less than the usual compliment of functional limbs.

Unfortunately, I was going to have ample time to empathize during the next eight weeks—six in the heavy, bent-arm contraption I was wrestling with now, and another two with a short arm cast.

Can you zip your pants with one hand? Even your good one? Try wringing out a washcloth, twisting the cap off a bottle of diet Coke, opening a letter.

Try earning a living waiting tables.

They tell me that in a couple of weeks the fingers on my right hand will be slightly more useful. But for now they have all the aesthetic and practical value of purple sausages.

"Look at it this way," Del said on the drive home from the hospital, "this'll give you lots of time to shop and read and do whatever else you like to do in the afternoons." She grinned.

"I'm not going to be able to afford anything if I can't work," I said. And what, exactly, I thought, would I be able to "do" (in Del's sense of the word) in this damn cast?

And who would I do it with? Stu, who didn't call, or visit, or send flowers after the accident? Not that I really expected such blatant signs of affection, but I was still a little hurt that he didn't even try.

"Hey, don't worry," said Del, who never worried about anything. "The hospital has no choice but to wait until you can pay. What are they gonna do? Take away your house?"

I didn't own a house. I paid rent to Del—in fact, I didn't have any possessions anyone could seize, unless a drawerful of homemade copies of James Taylor cassettes were valuable to anyone besides me. I'd already made arrangements to turn over what little savings I had, but that barely put a dent in the staggering total.

"I suppose they could take away your car, but that would net them a whole five or six hundred dollars," Del continued. "Maybe."

"I don't have a car," I said tiredly. My now-defunct savings account had been earmarked for a vehicle.

"Sure you do." She grinned. "Didn't anyone tell you? Ron pulled your name for the Pacer at the end of the Phollies on Sunday. You are now the proud owner of a dented, silver, manual transmission, high-mileage automobile. Luckily, you didn't have to be present to win."

Though they weren't the high-octane drugs I had taken yesterday, the painkillers I was on now sort of evened out the emotional bumps.

It was nice to win the car, but I couldn't get very excited about it.

"Standard tranny, huh?" I asked, wearied by the cast,

the inconvenience, and my life. "On the column or on the floor?"

If the gearshift was on the steering wheel, I just might be able to manage, even with the cast.

"On the floor, unfortunately," Del said.

I sighed. I didn't feel like driving anywhere anyway.

"You know, if you had to fall off something, why didn't you fall off the cafe roof? At least then you'd be eligible for Workman's Comp," Del said.

Though I was one of them, I'd never felt any commonality with the rest of the uninsured. Aphrodite truly couldn't afford full coverage for us, and we sure as hell couldn't pay for it on our own. We were healthy, and I, personally, avoided participating in anything that might result in injury—like sports or exercise.

It's hard to get hurt reading.

"Do you have a lawyer, dear?" the hospital accountant had asked quietly. "Not that I am trying to suggest anything, you know. But given your circumstances, it seems that these charges"—she poked a sheaf of alarmingly thick papers—"simply should not be your responsibility."

I agreed and said that it was nice of the hospital to feel that way, since I would probably never be able to find that much money.

"No, I think you misunderstand," she said, looking over her half-glasses at me. "You are ultimately responsible for payment. I just meant that it might be possible to recoup some of your expenses from those who caused your injuries."

Aphrodite was more to the point, "Sue 'em."

Though I hoped it wouldn't come to litigation, both the accountant and Aphrodite had a point. I didn't fling myself off that ferris wheel. At least not on purpose. And actually, even if I had, the carnival's liability insurance should cover accidents of that nature.

At first I was afraid that HBIE had packed up and left town—they were on a tight schedule, after all.

"They're not going anyplace until this whole Marko–Lily–ferris wheel thing is taken care of," Del explained.

"We heard that the DCI ordered them to stay put for the time being."

It was to that end, with a glimmer of hope, that I set out to have a chat with Hamilton Bogner, ignoring doctor's and friends' orders to stay put and rest.

Besides, I wanted to have another peek at that group picture on Good Old Ham's desk. In the hospital it had finally occurred to me that if Dr. William Aker was traveling with the carnival this summer only, he wouldn't be in *last* year's group shot. Process of elimination would pinpoint his identity, though I still didn't know if it mattered who he was.

I'm not fond of heat and humidity under normal circumstances. I liked them even less as I trudged down Delphi's main drag in the middle of the afternoon, bruised and limping and newly impoverished. Shouldering a two-thousand-pound cast.

"Come in, come in, Mrs. Bauer," Hamilton Bogner said jovially before I could knock. His smile did not reach his eyes, which were narrowed and mistrustful. "I'm glad you stopped in," he lied. "I'd like to offer my apology for your unfortunate, um, accident."

He didn't ask if there was anything he could do for me.

"Come in, sit down. Can I get you anything to drink? A beer, a glass of wine? I have an Oregon Riesling that is especially good. Knudsen Erath, 1991, not too sweet, crisp with a buttery finish."

"Thank you, no," I said as I carefully lowered myself onto the chair opposite his desk. "I'm not supposed to mix alcohol with the painkillers I'm taking."

"You don't mind if I have a glass, do you?" He tried not to stare at my bruised face or my broken arm or at how gingerly I moved and breathed. Eventually he didn't look at me at all, but busied himself moving papers and the picture frame (whose back was to me) to make room on the desk for the bottle of wine.

"Is there something I can do for you?" He looked up finally. Beads of sweat dotted the top of his bald head.

This was my opening. I took a deep breath, remembering at the last second to make it a little less deep.

"As a matter of fact, there is," I said. On the walk from my trailer to his, I'd decided to plunge right in. No pussyfooting. "The hospital needs your insurance information—you know, the name of your company, policy numbers, and that kind of thing."

He sipped from his glass but didn't say anything.

"You know, so the insurance company and the hospital can start processing my bills. It takes forever for these things to be resolved as it is; the sooner we get the ball rolling, the sooner it gets finished."

"I see," he said slowly, sitting up straight in his chair. "I'm going to need all of your insurance numbers too." He tore the top sheet off a small tablet and plucked a pen from his pocket.

"Why would you need my numbers?" I was indignant, but also stalling. I didn't have any numbers.

"So our insurance companies can communicate with each other while they sort out who's at fault in this accident."

"What do you mean, sort out who's at fault?" The pitch of my voice rose with every word. "It's obvious who's at fault—your employees kidnapped me and forced me to get on one of *your* carnival rides. They operated the ride negligently, and that negligence caused me to fall and sustain serious injuries."

I would have shouted that pseudolegal retort, but it hurt too much.

"I understand that is your contention," he said with an oily tone. "But my lawyer and I feel that an investigation will prove that you attempted to ride on my ferris wheel, without a ticket, and during hours when the carnival was officially closed. We think an investigation will show that my employees were only trying to remove you from the ride, and that your injuries were sustained when you resisted them."

I was so flabbergasted that I gasped, forgetting bruises and broken ribs.

Hamilton continued before I could find my voice. "And not only did you cause your own injuries, but you seriously"—he emphasized the word in a parody of my earlier statement—"injured one of my workers in the process.

"You *did* actually fall on one of my employees," he said, neither hesitant nor wary now.

"That's the biggest load of bullshit I've ever heard! You know goddamn well that's not how it happened!" Funny thing, anger works almost like a prescription drug.

Ribs? What ribs?

"I suppose that will be for the court to decide, won't it? And to get the ball rolling"—again parodying my own words—"my lawyer has asked that you sign this statement as a preliminary step toward filing the necessary paperwork."

He reached into the upper right drawer of his desk and pulled out a single-spaced document and handed it to me. It was a couple of pages long, stapled together in the upper left corner.

I scanned the first several paragraphs, which were densely written and nearly incomprehensible. I did catch a few phrases like "negligent action" and "release from all future suits" and "hold Hamilton Bogner harmless."

"I don't sign anything without reading it first," I said archly. "I'll take this with me and consult my lawyer."

Lawyer, I thought. How am I going to pay for a lawyer?

Ham reached over his desk and in a swift motion snatched the document from my hand. "I'm afraid that won't be possible. This is my only copy. I will be happy to make more after you've signed it and send them to you and your lawyer. And to anyone else you'd like."

"No way." I shook my head. "I'm not signing nothing."

I was pissed. Double negative pissed.

"Have it your way, Mrs. Bauer." He was smiling again. "Here's my lawyer's card. His number's on it.

Have your lawyer give him a call." He tossed the card in my direction. It landed on the floor.

"Fuck you," I said, and clumped out of the trailer, fuming.

"Slime," I muttered to myself. "All of them, every last one of them. Cheats. Thieves. Liars. Lawyers." I spat in disgust. It'd be a pleasure to sue Hamilton Bogner's big hairy ass.

I cursed them all, even poor dead Lily.

Why had I ever set foot on carnival ground to begin with? I hate carnivals. Stuart McKee, my mind answered. If it wasn't for him and his South Dakota Fucking Snail, and his slow dances and his green eyes, none of this ever would have happened.

Stu and pregnant puking Junior and her overripe chicken. Sex and salmonella.

I made it halfway home, fuming and swearing and blaming everyone in the world for a situation that was essentially my fault, before I realized that I'd left the card with Hamilton Bogner's lawyer's name on the floor of his trailer.

I stopped in the middle of the street, panting and exhausted. I didn't have insurance. I didn't have any money. But it appeared that I was going to need a lawyer. And soon.

I turned around and trudged back, prepared to suffer Bogner's smirk and ask for the card. Then I'd see about getting a lawyer who liked to work for free.

Forcing myself to be calm, I banged on his door with my left hand. There was no response. I banged again, leaning closer, ear cocked, to listen.

No sound came from inside. I called tentatively, with my mouth close to the hot sheet metal. "Mr. Bogner? This is Tory Bauer. I'd like to take that card with your lawyer's name on it. My lawyer's gonna need it before we get anything done."

I was shooting for conciliatory, but ended up sounding weak and whiny.

Who needs dignity anyway?

There was still no answer. I rattled the knob. The

door was unlocked. It opened. I poked my head inside. "Mr. Bogner? Are you here? I need to pick up your lawyer's card."

The trailer seemed empty. I stood on the step, open door in hand, considering my next move.

I squinted down the street toward our trailer and decided that I didn't want to come back later. In fact, it would be less embarrassing to slip in and pick up the card without talking to Bogner at all. He was now someone I would go out of my way to avoid.

"Yoo hoo," I said as I went inside, both as a cover in case anyone saw me and on the off chance that Ol' Ham really was inside, in the bathroom or something.

There was still no answer. There was also no card on the floor. I leaned over the desk and looked, careful not to touch anything. It wasn't there either.

I considered again, breathing as deeply as I dared. The trailer door was still open. I had a good view of the empty carnival grounds through the windows. No one was lurking outside.

Chewing the inside of my cheek, I sidled around the desk and opened the upper right drawer about halfway.

A small brown pill bottle rolled to the front of the drawer "Xanax" the label read. That triggered a memory of Hamilton Bogner slipping something small into his pocket before rushing out to deal with a furious Marko.

Something small, like a pill bottle full of tranquilizers. With the name William H. Aker prominent on the label.

I stared at the employee group photo on the desk, trying to memorize who was in it. Skinny Marko (presumably presteroid), Midge, Larry, Daisy, and of course Doc, were all there.

If I had remembered, earlier, that Doc was in the picture, I could have saved myself no small amount of grief.

Unfortunately, it looked like every single carnival employee, except Lily, was in that picture. Lily and Hamilton Bogner.

Remembering Bogner reminded me to hurry. The lawyer's card was also in the drawer, on top of the papers he'd wanted me to sign. I took both, suspicious at his insistence that I sign the papers immediately, without study.

Quickly, I pushed the drawer shut. The pill bottle rolled in the nearly empty drawer and struck something metal with a soft clunk.

Checking the window again for lurkers, I reopened the drawer, all the way this time, remembering as I did that Hamilton Bogner had also been in the fun house maze.

That he'd sent me out to call the police, alone.

That the necklace, which had been wrapped around Lily's hand when I left, wasn't there when Marko entered the maze just a few minutes later.

Before I saw it, I knew what I'd find in the back of the desk drawer.

34

....

The Good Doctor

In mystery books, when sleuths, amateur or otherwise, stumble across what appears to be a pivotal clue, no matter how surprising, they keep a cool head. They search for further clues. They risk exposure, and worse, in the single-minded pursuit of the truth.

They reconsider theories and reevaluate suspects, often on-site. And in traditional mystery epiphany mode, they suddenly understand the who/why/how and calmly go about wrapping the whole thing up.

The better to go and solve another puzzle in the next book.

It didn't exactly work that way for me. Instead of searching Ham Bogner's desk and the rest of the trailer for . . . what? For clues, for ideas, for a signed confession. The only epiphany I had was the definition of trespassing.

I hadn't exactly "broke," but I had surely "entered," and I was now in possession of papers that could be called stolen by a man who had already threatened me with a lawsuit. A frivolous one, I thought, but a lawsuit just the same.

Trespassing (and B&E and burglary) were not just civil matters, they were criminal.

So regardless of the deeper significance of finding Lily's turquoise cross, the one stolen and then purchased and restolen, in Ham Bogner's desk drawer, and doubly regardless of whatever other evidence might be hidden on the premises, I was seized by the overwhelming urge to get out of there. Immediately.

It is no small trick to fold papers one-handed, especially if you are in a hurry, and frightened to boot. The door to Bogner's office was still open, and the carnival, which by now was mostly a vacant lot dotted with loaded trailers and trucks, was quiet and deserted.

I stuffed the papers into a back jeans pocket and backed out, jarring my cast painfully on the jamb as I pulled the door shut. "Ow, dammit," I muttered aloud to myself.

"I don't think Mr. Bogner is in at the moment," a deep voice behind me said. "Shouldn't you be at home, resting?"

Carefully, trying to look as innocent as possible, I turned around. A vaguely familiar man stood in the dust at the end of the trailer. Tall with a fiercely peeling sunburn, he wore an HBIE T-shirt. The name above the pocket was "Hank."

"I know . . . well, I mean, I knocked and I wasn't sure if I heard an answer, so I stuck my head in to see if he was there. But Mr. Bogner isn't there. He's not home," I finished lamely, anxious to get down the steps and away.

I remembered Hank now. Hank had come into the cafe with Lily on Thursday, the day the carnival arrived in Delphi.

Hank with the illegible handwriting and pair of glasses stuffed in his breast pocket. Hank with the slightly Southern undertones in his voice.

I stopped for a moment.

"The *H* stands for Henry, doesn't it?" I asked, squinting at him.

Squinting at frowning Hank, who wasn't in last year's group shot of loyal carny employees.

Frowning Hank, who spent his summers incognito, being known by a short version of his middle name.

"Hello, I'm Tory Bauer," I said. "And you must be Dr. William H. Aker." With a self-deprecating shrug, I extended my useless right arm to shake, but instead he carefully grasped my fingers, peering at them closely before turning the hand over as far as the cast would allow to continue the examination.

"You're not experiencing any numbness in the thumb or fingers, are you?" He settled his glasses in place and picked up my other hand. To use as comparison, I guess.

"Unfortunately, I'm not numb anywhere," I said.

"Good." He nodded. "Pain is a good sign." The glasses went back into the pocket, and he looked at my face for the first time. "I'm extremely curious as to how you know who I am."

"It's a long story, and I'd like to talk to you too. About Lily Mitchell," I said. "But what I'd like more than anything is to get out of the sun and sit down."

"Yes, you shouldn't overexert yourself." He glanced up and down the shadeless street.

The cafe had reopened, but an appearance there would be an invitation for everyone inside to stop and chat about me and my accident, and what they were doing when they heard about it, and how they would have avoided the whole situation, and how I should have acted.

You know, Tuesday afternoon quarterbacking.

Though the reaction would probably be the same, there were apt to be fewer people in Jackson's, and therefore fewer interruptions.

"How about the bar?" I suggested.

He hesitated. "What meds are you on?"

"Don't worry—I know enough not to drink alcohol while taking painkillers. I'll just have a diet Coke."

"Make it caffeine-free," he said as we walked across the street. "Caffeine can react adversely with some kinds of medicines too."

The cool dark interior of the bar felt like heaven, even with the stale smoke and Garth Brooks on the jukebox.

"Hey, Tory." Mardelle waved from behind the bar where she was polishing glasses. "When I said 'break a leg' the other night, you weren't supposed to take me literally."

I glanced down at my cast and then back up at Mardelle. "Leg?"

"Or even figuratively." She laughed.

"Yeah, well, at least it kept me from singing. You have no idea how lucky you are to have been spared."

"Seems to me you're the lucky one," she said, and turned back to her work.

The bar was empty except for a scattering of weekday mid-afternoon drinkers. Mostly farmers, mostly men, each spent most of his time exploring his own beer-fueled universe.

Hank, or should I say Dr. Aker, steered us to a secluded table that was back by itself on the far side of the door that led to the Jacksons' upstairs living quarters.

He waited politely while I seated myself slowly in the chair that faced the door. It's a waitress rule—keep an eye on the door.

Waitresses and Mafia dons.

"Hey, Tory, how you feeling?" one of the Jackson twins asked, pad in hand, ready to take our order. "Tough break." He nodded in the general direction of my multiple injuries.

"Tell me about it." I hesitated. He was cheerful and not drunk, which made me decide he was Pat. On the other hand, his haircut looked fresh and his upper lip a little raw, as though unused to being shaved on a regular basis. "Pete."

He didn't correct me.

"What can I get you this afternoon?" He pulled a pen from the pocket of a cheap brown polo shirt.

"Coors Light for me, can," Hank said. "And a caffeine-free diet Coke for the lady."

Pete raised an eyebrow at me for confirmation. Women in Delphi usually order for themselves, and generally I would refuse to drink pop without caffeine. But one buzz at a time was sufficient.

"Now, I'd be pleased if you'd care to tell me how you know my name," Hank said as Pete walked away.

"You're fairly well-known in your field," I said. "You've published articles on steroid use and antidepressants." I sent a silent thank-you to Neil and his computer.

Hank sat forward and leaned his elbows on the table and said skeptically, "You read arcane medical journals?"

"Not really," I said, "but I have heard of you." That was true—Neil told me and I listened.

He accepted his beer from Pete, poured it into a frosted glass, and sprinkled salt on the foam. "Even if you've read every word I ever wrote, which I seriously doubt, how in the world did you recognize me? My picture wasn't published with any of the articles."

"Thanks, Pete, nothing else right now," I said, then turned to Hank. "To tell you the truth, I didn't recognize you. At least from a picture. I knew you were traveling with the carnival and it was a simple process of elimination to discover who you were."

Well, sort of simple.

"That's what puzzles me." He drank and continued. "How did you know I was even with this carnival this summer?"

"Easy," I said, sipping the flat pop. "Hamilton Bogner, himself, told me."

He shook his head, confused. "You know Hamilton Bogner well enough to discuss personnel matters?"

"We were talking about carnivals in general, and I asked about health care for his people and he mentioned that you were traveling with them for the summer."

"Did he mention that I wasn't with them in a medical capacity?"

"Actually, no. In fact, he specifically told me that you were available to treat any medical emergencies."

Hank turned away with a pained look on his face. "I

am here on hiatus. Every summer I work somewhere
different just to see another part of the country. In some
states I am allowed to practice medicine and I hire on in
that capacity. But Hamilton Bogner's International Extravaganza," he pronounced the name with disgust,
"crosses several state lines. It was not possible to be
certified in all of them. So I am officially not a doctor
until I get back to my office in late August.

"I have a high-pressure job which demands periodic
relief. I go back to my practice spiritually and physically
renewed. Can you understand that?"

"Just passing time with the little folk, is that it?" I
asked.

He ignored that. "You've talked to Bogner, you know
him. Tell me, how did he strike you?"

This was interesting—a doctor asking for my
opinion.

"I think he's a creep and a scumball. He's threatening
to sue me for having the audacity to fall off his ferris
wheel."

"You're kidding."

"Not at all. Personally, though"—I leaned over the
table and lowered my voice—"I think it might be a
bluff." A comforting theory had occurred to me. "I
asked about his liability insurance and he went on the
attack."

"You may have a point." Hank signaled for another
beer. "I haven't seen any figures or anything, but I'm
pretty sure the whole outfit is running in the red. I think
Bogner is on the edge of bankruptcy. I know his backers
are worried. He might not even have any insurance. It's
pretty expensive, you know."

I presume a doctor would know whereof he spoke on
the subject of insurance premiums.

Hank continued, "He's probably trying to scare you
off with the threat of a countersuit, since obviously you
weren't at fault."

I groaned. If HBIE wasn't insured, I was in deep
trouble.

"Add to that the complication of an employee found

dead—and in mysterious circumstances." He frowned at the used glass in front of him, then carefully sprinkled salt directly into a new can of beer and saluted me. "Found, incidentally, by the same woman who was seriously injured on carnival grounds. A perfect reason for surliness, no?"

A good opening to turn the conversation back to Lily.

"You worked with Lily, you knew her. What was she like?"

I'd heard so many contradictory versions, I wanted his take.

"She wasn't very well equipped to deal with real life. Numerous problems dating back to her early childhood—with authority, with substance abuse. With reality."

"She lied a lot, I heard."

He raised an eyebrow. "There's an understatement. Though she seemed to be getting a better handle on her life, and we all thought she was improving."

I'd heard that one too. From Marko.

"She said she was fired for turning tricks. Hooking," I explained, as if he needed a definition. "Any truth to that?"

"Are you asking if she was hooking or whether that was really why she was fired?"

"Either one," I said. "Bogner told me, off the record, that her days with HBIE were numbered, though he didn't say why."

"I don't know. HBIE wasn't operating profitably, and that's one tax-free way of bringing in some spare change. As to whether or not Lily was hooking, either with or without the tacit approval of the management, I also couldn't say. However, with her history of possible child molestation and abuse, anything's possible."

He drained his glass and looked around for Pete, who was busy taking pitchers to another table.

Hank stood and stretched. "I believe I'll get me another one of these," he said. "You should go home and get some rest—you need it."

"I thought you couldn't practice medicine in South Dakota," I said.

"I'm not ordering, I'm advising. I can do that anywhere. Go home."

There was no point in staying. I'd heard everything I needed from the good doctor, and he was right. I was beat.

He walked with me toward the door.

"Say," he said quietly, "I'd appreciate it if you wouldn't broadcast who I really am. The summer is almost over and I'd like to finish it anonymously."

Easy enough. Only one person would be interested anyway, and Neil could keep secrets.

I turned to agree and found that he was already over at the bar, ordering another beer from Pete.

The sight of him, standing there in his black shirt, with his back to me, head red and peeling and can of beer in hand, froze me in place.

My mind's eye formed a scene from the street dance with absolute clarity. Just beyond the alley and over Stu's shoulder, a tall man in an HBIE shirt took a swing at Lily.

And I saw her empty, outstretched hand, and the silver arc of a beer can as it flew through the air.

35

....

Filling in the Picture

It would not be an understatement to say that I was depressed, worn out, and just plain confused.

It wasn't that I'd jumped to the wrong conclusion about Marko. That was a legitimate wrong conclusion, based on information at hand, processed under fairly trying circumstances. I've run the scenario in my head over and over, and outside of letting Marko fall to what seemed a certain death, I can't imagine what I'd have done differently.

It wasn't even that I stepped in it by thinking that Doc, with the scrunched-up cowboy hat and his fat complex, was a real doctor. From Harvard, no less.

Neil bought that one too.

No, it was that I'd drawn so many wrong conclusions and now had to deal with even more confusing, conflicting information, and was no closer to an answer than before.

Only, now I knew better than to rely on my own flawed deductive reasoning.

It was past time for more magic pain pills, but they fuzzed my mind. And as much as I longed for that floating sense of well-being, I needed a clear head.

Hamilton Bogner had Lily's (and Marko's, Mobridge's) turquoise cross necklace in his desk. He took it from her body, that much was clear. He was tall; he probably just reached up and unwound it from her hand after sending me out to call the authorities.

And obscure Hank, the mysterious Ivy League Dr. William H. Aker, where did he fit?

A successful, published, professional man spending his summers slumming, the better to treat Beltway bipolar syndromes in the winter months?

Evidently Dr. Aker was the physician and Hank was the working man.

And HBIE had employed Hank, not the doctor, since Dr. Aker couldn't practice in South Dakota.

But what about the bottle of pills in Bogner's desk? With our Dr. Aker's name on the label.

And what about the blurry face wearing glasses that hovered over me after I fell? It wasn't Neil, it wasn't Marko, and it sure as hell wasn't Doc. It had to have been Hank.

Practicing medicine in South Dakota.

I remembered again Lily and Hank in the cafe the morning the carnival came to town. She ordered lunch and shook a small pill out of an envelope and swallowed it with a gulp of water.

Lily and Hank had argued at the dance. And seemingly gentle and compassionate Hank took a full-arm swing at Lily. He missed, but in that case intent mattered more than aim.

Of course, the whole thing revolved around Lily. Lily the liar? Lily the prostitute?

Nothing was certain about her, except that she was dead.

Even Del, whose most complicated reading came from "The Playboy Advisor," knew that you couldn't draw the proper conclusions without looking at the whole picture.

And Lily, arguably the most important person of all, wasn't in the picture.

The newspapers had listed Lily's parents as Harold and Virginia Waltman of Cody, Wyoming. Directory assistance provided the phone number of one Waltman, H., the only Waltman in the area.

Knowing that what I was about to do was an invasion of privacy and a terrible intrusion on this family's grief, I sat at the kitchen table and dialed the phone.

A woman with a quiet middle-aged voice answered.

I introduced myself, said where I was from, and apologized for bothering her.

"I know this is a hard time for you and your family, and if you don't want to talk to me, I'll understand," I said. "But I met your daughter shortly before her death. And I'd like to ask you a couple of questions, if you're up to answering."

That was lame, heartless, and cold. Mrs. Waltman would probably hang up on me, and I'd deserve no better. She was the one who lost a daughter. She owed me nothing.

The line was quiet for a long pause.

"You're the one who found her, aren't you?" she asked finally, sounding weary beyond recovery. "I recognize your name. The police said you were a waitress."

"Yeah, that's sort of how I met Lily," I said. It wasn't quite the truth, but it'd do. "I don't know if you'll understand this, but I feel a kind of connection to Lily and I want to know more about her life. Does that make sense?"

"Actually, it does," she said. "Lily had a way of making others want to take care of her." She chuckled sadly. "Not that it ever helped. In her whole life, Lily never once made a good decision, or listened to advice no matter how well-meaning."

"People here seem to think she had a troubled childhood," I said carefully. Hank had mentioned child abuse and molestation.

"You could say that," Mrs. Waltman said. "As a child Lily was often depressed—not just blue or unhappy, but the real thing. Clinical depression. She had low self-esteem a long time before it was popular. She was anxious and mistrustful. She lied constantly and was uncontrollable. We tried to deal with it by ourselves. For years."

She paused, sorrow thickening her voice. "After the third suicide attempt, when she cut up her wrists with Harold's Swiss army knife, we went to a therapist. He said she had something called a 'borderline personality' and suggested therapy for Lily and the whole family."

I knew that for therapy purposes, there were no "bad" children in "good" families. Everyone contributed to the problem and could only find resolution by working together. At least that was the theory.

"And did you all go? To therapy, I mean?" I asked gently.

"Of course," she said shortly. "We wanted Lily to get better, and would have done anything to help. But Lily's problems started long before she came to us. And nothing, not therapy, not community service like the judge ordered, not even medication, helped. Until lately."

"You say she took medicine? Different kinds?"

That was the kind of information I was after.

"They'd had her on all kinds of antidepressants, which played hell with her moods and sleep patterns and did absolutely nothing to help her to cope with her life. At least until this summer. She started on a new one that finally seemed to make a difference. She was already traveling with that carnival so we didn't get to see the changes in person. But on the phone she sounded light-hearted and happy."

Mrs. Waltman stopped for a moment. She was either crying or trying very hard not to.

"We were so happy for her and so hopeful for her future," she finally continued. "We'd given up a long time ago on drugs. And then Parnate gave Lily back her life. It seemed like a miracle."

Again, a lengthy pause.

"And maybe it would have given Lily back to us.

Maybe we could have made up for all the bad years . . .
if she hadn't insisted on going to Delphi. In fact, that's
the only reason she took that stupid job—she saw the
carnival itinerary and applied on the spot.

"She had enough trouble coping as it was; going to
Delphi seemed like tempting fate.

"Looks like we were right. It was the worst decision of
her life."

I said slowly, "Lily also mentioned that you were
against her coming here specifically. I guess what I don't
understand is why it mattered so much for your daughter to avoid a town that she'd never been to before."

"Oh," she said. "I thought you knew. I thought that's
why you called."

"Knew what, Mrs. Waltman?"

Whatever was coming, this was the key.

"Lily wasn't our daughter. Not a biological one,
anyway. Her real family was killed when she was a
toddler. She lived with her only remaining blood relative for a few years, but her grandmother was unstable
too. It ran in the family, I guess. The grandmother killed
herself when Lily was about seven.

"For a while Lily bounced from foster home to foster
home. Some of them were pretty awful, I heard. She'd
certainly been abused by the time we got her. Even
though she was just a kid, she was already in trouble
with the law and suffering from periodic bouts of
depression.

"We did our best by her. We loved her like our own
and eventually adopted her, though she kept her parents' last name. We loved her," she said again sadly.

I'd assumed the differing last names were the result of
divorce and remarriage. Adoption hadn't even occurred
to me.

But I was still confused.

"I don't understand. What does all that have to do
with Delphi?"

"Lily was obsessed with Delphi and with confronting
her past. We didn't think she could handle being there
alone. We thought it would be too much for her." She

sighed. "And we were right, though not in any way we could have foreseen."

"But why Delphi, Mrs. Waltman?"

"You see, that's what I thought you already knew, why you called.

"Delphi's where her whole family died. Over twenty years ago. Lily was the only survivor of a car accident just outside of town."

36

....

Phone Secs

As embarrassed government officials have been known
to say after being caught in compromising positions o
their own making: Mistakes have been made.

It's a tidy admission that allows for public declara
tions of wrongdoing without actual acceptance of guilt

It applies to private situations too. Mistakes had bee
made. My mistakes. Lily's mistakes. Everyone's mis
takes.

Easing back and propping my broken arm on a pile o
books, I thought through what I needed to know, the
dialed the phone again.

"Hi there, got a sec? Got a couple of short question
for you."

"The joint is hopping," Neil said, "but I think I ca
work you in if you're really fast."

Talk and laughter echoed in the background.

"Quickly then, do you have, somewhere in you
reference section, a book describing prescriptio
drugs?"

"Of course," he said. "What kind of library do you think I run?"

"How silly of me. Will you go and look up a drug called Parnate and read me the poop? I'm pretty sure it's an antidepressant."

"No problem." I heard him tell someone he'd be right back. "Considering addiction, or perhaps the retail sale of restricted pharmaceuticals?"

He carried the cordless phone with him. I heard footsteps and the heavy thud of a book on a table.

"Both, probably," I said. "Waiting tables is going to be a tad difficult for the duration."

"No kidding," he said. Pages ruffled.

"Ah, here we go. Yes, Parnate, generic name tranylcypromine, daily recommended dose thirty to fifty milligrams, ten milligrams per tablet. General psychiatric drug, officially a monoamine oxidase inhibitor, or MAOI for short."

I scribbled notes. Extremely slowly. With my left hand. I hoped I'd be able to read them later.

"What's it used to treat?" I asked.

"Chronic or severe depression and anxiety, sometimes beginning in early childhood. Apparently good for disorders that don't respond well to conventional psychotherapy."

He paused, skimming, I heard another page turn. "Often has a dramatic effect. Patients report feelings of well-being and marked, observable, personality changes for the better, almost immediately.

"Any of this what you're looking for?" Neil paused.

"That's exactly what I need. Go on."

"Hokay." He continued to read. "MAOIs cause very few side effects as long as certain dietary restrictions are followed. You want to hear the restrictions and effects?"

"Just give me a rundown."

He did and I wasn't surprised.

"What's this all about?" he asked.

"How busy are you?" I asked. "It's a long story."

"Unfortunately, too busy for anything but the highlights right now," he said.

"You'll have to wait, then. It's too complicated for condensation. One last thing, though." I'd remembered another question. "Can you quick check Dr. William Aker's articles on antidepressants to see if either Parnate or MAOIs are mentioned?"

"Let's see." He hummed a melody I sort of recognized. Probably more Beatles á la Bach. "Ah, here we go. Boy, are you psychic or what? Both of them right there on the printed page. In fact, one entire article is about Parnate and its effects. Want a summary?"

"Nope," I said. "Got everything I need for now. Talk to you later."

I sat for a minute, working up courage for the next call.

"McKee's Feed and Seed. This is Stu, how can I help you?"

"Uh, hi, Stu, this is Tory," I said, heart pounding.

Damn, he still does it to me.

"Ah, how can I help you?" Stu asked, wary. I never call him. At work or at home or anywhere else. And wouldn't have called now, except I thought he might have a piece of the puzzle.

"I won't keep you for more than a minute, I know you're busy, but I need to ask you something."

"Uh, sure." He sounded so uncomfortable, I wondered if Renee was standing in front of him. Not that mattered—there was nothing untoward in this call.

Studiously forgetting our relationship, I asked Stu my question, which he answered as quickly as possible, then hung up.

I stared at the phone a second and then sighed. Maybe Renee *was* standing in the feed store. That would explain Stu's reticence. She'd been in some pretty odd places during the last week.

Or maybe he was just starting to realize that all the secrecy and sneaking exacted a price too high for the goods received. For either of us.

I sighed again, then dug the papers out of my back pocket and made another very quick call, and was again not surprised by the answers I got.

I reviewed the phone calls and realized I'd learned a couple of new things. But mostly, I'd just confirmed what I already knew.

I thought again and made one more call to Lily's mother, to ask one more question.

The last important piece, or at least what I thought was the last important piece, fell into place when I saw Presley wearing his Carpe Wiener shirt, and Chainlink and John Adler, in their new black T-shirts, goofing around in the street.

I sat for another minute, ticking off facts in my mind, arranging them in proper order. When I finished, I knew who killed Lily Mitchell.

And why.

And how.

37

....

Whine and Ham

It wasn't five o'clock, but as we like to say in South Dakota, it's happy hour somewhere.

Trusting that the carny folk, unable either to work or to leave town, felt the same way, I headed straight for Jackson's.

The walk was slow going because the heat and my injuries severely restricted speed. And because I was stopped at least four times to explain to concerned folk in pickup trucks that yes, it sure did hurt, and no, I didn't kill the other guy, and yes, I expected to make a full recovery, and no, there wasn't anything they could do to help but thanks for asking anyway.

The bar was considerably more crowded than before. I saw, as my eyes adjusted to the dim interior, that everyone I needed was in the room. The noise level had risen to a Saturday-night pitch with much clinking of glasses and sloppy singing along with Alan Jackson as he water-skied down the Chattahoochee.

There were so many customers that Mardelle had

been pressed into illegal service carrying overflowing beer mugs to slack-jawed greaseballs who'd opted to employ their free afternoon drinking rather than showering.

The twins scuttled behind the bar, between the sink and the taps. And Pat, her beady eyes glittering at the sight of all that profit, hovered near the cash register.

I suppose the noisy spectacle should have been enough to make me take a vow of sobriety. Unfortunately, I would have killed for a beer. But what I'd learned convinced me to abstain for a while.

The crowd was so boisterous and the smoke so thick, that no one noticed me until I pulled up a chair next to Hamilton Bogner and clumsily sat down. The silence was immediate.

Midge, eyes narrowed and solidly drawn eyebrows knitted, pointedly stood up and moved to another table. As did Larry and a few others.

It didn't bother me. I wasn't out to win any popularity contests, and besides, it'd be easier to talk seriously with fewer people close by.

Ham emptied his wineglass in one swallow, grimaced, then poured another swig from the bottle on the table.

Around here, if you order wine you have your choice of red, white, or pink, all prime Gallo vintages from sometime in the last three months.

I'm no expert, but even to me, Ernest and Julio's finest tasted like piss.

Evidently Ham agreed, though at the rate he was sucking that bottle down, I doubted taste was much of a factor.

"Ah," he finally addressed me slurrily. "The good doctor and I were just talking about you."

I could well imagine.

Hank, who'd evidently continued drinking beer since I left earlier, saluted me with an empty glass. "Barkeep." He waved at Pete. Or Pat. "Another round for the table and a glass of water for the lady."

Drunk or not, he was still a doctor.

"So"—he leaned across the table—"have you something to discuss with us?"

"Just a few things to clear up," I said. "I won't take up much of your time. You first, Mr. Bogner."

Ham eyed me warily.

"You should be ashamed of yourself, trying to badger me into signing a piece of shit like this." I pulled the papers from my pocket.

I'd called a random lawyer and asked about standard release forms and their validity when retroactive.

"Hey, how'd you get that?" he asked, alarmed.

"You should lock your doors," I said. "Especially if you're going to threaten me with frivolous lawsuits and try to coerce me into signing a release form that wouldn't hold water, even if I'd signed it *before* I fell."

"Well, um, sorry about that," Ham said defensively. "But you barged in with no warning, asking about insurance premiums and talking about liability and all I just sort of panicked."

My heart sank.

"You mean, you really don't have any insurance?" I asked. "Any at all?"

"Unfortunately, no," he said. "We're barely surviving as it is, and there just wasn't enough money to make the premiums and payroll both."

"Don't you have to present certificates of insurance before you can get hired?" I asked.

"Certificates can be forged," Ham said with a shrug. "I was only trying to keep the troupe going."

"Is that why you took the necklace from Lily's dead body before the police arrived?"

Hank spit beer on the table. And my shoulder.

"Oh, you know about that too, huh?" Ham asked. He sighed, and continued. "I recognized the necklace as soon as I saw it. Some of our workers are not entirely trustworthy," he understated, "and I've found it's good practice to monitor each town's newspapers after we leave."

The *Mobridge Tribune* had been in Ham's desk drawer.

"I knew there was going to be trouble as soon as I saw her, um, up there, you know. And I knew it was going to fall back on me, so I decided on the spot to take the necklace.

"It seemed obvious that someone on my staff had stolen it from that town back a couple of weeks. Lily Mitchell was nothing but trouble from day one. Alive she was bad enough, and dead, she'd be even worse. I honestly figured it couldn't hurt her, and it might save us some grief if I quietly removed the necklace. Guess I was wrong."

There wasn't much to say to that. I turned to Dr. Aker.

"You're something of an expert on MAOIs in general and Parnate in particular, right?"

"Well, I wouldn't go so far as to call myself an expert, but I've studied them a little." He took a drink. "Over the years."

"You're being modest," I said. "Several articles in respected journals on the use and effect of monoamine oxidase inhibitors make you pretty much of an expert, I'd say."

"I try not to blow my own horn, but if you insist, okay, I'm an expert."

Though Ham continued to drink steadily, he was intently listening to the conversation.

"So you definitely know all about the cautions against mixing those drugs with certain foods and other medicines."

"Any first-year medical student knows that."

"And do you tell your patients about those dangers?"

He was indignant. "Of course I do. I'm very careful to explain drug interaction to all of my patients."

I paused and tilted my head. "And did you explain it also to Lily Mitchell?"

"Lily Mitchell wasn't my patient," he said into his glass. "I told you already, I'm not practicing medicine this summer."

"Oh yeah?" I pounced. "What about helping to stabilize me after I fell? Before the ambulance came?"

"That's not practicing medicine. I didn't perform any invasive procedures or prescribe anything. I only did what any compassionate human being with specialized skills would do."

"And I'm grateful for the help," I said. "But what about the bottle of Xanax in Ham Bogner's desk? The one with your name on it?"

"How'd you know about that?" Ham interrupted.

We ignored him.

"Xanax," I continued, "prescribed by you to help keep Marko Parker in line whenever he went into his frequent steroid-induced rages."

"It's Marko," Doc had said, "again."

"If you knew anything about medicine at all, you'd know that Xanax has no effect whatsoever against extreme emotional outbursts. Especially as they occur," Hank said sharply. "And if you'd been a little more observant, you'd have noticed that the prescription was written *for* me, not *by* me. By my own physician, more than five months ago."

"Then what was the pill bottle doing in Ham Bogner's desk along with your prescription pad?"

"Why don't you tell her, Ham?" he said with an expansive gesture. "Since she's so curious."

"Well." Ham swallowed a belch. He was pretty seriously lit. "My good friend here generously offered to share his own personal tranquilizers with me. The stress of keeping this operation together on the road is pretty high sometimes . . ." He trailed off.

He had my grudging sympathy for courting bankruptcy while relying on a crew of thieves, druggies, and prostitutes. Even if he had to cope by borrowing drugs.

However, this was not leading exactly where I'd thought it would. Ham had taken the pill bottle, all right, not to deal with a furious Marko but to calm himself down.

"And the prescription pad?" I asked weakly.

"I'll take that one, Ham old buddy," Hank said. "You see, security at Bogner International is not exactly top notch. Locks, when they work at all, are a small chal lenge to the larcenous, occult-worshiping, highly creative individuals we travel with."

So Junior had been right about the Satan stuff. I didn't think I'd tell her.

"I was aware that several of our merry band were busily engaged in the consumption of illegal drugs," Hank continued. "Some of which could be easily obtained with forged prescriptions."

Steroids are a prescription drug.

"I was worried that the pad might be stolen from my quarters, so I gave it to Ham for safekeeping."

Hank barked a beer-swelled laugh. "Rather silly of me, I realize, in retrospect."

Giving up, I said, "So how did Lily get the Parnate?"

"I accompanied her to a doctor a couple of states back and consulted with him about her case. He happened to agree with me, and prescribed the medication for her. We were right—it made an amazing change in her."

He emptied another glass.

"Unfortunately, what we all overlook sometimes is that there are no fundamental personality changes, no miracles wrought by Parnate or any other drug. A wild, reckless, ungovernable person who takes Parnate is happier and somewhat more tractable, but still the same person. Still wild and ungovernable.

"We forgot that with Lily," he said.

38

....

One Little, Two Little, Three Wrong Conclusions

I warned you from the very start that I would come to a couple of wrong conclusions before the end of this story.

All right, all right, so there were more than a couple. But given the information at hand, I think most of them were *logical* wrong conclusions. Anyone could, and maybe would, have made the same mistakes.

Regardless, those were pretty small potatoes compared to the three major misapprehensions I'd labored under all along. Each of the three forced me to rethink the whole shebang. Each one changed my perspective just a little.

I had recognized the first almost immediately after I left Hank and Ham boozing it up across the room.

"Can I get you something, Tory?" Pat Jackson asked. I knew he was Pat because Pete still wore the brown polo shirt he'd had on earlier, and Pat had on a custom-made HBIE shirt with "Pat" stenciled above the pocket. Besides, I just knew.

Finally, when the whole thing was just about over and

it didn't matter at all, I could tell the Jackson twins apart.

I slowly sat myself on a bar stool down by the cash register.

"Nothing right now," I said, considering how to bring the subject up. "How about that wreck on Highway 12 last Wednesday? You had to have seen it when you drove Pete's pickup back from Webster. Nasty one, wasn't it?"

Actually, Stu and I didn't see any wrecks, but it was a safe question. On any given day, there were always one or two.

Pat frowned and shook his head. "Wednesday? I wasn't in Webster last Wednesday. I'm taking an accounting class in Aberdeen and I've spent every Monday, Wednesday, and Friday up there at the college all summer long."

He turned to his wife, who was hovering, listening. "That musta been you, hon. Isn't Webster where you picked up that used popcorn machine you found a couple of weeks ago? You and Pete?"

There it was, the first wrong conclusion.

While I was trying to hide behind the ice machine, Pete Jackson, still readily identifiable with a Fu Manchu mustache and scraggly ponytail, had said to the person in the Super 8 Motel room "Pat, why don't you straighten this mess up?" shortly after Lily burst from their room in tears.

And later, down by Stu's truck in the hot parking lot, he'd said, "Pat can drive the truck home later."

Mardelle had told me her father was taking an accounting class. But Stu's carnival hooker narrative had been fresh in my mind and I'd assumed that the boys, Pete and Pat, were up to old tricks, no pun intended.

It seemed that Pete and Pat were up to tricks all right, but it wasn't Pete and his brother, but Pete and his brother's wife. Pete and Mrs. Pat. Mrs. Pat, the former Patricia Rhorbach, the former girlfriend of Pete Jackson.

Evidently not so former after all.

Arranging, together, for Lily's services?

"Hey, Pat," a couple from the nearby table called. "Can you get us another pitcher over here?"

"Comin' right up," he answered. "Duty calls, gotta go," he said to me.

I saw that Mrs. Pat was eyeing me narrowly. "You must think you're pretty smart," she said quietly. "Got it all figured out, huh?"

"Actually, no. On all counts," I said. "Can I ask you a couple of questions?"

She shrugged, massive shoulders and thick neck tense.

There was no gentle way around it. "You and Pete?"

"We were together a long time ago, long before . . ." She hesitated.

"Before the car wreck," I filled in. "The accident that killed Lily Mitchell's whole family."

She raised an eyebrow.

"The accident that sent Pete to prison for the first time," I finished.

There. The second wrong conclusion—that the whole saga began only last week. For Lily and the Jacksons, the beginnings were long ago. And if I'd realized that, I would have understood it all much sooner.

For Lily, especially, it started in Delphi. And for Lily it ended here.

"I was supposed to go with them that night, you know," Pat said quietly. "But I was sick, ate some bad potato salad or something. Food poisoning, not that it matters. So the boys went out alone."

The rest was Delphi history. The twins stole a car and some liquor, got drunk, and committed vehicular homicide.

"Pat"—she nodded at her husband, who was laughing with Mardelle at the other end of the bar—"Pat, he's always felt guilty. Always felt like the whole accident was his fault."

"But he wasn't driving, was he?" I asked.

"No, but it wasn't who was driving that was important. They were fighting, you see. Over a girl."

"You?" I was starting to see where this was headed.

"I was still going out with Pete, you know, but I had a one-nighter with Pat. I mean, they're identical. It really shouldn't have mattered. But that night, I was just too sick to go with them and explain."

Sex and salmonella. Again.

"But Pat, he had this guilty conscience, and it was eating away at him—the fact that he'd screwed his brother's girlfriend."

"So he confessed," I said.

"And they were swinging at each other, driving stupid. They woulda got over it eventually. We all would have worked it out. But they hit that car full of people, and everything changed."

"So Pete went to jail, and you married Pat," I said, sorting it out.

"And Pat has felt guilty every minute since. That's why he didn't mind about Pete and me. He felt he owed Pete something. And that girl."

And I had worried about how Mrs. Pat would feel about her husband's infidelity.

"When Pat finally traced her down, the one who survived the wreck, and found out she was actually coming to Delphi, he went a little nuts."

"Nuts, like how?"

"Nuts like wanting to empty out all of our savings accounts as some kind of settlement for the kid. To try to make up for taking away her family when she was so little," Pat said in disgust. "As if money could do that."

A good many lawyers and judges think it can, I said to myself.

"You knew she was in Webster," I said.

In my last call, Lily's mother had told me she'd been contacted by the brother of the man who had been driving the car. He'd asked for Lily's whereabouts.

Virginia Waltman had said, "I knew it'd be difficult for Lily. But as long as she insisted on going to Delphi in the first place, I thought it might be good for her to meet

with that man. Besides, he wanted to give her some
money. She was excited about that."

"So you pretended to hire her as a hooker,"
prompted.

Pat grinned. "It got her to our room. She was a girl
who liked making money. Unfortunately, Pat had al
ready contacted her and told her his nutty settlement
idea."

"Which she liked just fine," I said.

"She was full of grand ideas," Pat said. "Until we told
her there wasn't any money, there was never going to be
any money. She came unglued, trashed the room, and
ran out."

Which was when I'd seen her.

"Pete and I realized she wouldn't give up that easily
that we would have to get rid of her or Pat would
bankrupt us.

"We found out she was in trouble at work; we though
it'd be pretty easy to get her fired."

"How'd you know she was in trouble?"

Pat grinned evilly. "You told us."

"*Me*? I never told you anything."

"Sure you did." Pat fished in a drawer behind the ba
and pulled out a wrinkled slip of green paper and
handed it to me.

I smoothed it out. Written on it was a short note in
sloppy handwriting: "Went back to Delphi with S
McKee. You drive truck home when you finish."

That made no sense. I shrugged.

"Turn it over," Pat suggested.

It was a Delphi Cafe ticket. On it, in my handwriting
were, among other things, the words "Lily Mitchell—
trouble—gone soon."

The notes I'd taken during my ersatz interview with
Hamilton Bogner in Webster. The top page of the pad—
the one I'd inadvertently torn off so Pete could write his
own note.

"As I said, we knew she was already in trouble," Pat
said smugly. "And what exactly were *you* doing in
Webster with Stu McKee?"

"Checking out the carnival for my cousin Junior," I said testily.

"Sure," Pat said. "Anyway, we decided to circulate a couple of stories about Miss Lily White hooking. Pete made sure to tell the old bat at the T-shirt booth when he had special ones made for him and Pat. He also told that guy at the ticket booth."

Doc, I thought. And then Doc, or more likely Midge, had reported the stories directly to Ham Bogner, and Lily had been fired.

She'd lied about that too, but what did that matter? I was beginning to realize, late in the game, that Lily Mitchell had lied about everything.

"But it didn't work, did it?" I asked. "I mean, firing Lily didn't make her go away. I talked to her Friday night. She was even more determined to stay in Delphi, and she knew who would help her."

"No shit. First she came to us, threatening to tell everyone about Pete and me," Pat said.

If prostitution was the world's oldest profession, blackmail must be the second.

"Why would that matter?" I asked. "You already said that Pat knew."

"Pat knows," she said. "But Mardelle doesn't."

She watched her lovely daughter, who'd inherited none of her mother's build or coloring, with the first soft look I'd seen. Then she frowned. "And the town doesn't know. And there's no reason for either to find out.

"Something you might want to keep in mind," she said darkly. "For your sake too. Carnival checking, my ass."

No shit, as someone recently said.

"So, Lily came to you Friday night after the dance?"

"Yeah, to try to extort, whine, and wheedle anything she could out of us. I think she would have raided the till if we'd let her out of our sight."

"Our?"

"Me, Pete, and Pat. All in the back room. Mardelle was upstairs asleep, thank God."

So all three were there.

"And Pat would have given her everything, gladly," said Mrs. Pat wonderingly, and then clamped her mouth in a tight line, reliving the night, a slight look of horror on her face.

"And we probably *would* have given her something, just to shut her up. But she collapsed. Fell to the floor.

"Died right there in front of us, before we could do anything or call anyone or help her," Pat finished.

By now, her husband had noticed our intense conversation and had come to stand behind his wife. From the back room, Pete also joined her. The three of them, bound together by history and horror.

A family.

"She ate something, didn't she?" I asked. "She was drinking too, right?"

Pete said, "She ate like a horse. There was a cheese-and-deer-sausage platter left from the Rocky Mountain oyster feed in the fridge. She musta stuffed eight or ten pieces in her mouth in less than five minutes."

"And she guzzled at least three beers, talking and laughing about what she was gonna do with all her money," Pat, Mr. Pat, said.

"Her face got really red, and she started sweating and her eyes kinda popped a little, and then she died," Pete said. "Just like that."

I remembered Lily wolfing a toasted cheese sandwich in the cafe after she'd specifically told Hank she was having a cheeseless hamburger. Her face was flushed then too, and she broke out in a sweat.

Flushing and perspiration are symptoms of high blood pressure. Neil had read over the phone, "MAO inhibitors can cause sudden, dangerously elevated blood pressure when they are combined with certain other drugs and food."

Like fish and fava beans and liver and overripe bananas. Like fermented sausage, such as deer. Like cheese.

"Combining some foods and drink can be extremely dangerous for persons taking monoamine oxidase inhibitors," Neil had continued. "Extreme high blood pressure can result in potentially fatal episodes such as stroke. Patients are especially cautioned against combining MAOIs with alcohol."

I had seen Hank take a swing at a red-faced, sweating Lily at the dance. I thought he was swinging at her and missed. But I was wrong. He'd aimed for the beer can and knocked it out of her hand and into the air.

Hank, the good Dr. Aker, had been trying to save Lily's life.

And there was the third wrong conclusion. The biggie. The only one that mattered: No one murdered Lily Mitchell.

Foolish, headstrong, willful Lily. Lily who had a problem with authority. Lily who never, ever did what she was told.

Lily who knew that eating certain foods and drinking certain liquids was dangerous.

Lily who ignored good advice and died of her own stubbornness.

Lily who took Parnate, but still remained the same person, only happier.

The rest was easy. I could imagine the panic.

"I'm on probation," Pete explained. "I don't want to go back to jail. We didn't know what happened to her, but we knew no one'd ever believe us. And I'd be blamed."

"We were sitting there with a dead girl. That kind of thing gets noticed in Delphi. Someone would eventually remember that car wreck," Pat said. It didn't matter which one.

"So you trucked her over to the fun house. Pete picked the lock and you put her inside and just waited," I said.

That was the call to Stu—What were most of Pete's convictions? Breaking and entering.

"Both of you wore your HBIE shirts, so no one would think anything was out of the ordinary if you were seen," I said.

Once they'd stashed the body, anyway.

"And the necklace?" I asked. It was the very last thread.

"Lily hinted that the muscle guy gave it to her," one of them said. "We figured if we wrapped it around her hand like that, it'd at least throw suspicion back at the carnival and away from us."

It worked.

The autopsy toxicology reports would eventually show how, and why, young Lily Mitchell died of a stroke. Just like the medical examiner said. Just like Agent Ingstad thought.

I reluctantly realized that Lily's death truly wasn't murder.

I did, however, make a mental note never to look closely at the Jacksons' bookshelves. I did not want to know if a drug interaction manual was nestled among the volumes.

Epilogue

LATER THAT WEEK

I was on the couch, blissfully whacked on painkillers, trying, fruitlessly, to make one-handed sense of the Carl Hiaasen novel Neil sent over. Those Florida people are even weirder than the folks in Delphi.

And that takes some doing.

Presley had been moping around all day.

"Where's your mom?" I asked. It was Del's day off and I hadn't seen her at all.

"She's in Aberdeen, I think," he said with a sneer. "On a date."

"Oh yeah?" I asked. That was news to me. "With who?"

Strong painkillers tend to nullify the grammar instinct.

"That doctor, the one you had in the hospital. The one from India or wherever."

He was genuinely upset.

"Does it bother you that he's from India?"

He made a jeez-you're-dense face. "Of course not. But that's all she thinks about."

"Dating?" I asked. "Doctors? India?"

"No, dummy. Sex," Pres said, disgusted. "She doesn't even care if the guy is married."

Ah, that was why he'd been so crabby lately. No male deals well with the notion that his mother likes sex.

Though in Del's case, Presley had a valid point.

"Do you need me for anything?" Pres asked. The conversation clearly made him uncomfortable, and he was looking for an escape.

I suppose if I'd had my wits about me, I would have tried to talk to him about it a little. Shared feelings, explored vulnerabilities. You know, nineties bullshit.

On the other hand, what could I say? Del's habits made me uncomfortable too. Not that I had any room to talk.

"Nah," I said. "Go on."

"Thanks." He grinned, pausing at the door. "At least I don't have to worry about you. You'd never sleep with a married man. Right?"

He ducked out with a wave before I could come up with an answer.

Well, maybe neither of us would have to worry about it.

Stu still hadn't called.

There was a knock at the door.

"Come in," I shouted. Probably another kind soul with a casserole. We already had enough to feed us for the next month.

Renee McKee came in.

Without a casserole.

She picked her way to the recliner, trying to mask a delicate look of distaste.

I was dumbfounded. Literally.

"I suppose you're wondering why I'm here," she said.

You could say that. Although I couldn't.

"I thought I'd tell you that I'm leaving Stuart. I'm taking our son and going back to Minnesota. I hate this state."

I found some words. One anyway.

"Why?" I croaked.

"Not because of you," she said, "although you probably won't believe that." She continued, mostly to herself. "I tried, I really did. Especially lately. But honestly, there are no restaurants here, no theaters, no shopping. You have to drive thirty miles just to see a movie."

I swallowed painfully.

I've always thought that South Dakota was a great place to live, but I wouldn't want to visit.

"I'm going and it remains to be seen whether or not Stuart will follow," Renee said. "However, I give you fair warning—I expect he will follow me eventually. And I will probably even take him back."

Try as I might, I could think of no suitable reply.

"Well," she said, standing. "I can see you're overwhelmed at the prospect, so I'll leave you to your book.

"Oh." She paused at the door on the way out. "I do have one caution: Watch out for the Minnesota Snail." She grinned wickedly. "It's a killer."

I sat there astonished, unsure whether to laugh or cry. Or scream.

I only knew that I needed a drink, though after what I'd learned last week, it seemed wiser to wait.

A native of the Pacific Northwest, KATHLEEN TAY-LOR has lived and worked in the same rural South Dakota town for the last twenty-five years. She resides in a restored Victorian house with her building contractor husband, two dogs, and two cats. She has two grown sons; the elder is married and both are graduates of the University of South Dakota.

For fourteen years Taylor wrote reviews and designed needlework for craft and women's magazines. The Tory Bauer Mystery series is her first foray into fiction.